'Something appears to be troubling you, Miss Mortimer. I trust you are not concerned about being in here alone with

'You are in no da... ed. 'And if, for any ... ence an overwhelming de... violent hands upon you, I'm sure your trusty hound would come to your rescue.'

'Ha! I'm not so very sure he would!' Isabel returned, quite without rancour. She was more amazed than anything else that Beau had taken such an instant liking to someone. Which just went to substantiate her belief that his lordship was not the black-hearted demon he had sometimes been painted.

'So, what were you thinking about a few minutes ago that brought such a troubled expression to your face?'

Lord! Isabel mused. Was he always so observant? Had she not witnessed it with her own eyes she would never have supposed for a moment that those icy-blue orbs could dance with wicked amusement. He really was a most attractive and engaging gentleman when he chose to be. And she didn't doubt for a second a damnably dangerous one, to boot, to any female weak enough not to resist his charm! Was she mad even to consider remaining with him a moment longer?

Anne Ashley was born and educated in Leicester. She lived for a time in Scotland, but now makes her home in the West Country, with two cats, her two sons, and a husband who has a wonderful and very necessary sense of humour. When not pounding away at the keys of her computer, she likes to relax in her garden, which she has opened to the public on more than one occasion in aid of the village church funds.

Previous novels by the same author:

A NOBLE MAN*
LORD EXMOUTH'S INTENTIONS*
THE RELUCTANT MARCHIONESS
TAVERN WENCH
BELOVED VIRAGO
LORD HAWKRIDGE'S SECRET
BETRAYED AND BETROTHED
A LADY OF RARE QUALITY
LADY GWENDOLEN INVESTIGATES
THE TRANSFORMATION OF
  MISS ASHWORTH
MISS IN A MAN'S WORLD

*part of the Regency mini-series
 The Steepwood Scandal

THE VISCOUNT'S SCANDALOUS RETURN

Anne Ashley

First published in Great Britain 2011
by Mills & Boon, an imprint of Harlequin (UK) Limited.
Harlequin (UK) Limited, Eton House, 18-24 Paradise Road,
Richmond, Surrey TW9 1SR

© Anne Ashley 2010

ISBN: 978 0 263 88812 6

Harlequin (UK) policy is to use papers that are natural, renewable and recyclable products and made from wood grown in sustainable forests. The logging and manufacturing process conform to the legal environmental regulations of the country of origin.

Printed and bound in Spain
by Blackprint CPI, Barcelona

THE VISCOUNT'S SCANDALOUS RETURN

Chapter One

September 1814

Miss Isabel Mortimer's return to her farmhouse-style home coincided with the long-case clock's chiming the hour of eleven. She had been out and about since first light, and so might reasonably have expected a more enthusiastic welcome than the decidedly reproachful glance her ever-loyal housekeeper-cum-confidante cast her.

'Oh, Lord, miss!' Bessie exclaimed, as she watched her young mistress deposit the gun and the fruits of her labours down upon the kitchen table. 'You've never been a'wandering over Blackwood land again? I've warned you time and again that there steward up at the Manor will have you placed afore the magistrate, given half a chance. Heard tell he weren't best pleased back along, when them there high-and-mighty legal folk came up from Lunnon, asking questions about the night of the murders, and he discovered it were you had stirred things up again after all these years.'

'No, I don't suppose he was pleased.' Not appearing in the least concerned, Isabel collected a sharp knife from a drawer and then promptly set herself the task of preparing the rabbits for the stew-pot. 'What's more, young Toby told me, this very morn as it happens, there's been no sign of Master Guy Fensham these past two weeks. Which I find most revealing in the circumstances. After all, what had he to fear if he told the truth about the happenings on that terrible night?'

'Well, that's just it, miss. He couldn't have done, now could he, if what the old master set down on paper be true? And I would far rather believe the old master, 'cause there were nought wrong with him at the time of writing.'

'Well, I, for one, never doubted the truth of Papa's version of events. As you quite rightly pointed out, he wrote his account before he suffered that first seizure.'

Whenever Isabel thought of her late father she experienced, still, an acute sense of loss, even now, after almost two years. They had always been wondrous close; more so after he had become infirm and had come to rely upon her for so much. Yet nothing in her expression betrayed the fact that she had nowhere near fully recovered from his death. If anything, she seemed quite matter-of-fact as she said,

'So you've no need to fear I shall fall foul of Fensham, especially as I didn't take one step on Blackwood land. I've been in the top meadow, as it happens. Besides...' she shrugged, emphasising her complete unconcern '...what would it matter if I had been trespassing? If and when his lordship does return, I shall make it perfectly plain that he owes me a deal more than the few fish I've removed from his trout stream for all the damage his overgrown ditch has done to my vegetable garden during his long absence. Why his father ever employed such a lazy ne'er-do-well as Guy Fensham as steward up at the Manor, I shall never know!'

Thoughtfully drying her hands on her apron, Bessie joined her young mistress at the table. 'Well, miss, no matter what folks may say about the old Viscount—and you'll find plenty hereabouts who never liked him—you'll never hear anyone say he neglected either the land or the Manor. When the old Lord Blackwood were alive the steward did his work, and toed the line.' She shook her head sadly. 'Now look at the place! It's a year and more since you went to Lunnon to seek out Mr Bathurst,' she reminded her mistress. 'And never a word since!'

'Now, that isn't strictly true,' Isabel corrected, striving to be fair. 'We've never been precisely kept abreast of developments, I'll agree. Even so, Mr Bathurst did take the trouble to send that one letter, confirming he'd set the wheels in motion, as it were, and thanking me once again for the trouble I'd taken in seeking him out personally in order to pass on Papa's written account. And he fully reimbursed me for all the expense of travelling to London and remaining there for those few days. He was most generous, in fact!'

Isabel cast a long, considering look at the large dresser that almost covered the entire wall opposite. 'How very fortunate it was that so many hereabouts recalled that it had been none other than Mr Bathurst himself who had sold this very property to my father, and had gone to London to study law. Fortunate, too, that so many remembered he and the Honourable Sebastian Blackwood had been upon the very best of terms in their youth. He was the ideal person for me to seek out and pass on what Papa had revealed about the Viscount's younger son.

'And you must remember,' Isabel continued, after a further few moments' consideration, 'Mr Bathurst was in something of a precarious position. Just how much of a hand he had in effecting his friend's escape from the authorities, after Sebastian Blackwood had been accused of murdering both his father and brother all those years ago, I can only speculate. All the same, for some considerable time Mr Bathurst has been a well-respected barrister, a veritable pillar of the community and a staunch upholder of the law. He would need to be circumspect and surely wouldn't wish his name to be too closely connected with a man who, as far as we know, is still accused of committing the atrocities.'

After listening intently to everything her young mistress had said, Bessie nodded her head in agreement. 'But do you know, Miss Isabel, long afore you found your father's papers about the happenings on that terrible night, I never for a moment thought young Master Sebastian had gone and done that wicked deed. And I weren't the only one who disbelieved it, neither. Now, I ain't saying he were a saint, 'cause he weren't. For a start, he were a devil for the ladies, young as he was. Not that I ever heard tell he got any round these parts into trouble—think he preferred painted doxies, or maybe those nearer his own class.

'Oh, but he were right handsome, so he were.' Bessie continued reminiscing, her plump cheeks suddenly aglow at some private thought. 'I can see him now—so tall, so proud, riding by on that fine horse of his. Why, he used to send my heart all of a-flutter, to be sure!'

'Get a hold of yourself, woman!' Isabel admonished lovingly. 'I remember him too. And I'll tell you plainly we're far beneath his touch. Why, he'd never give the likes of you and me a second glance!'

'Not me he wouldn't, that's for sure,' Bessie acknowledged a moment before a surge of loyalty, borne of an ever-increasing loving respect, prompted her to add, 'But you're quite another matter. Well, you would be, if you'd trouble yourself about your appearance once in a while,' she amended, frowning at her mistress's shabby, worn attire, and windswept chestnut locks, numerous strands of which had escaped the confining pins.

Isabel responded with a dismissive wave of one hand. 'I've better things to do than sit before a mirror for hours on end preening myself. I might have been born the daughter of a gentleman, and raised to be a lady, at least when dear Mama was alive, and had a hand in my upbringing, but even so I never was the sort to attract the attentions of any aristocratic gentleman, least of all one so high on the social ladder as the son of a viscount. And I've always had sense enough to realise it! I'm far too managing for a start. Besides...' she shrugged '...I'm not altogether sure I really wish to marry. I'm happy enough as I am, and I enjoy my independence. No, if and when Lord Blackwood does return to take his father's place up at the Manor, my only interest in him will be to see how long it takes him to improve the drainage on his land, and to improve, too, the lot of those unfortunate wretches who rely upon the estate for a living, not least of which, as you very well know, is poor old Bunting.'

At this Isabel became the recipient of a hard, determined look. 'Now, miss, the old butler up at the Manor be none of your concern. I know 'tis a sinful shame he weren't pensioned off years ago, and given one of the estate cottages promised to him by the old Lord Blackwood. I think it's wicked, too, that a man of his years should be alone up there in that great house, hardly seeing a soul. Why, if it hadn't been for you and the young curate visiting him so regular last winter, I swear the influenza would have taken him off.'

'You did your share of nursing too,' Isabel reminded her.

Bessie, however, steadfastly refused this time to be won over by the warmth of her mistress's lovely smile. 'I know I did. But that don't change matters. You simply can't afford to take on any more waifs and strays. You've too many folk depending on you as it is.

'And it's no earthly good you looking at me like that!' Bessie exclaimed, totally impervious to the reproachful glance cast in her direction. 'I know you feel grateful to Troake for all the care he took over your father during those last years. And there's no denying he worked well enough when the old master were alive. But even you can't deny he's become dreadful slow of late, not to mention a bad-tempered old demon. And then there's young Toby. Now I ain't saying the lad ain't worth his weight in gold,' Bessie went on, thereby successfully cutting off the protest her mistress had been about to utter. 'The boy's nothing less than a godsend, so he is, the way he repaired the barn roof last winter. But the wages you pay him could be put to better use.'

Bessie's brown eyes slid past her mistress to the large shaggy dog lying sprawled on the floor, close to the range. Before she could voice any condemnation of the hound, which had been saved from a watery grave in the millpond, and which had become totally devoted to the mistress of the house, his rescuer forestalled any criticism by announcing,

'Don't you dare say a word against him! I won't deny there is some justification in what you've said about both Troake and Toby Marsh. But I would never be without my darling Beau! Why, if it hadn't been for him the house would have been broken into on at least three occasions that we know of these past months. Furthermore, but for him, we wouldn't be having rabbit stew for supper. He managed to root out half a dozen in the top meadow.'

Bessie, ever sharp, wasn't slow to pounce upon this interesting snippet. 'In that case, where be the other two?'

Isabel had the grace to look a little shamefaced in view of what had been mentioned already. 'I let Toby take them home to his mother.'

Bessie cast a despairing glance up at the ceiling. 'Now, why doesn't that surprise me none, I wonder! I don't suppose you took a moment to consider we've an extra mouth to feed, now that young cousin of yours has taken refuge in the house. Now, I ain't saying you shouldn't have taken her in the way you did, she being the only child of your papa's dear sister, and the only

close kin you've left in the world that's ever had any
dealings with you. And there's no denying she, too, be
worth her weight in gold,' she hurriedly conceded. 'I do
declare the house has never looked so clean and tidy for
many a long year. I defy anyone to find a speck of dust
about the place! And sew…? I've never known anyone
set a neater stitch than Miss Clara, not even your sainted
mother. It's a pleasure to show folk into the front parlour
nowadays, what with the new curtains, and all.'

It was clear that Bessie was at least a staunch sup-
porter of the young woman who had surprisingly turned
up on the doorstep late one evening a month before,
almost begging sanctuary. Isabel hadn't recognised the
beautiful stranger as the young cousin she had seen only
a few times in her life, and then many years ago, when
her aunt and cousin had paid the occasional visit to
London. None the less, she hadn't doubted her authenticity. Nor did she regret for a moment the decision she
had made to help her hapless relation, who had been
fleeing from a forced union with a man old enough to
be her father. All the same, she couldn't help feeling that
her act of kindness might bring trouble in the future.

She tried not to dwell on this uncomfortable possibility as she enquired into the whereabouts of her relative,
and by so doing gave rise to a look of comical dismay
in her ever-faithful companion.

'The young curate were round here again, bright and
early this morning, with a few more newspapers from
up at the vicarage. It's good of him, I suppose. But it do
put queer notions into your cousin's head. Now, I ain't
saying Miss Clara ain't in the right of it not wishing to
be a burden on you,' Bessie went on, somehow manag-

ing to preserve a serious countenance. 'But what wife and mother in her right mind would ever employ such a beautiful girl as a governess? She seems to suppose someone will, though, and begged a lift with the local carrier into Merryfield so that she might visit the sorting office with her reply to an advertisement she spotted in one of them there journals.'

Smiling wryly, Isabel shook her head. 'Yes, you're right. Clara has the sweetest of dispositions. She's hard-working, can set a stitch better than most, and she is far from dull-witted. Sadly, though, she isn't very worldly.'

She was suddenly thoughtful. 'I just hope she doesn't come to regret this determination of hers to find employment. I cannot help but feel that the fewer people who know her present whereabouts the safer it will be for her. Should her stepmother discover where she is, I'm not altogether sure I could prevent her from removing Clara from under this roof.'

The application of the front-door knocker success-fully brought an end to the conversation. The house-keeper made to rise from the table, but Isabel forestalled her by saying she herself would go. Although mistress of the house, she had never been too proud to answer her own front door, should the need arise.

Consequently, as soon as she had washed her hands, removed her soiled apron and made herself reasonably presentable by repositioning a few wayward strands of hair, she went along the passageway to discover a man of below-average height awaiting her on the other side of the solid oak barrier.

Everything about him suggested a professional man, so Isabel wasn't in the least surprised to have a business card thrust into her hand bearing the names of Crabtree, Crabtree and Goodbody, a firm of lawyers based in the metropolis.

'And you are?' Isabel enquired, her great fear that he might have come in connection with her cousin Clara's present whereabouts diminishing somewhat by the fact that the notary was flanked by two young children. By their clear resemblance to each other, Isabel felt they must surely be brother and sister.

'Mr Goodbody, ma'am,' he answered promptly, doffing his hat, whilst all time favouring her with a scrutiny that was no less assessing than her own had been. Evidently he had decided that, although not in the least stylishly attired, she bore all the other characteristics of a young woman of refinement, for he added, 'Would I be correct in assuming I have the pleasure in addressing Miss Mortimer, daughter of the late Dr John Mortimer?'

Isabel would have been the first to admit that she had been reared to conduct herself in a genteel manner, at least for as long as others had had an influence on her behaviour. Years of increasing responsibilities had tended, however, to persuade her to disregard social niceties, and adopt a more forthright approach when dealing with her fellow man. Some, it had to be said, found her abrupt almost to the point of rudeness, whilst others considered her no-nonsense approach commendable.

Seemingly Mr Goodbody fell into this latter category, for he betrayed not a modicum of disquiet when she demanded to know precisely why he had called, and answered promptly with, 'I am here at the behest of the present Lord Blackwood, ma'am.'

Although intrigued, and quite naturally interested to discover the seventh Viscount Blackwood's present whereabouts, Isabel couldn't help experiencing a feeling of disquiet where the two children were concerned. She could detect no resemblance whatsoever to the dapper little lawyer, which instantly begged the question of whose children they were. An alarming possibility instantly sprang to mind. None the less, although renowned for her no-nonsense manner, she was also known for her innate acts of kindness. The little girl, clearly weary and afraid, clung to the older child like a limpet, instantly rousing Isabel's sympathy.

'In that case, sir, you'd best bring the children into the house, and we'll discuss the matter which has brought you here in the comfort of the front parlour.'

Bessie had not exaggerated about the transformation that had taken place since Clara's arrival in the house. Tirelessly she had worked on making new curtains. She'd repaired all the upholstery where she could, and had even taken the trouble to embroider new covers and cushions to place over those worn areas that had been beyond her skill to repair. Clearly Mr Goodbody was favourably impressed, for he cast an admiring glance about him the instant he entered the largest room in the house.

After settling the two children on the sofa, and furnishing the lawyer with a glass of Madeira, Isabel once again asked for an explanation for the visit, adding, 'And would I be correct in assuming that his lordship's whereabouts is no longer a mystery, and he is presently in the country?'

All at once the little man's expression became guarded. 'I'm afraid I am not in a position to divulge his lordship's current whereabouts, Miss Mortimer. All I am able to reveal is that a successful outcome to the enquiries regarding past—er—unfortunate happenings will not be long delayed now. In the meantime, his lordship feels himself unable to take up his responsibilities with regard to these two young persons.'

There wasn't so much as a flicker of compassion in the glance Isabel cast the children this time, before fixing the notary with a haughty stare. 'And what, pray, has that to do with me, sir?' she enquired in a voice that would have frozen the village pond on the warmest summer's day. 'His lordship's private domestic arrangements are entirely his own affair.'

'Indeed, yes, Miss Mortimer,' he readily concurred, having seemingly realised in which directions her thoughts were leading. 'Perhaps if you were to read his lordship's letter first,' he added, delving into the leather bag he had carried into the house. 'It might set your mind at rest on certain matters.'

Still very much on her guard, Isabel, with some reluctance, took the missive from the notary's outstretched hand, and broke the seal to read:

My dear Miss Mortimer,
I am fully cognisant of the debt of gratitude I already owe you, and the charge I would settle upon you now. Believe me when I tell you the decision to place my wards into your care was

not taken without a deal of consideration, and I
can only trust to your forbearance in this matter.

The estimable Mr Goodbody is in a position to
answer any questions you might have with regard
to my wards, and has been instructed to reimburse
you in advance for the expenses you will undoubtedly incur whilst the children are in your care. If,
however, you feel unable to burden yourself with
the responsibilities of a surrogate guardian, I shall
perfectly understand.

And will have the honour to remain,

Your obedient servant,

Blackwood

Although there was a certain familiarity in the tone
of the missive, Isabel couldn't find it within herself to
be offended. At least it had vanquished the idea that she
was being asked to care for the Viscount's by-blows!

After reading the letter through again, she raised her
eyes. 'So these children are Lord Blackwood's wards.'

'Indeed, they are, ma'am,' the lawyer duly confirmed, before instructing the boy to stand and make
his bow. 'This is Master Joshua Collier, who has recently celebrated his ninth birthday, and his young sister,
Alice, who is six.'

Isabel, having had little experience of children, was
at a loss to know what to say to the siblings to put them
at their ease, while she considered more fully the errant
Viscount's request. The boy stared back at her now with
an almost defiant gleam in his dark eyes, as though he
was more than ready to challenge any authority she
might in the future attempt to exert over him, while his

little sister merely stared, awestruck, as though she were looking at a being from another world. Fortunately the slightly embarrassing silence was brought to an end by Isabel's cousin unexpectedly entering the room.

'Oh, I'm so sorry. Bessie quite failed to mention you had visitors.'

'No need to apologise,' Isabel assured her. 'Your arrival is most timely.'

She was now quite accustomed to the effect her strikingly lovely cousin always had on members of the opposite sex, most especially those who came face to face with her for the very first time. And Mr Goodbody was no exception! Although he refrained from gaping, there was no mistaking the look of appreciation he cast the stunningly lovely girl who glided towards him in order to clasp his outstretched hand.

Few gentlemen, Isabel suspected, would be proof against such wide, brilliant blue eyes, and the sweetest of smiles, set in a heart-shaped face. It was a countenance truly without flaw, and crowned with the brightest of guinea-gold curls.

'Would you be good enough to take Master Joshua and his sister into the kitchen and provide them with something suitable to eat and drink, Clara? I'm sure they must be hungry after their journey.'

'Of course,' she obligingly replied, holding out her hand to the little girl who, after a moment's hesitation, seemingly decided she would be happy to go with the pretty lady with the kindly smile. Her brother, evidently less impressed by Clara's physical attributes, frowned dourly up at her before following them from the room, the prospect of plum cake and apple tart seemingly having won the day.

'Now that we are able to discuss the matter more freely, Mr Goodbody,' Isabel began, the instant they were alone, 'perhaps you would be good enough to enlighten me as to why his lordship felt himself unable to place the children with a relative or friend? After all, I am neither. His lordship and I have never exchanged so much as a pleasantry.'

'And that, I strongly suspect, is one of the main reasons why he chose you above anyone else.' Frowning, the lawyer considered more fully for a moment. 'Given what you have unselfishly done on his behalf, his lordship must be satisfied as to your integrity. Naturally, he has the children's best interests at heart. Until such time as he is able to undertake the duties of his guardianship, he wishes his wards kept well away from their uncle's sphere—their late mother's brother, that is.'

'Does his lordship believe the children's uncle means them harm?'

'I shall be diplomatic here, Miss Mortimer,' he responded after a further moment's consideration, 'and say that neither his lordship nor myself believe the gentleman to be in the least trustworthy. He resided with his sister throughout the last year of her life, during which time certain irregularities came to light with regard to her finances. One can only speculate as to why so many large sums were withdrawn from her bank during this period. Furthermore a letter, supposedly written by the children's mother, unexpectedly came to light shortly after her death. In it she requested an adjustment to her will, naming her brother sole guardian to her children, and sole beneficiary in the event of their deaths, giving the reason for the changes as a staunch belief that the present Lord Blackwood would be an unfit guardian. I am now in possession of certain letters written over the years by Sarah Collier to his lordship, the last one penned no more than three months ago, that clearly refute this. Therefore, it is my belief that either pressure was brought to bear upon the lady, when she was not in full possession of her faculties, to make adjustments to her will, or the letter is a complete forgery. I strongly suspect the latter.'

'There was nothing suspicious about her death, though, surely?' Isabel asked gently.

'Nothing whatsoever, Miss Mortimer,' he assured her. 'She died of typhus.'

Isabel was far from sure that she wished to burden herself with the responsibilities of caring for two recently orphaned children. After all, what would happen if the uncle should happen to come to Northamptonshire in search of his niece and nephew?

'I think that most unlikely, Miss Mortimer,' the lawyer assured her, after she'd voiced this fear aloud. 'The uncle, Mr Danforth, is completely unaware of his lordship's present whereabouts. If he chose to make enquiries, all he would discover is that the Manor and his lordship's town house are still unoccupied, as they have been for more than eight years, save for one reliable servant in each. Furthermore, Danforth knows I removed the children from their home. I know for a fact that my own house has been watched during this past week. I strongly suspect that he believes, you see, I have the children safely hidden in London. By the time he has exhausted every possibility, and I have several sisters residing in the metropolis, it is fervently hoped that his lordship will have been cleared of all charges against him, and I myself shall have proved beyond doubt that Sarah Collier's supposed adjustment to her will is entirely fraudulent.

'But until such time, and if you are agreeable,' he went on, when all Isabel did was to stare at him in thoughtful silence, still unsure what she should do, 'his lordship has instructed me to give you this, in advance, in the hope that you will accept the responsibility he would place upon you.'

Delving into his bag once again, he drew out a bulging leather purse, which he promptly deposited on the low table between them. Isabel could only speculate on how much it contained. None the less, she suspected it held a considerable sum, perhaps more than she'd seen at any one time in her entire life.

'His lordship will ensure that a draft on his bank is sent to you at the beginning of each month, until such time as he is able to make alternative arrangements. He wishes the children to be as little trouble to you as possible, and therefore requests that a governess be engaged, and any other help you deem necessary. I had no time to engage a suitable person, but if you are happy to accept the responsibility, I shall gladly do so on my return to London.'

'No, there's no need for you to trouble yourself, sir,' she countered. 'I happen to know of the very person.'

'Do I infer correctly from that, Miss Mortimer, that you are agreeable to his lordship's request?'

'Yes, sir, you may be sure I am.' The bulging purse on the table having comprehensively silenced the voice of doubt.

Although Clara had little difficulty in winning the trust and affection of little Alice Collier, her stronger-willed brother proved a different matter entirely. As Isabel had suspected, young Joshua had little appreciation of Clara's beauty and, as things turned out, he wasn't above taking wicked advantage of her innate good nature either.

On several occasions during those first weeks, Isabel was called upon to restore order to the upstairs chamber that functioned as a schoolroom-cum-nursery. Which she did in a swift and very effective fashion. Whether it was because she would tolerate no nonsense, or the fact that she was happy to take him along with her whenever she went out hunting or fishing that quickly won the boy's respect was difficult to judge. Notwithstanding, by the time autumn gave way to winter, it was clear to all at the farmhouse that Master Joshua Collier had grown inordinately fond of the mistress of the house.

Naturally, having a young boy and girl residing under the roof resulted in a much more relaxed and cheerful atmosphere about the place. Bessie, however, considered there was more to it than just having two very contented children round the house.

The prompt payments sent by Mr Goodbody early each month had brought about numerous beneficial changes. Clara's employment as governess had resulted in her feeling a deal happier knowing she was able to contribute something towards household expenses.

The extra money had meant that items, once considered unnecessary luxuries, had been purchased, making life at the farmhouse so very much easier and agreeable. Most gratifying of all, as far as Bessie was concerned, was the non-appearance of those troubled frowns over financial matters that had from time to time creased her young mistress's intelligent brow during recent years, whenever money for large bills had needed to be found.

Although he made no attempt to return to the farmhouse to see how the children fared, Mr Goodbody never failed to enquire after their welfare in the accompanying letter he always forwarded with the promissory note; Isabel duly replied, attesting to their continued well-being, and assumed he must surely pass these assurances on to the children's guardian.

Of his lordship himself, however, Isabel saw and heard nothing; until, that is, the arrival of Mr Goodbody's December letter, wherein he apprised her of the fact that the seventh Viscount Blackwood had finally been cleared of all charges against him, and was now at liberty to take up his rightful place at the ancestral home.

Isabel received this news with decidedly mixed feelings. On the one hand she knew it would greatly benefit many in the local community to have the Manor inhabited again; on the other, she would miss the children, most especially Josh. She was honest enough to admit, too, that she would miss the generous payments she had received over the past months for taking care of the orphans.

The New Year arrived with still no sign of the Viscount. Nevertheless, it was common knowledge that an army of local tradesmen had been hired to work in the Manor. So it stood to reason that Lord Blackwood was planning to take up residence at some point in the near future.

An unusually dry January gave way to a damp and dismal February, and brought with it no further news of his lordship. Then, in the middle of the month, an unexpected cold spell struck the county, making travel virtually impossible, even the shortest journeys, for several days. The vast majority of people, of course, were glad when at last the thaw set in, and they could go about their daily business unhindered; but not so Josh and Alice, who returned to the farmhouse with their governess, looking most disgruntled.

'My snowman's dying,' Alice lamented, close to tears.

Both Isabel and Bessie, who were busily preparing the luncheon, tried to appear suitably sympathetic, unlike Alice's brother, who was far more matter-of-fact about it all.

'He's not dying, you goose!' Josh admonished. 'He's just melting. Snowmen aren't alive, are they, Miss Isabel?'

She was spared the need to respond by Beau's timely intervention. He had risen immediately the children had entered the kitchen, and was now receiving his customary pats and strokes.

It never ceased to amaze Isabel how differently the hound behaved towards the children nowadays. When they had first arrived at the farmhouse, it had to be said that he hadn't been at all enthusiastic and had growled at them both whenever they had attempted to venture too close.

Quite understandable in the circumstances when one considered his life had very nearly been terminated by a group of village urchins, she mused. It hadn't taken Beau very long, though, she reminded herself, while continuing to watch the by-play, to realise that children divided into two distinct factions—those who would cruelly tie a brick round his neck and hurl him in a pond; and those who offered tasty treats, and threw sticks in lively games.

Beau, now, was quite happy to accompany Josh and Alice whenever they went out to get some exercise under the watchful eye of their governess. More often than not, though, he would return in search of the mistress of the house, if she failed to put in an appearance after a short time.

'Come, children, let's go back upstairs to the school-room,' Clara announced in her usual gentle way, making it sound more like a request than a command. 'We've time enough, before luncheon is ready, to finish reading the story we began earlier.'

Both children obediently rose to their feet, and were about to accompany their governess, when there was an imperious rat-tat-tat on the kitchen door.

It wasn't unusual for callers to use the rear entrance. More often than not it was the young lad whom Isabel employed to help her about the place seeking instructions on what work needed to be done. Toby Marsh had quickly become a firm favourite with Josh, who rushed across the kitchen to answer the summons, only to discover a forbidding-looking female standing there, dressed from head to toe in sombre black, accompanied by an equally unprepossessing gentleman, standing directly behind her.

Confronted by two such daunting strangers, Josh quite naturally fell back a pace or two, as did his governess, who also let out a tiny whimper, which not only captured Isabel's attention, but also that of the unexpected female caller.

'So there you are, you wicked, ungrateful gel!' the visitor exclaimed, striding, quite uninvited, into the kitchen, with much rustling of wide bombazine skirts.

Although Isabel had never seen the middle-aged matron in her life before, her cousin's suddenly ashen complexion and wide terrified eyes, as she fell back against the wall, gave her a fairly shrewd notion of who the harridan must surely be. Unless she was much mistaken, this was Clara's stepmama, the woman her cousin's loving father had married in the hope of replacing his beloved first wife. Well, it might have been beneficial for the late James Pentecost to remarry, but from things Clara had revealed during recent months her lot had not been improved by her late father's second marriage, and the arrival in the family home of a selfish stepsister.

After calmly wiping her floured hands on her apron, Isabel placed herself squarely between her cowering cousin and the woman who was causing her young relative such distress. Evidently her resentment at having her home invaded by two complete strangers had conveyed itself to her faithful hound. Beau's hackles rose as he let out a low, threatening growl, which had the effect of bringing the fleshy-faced man to a stop, as he made to follow into the kitchen, and even induced his equally unwelcome companion to retreat a pace or two.

'My name is Isabel Mortimer, Clara's cousin and mistress of this house,' she said, managing to convey a calmness she was far from feeling.

Although she detected the sound of the front door-knocker being applied, Isabel considered she had more than enough to cope with at the present time without becoming sidetracked by a further caller, and so ignored the summons, as she turned to her cousin.

'Would I be correct in assuming this female, who has dared to invade my home without the common courtesy of at least introducing herself first, is none other than your stepmama?'

'Yes, I am Euphemia Pentecost,' the woman responded, when all her stepdaughter did was to nod dumbly, and stare at her strong-willed cousin in awestruck silence for daring to remind such a formidable matron of basic good manners.

If Mrs Pentecost had been slightly taken aback, her discomfiture was not long lasting. 'If I seem rude, miss, then I apologise!' she snapped, sounding anything but chastened. 'But let me tell you I have been sorely tried these past months in attempting to trace this wicked, ungrateful gel, who left her loving home without so much as a word to anyone!'

She gestured towards her companion who, keeping a wary eye on Beau, had been attempting to edge ever closer to her. 'And poor Mr Sloane, here, has been almost out of his mind with worry over his fiancée's well-being.'

'Really?' Isabel raised her finely arching brows in

mock surprise as she studied the fleshy-faced gentleman closely for the first time, noticing in particular the
lack of neck and wide, thick-lipped mouth. 'Now, that is
most interesting, because I have been led to believe that
my cousin flatly refused to marry Mr Sloane, and that
she was obliged to flee the family home because of the
pressure being brought to bear upon her by you to form
the union, ma'am,' Isabel countered, the accusing note
in her voice all too evident. 'Which begs the question,
does it not, of who is speaking the truth?'

Having seemingly appreciated already that she was
having to deal with a young woman of character and
determination, the antithesis of her stepdaughter, in fact,
the widow adopted a different tack, becoming nauseat-
ingly apologetic and ingratiating as she bemoaned her
widowed state, and the extra burdens placed upon her
since her husband's demise.

'Believe me when I tell you, Miss Mortimer, it is
my one cherished wish to do everything humanly possible to ensure my stepdaughter's future happiness,'
she continued in the same fawning tone, 'and I would
be failing in my duty if I didn't attempt to arrange the
best possible match for dear Clara. I'm sure a sensible
young woman like yourself must appreciate that it is
much better to marry an upright gentleman of property,
like Mr Sloane here, who can offer a future wife most
every creature comfort in life, than to retain foolish,
girlish dreams of meeting a dashing knight in shining
armour whose interest would very soon wane.'

'I couldn't agree more, ma'am,' Isabel quickly intervened before the widow could develop the theme. 'But
that doesn't alter the fact that Clara doesn't wish to

marry Mr Sloane. Nor, indeed, any profligate in armour,
as far as I'm aware. Let me assure you that she is more
than happy to make her own way in the world, and not
be a burden on you any longer, by engaging in a genteel
occupation.'

Hard-eyed and tight-lipped, the widow transferred
her gaze to her stepdaughter. 'I am fully aware of it,' she
unlocked her nutcracker mouth to acknowledge, thereby
clearly heralding the return to her former inflexible
stance. 'How do you suppose we managed to locate
your whereabouts, you foolish girl! The gentleman
with whom you attempted to attain employment several
months ago just happened to read the notice we were
eventually obliged to place in the newspapers regarding
your disappearance and, recalling the name, wrote to
Mr Sloane, providing us with this address.'

She looked her stepdaughter up and down, the
contempt in her eyes all too discernible. 'Governess,
indeed! Who would ever employ you as a governess?'

'It might surprise you to learn, ma'am, that somebody
already has,' Isabel informed her, experiencing untold
delight, before she turned to her cousin, who was holding a now, tearful Alice to her skirts. 'If you have no
desire to accompany these persons back to Hampshire,
Clara, perhaps you would be good enough to return to
the schoolroom with your charges.'

'You stay precisely where you are!' the widow
instantly countered as Clara made to leave the kitchen.
'Until you attain your majority, my girl, you remain
under my control, and you will do precisely as I tell
you.'

Whether this was true or not did not alter Isabel's

resolve to protect her cousin at all costs from such a harridan. Very slowly she moved across the kitchen and, by dint of using a low stool, was able to reach up far enough to remove the pistol that she always kept ready for immediate use on top of the dresser, much to Josh's evident astonishment.

'No, you didn't know I had this, did you, Josh? I keep it primed and ready for just such an unfortunate occurrence as this.' Smile fading, Isabel turned to face her unwelcome visitors again. 'You shall both leave my house at once, otherwise I shan't hesitate to use this.'

Even the case-hardened widow fell back a further pace or two when the pistol was levelled in a surprisingly steady hand. 'You've not heard the last of this, young woman,' she threatened in return, though keeping a wary eye on the firearm. 'You may force us to leave now, but we shall be back with the constable, you mark my words!'

'Spill her claret, Miss Isabel,' Josh urged with bloodthirsty delight.

A moment's silence followed, then, 'I sincerely trust you will refrain from doing any such thing, my dear young woman,' a softly spoken voice from the doorway strongly advised.

Chapter Two

Apart from his superior height and faintly haughty bearing, Isabel could detect no resemblance whatsoever to the handsome young aristocrat whom she had glimpsed all those years ago riding by on a fine bay horse. Yet instinctively she knew that the elegantly attired gentleman framed in the doorway was none other than the late Viscount Blackwood's younger son, home at last to claim his inheritance and take his rightful place up at the Manor.

His unexpected arrival had an immediate effect upon all those present. Silence reigned as all eyes turned on the distinguished gentleman who came sauntering languidly into the kitchen, removing his gloves as he did so. Out of the corner of her eye Isabel saw Bessie check in the act of reaching for the rolling pin, which undoubtedly her trusty housekeeper had intended brandishing as a weapon. Surprisingly, even Beau ceased his growling to turn his head on one side to study the new arrival, and Isabel found herself automatically lowering the pistol on to the table, somehow sensing that its use now would not be necessary.

She continued unashamedly to study him intently as his ice-blue eyes, betraying no emotion whatsoever, flickered briefly over the two unwelcome visitors. Even when he turned his head to study her cousin, still clutching the little girl to her skirts, incredibly there was nothing to suggest that he was possibly viewing one of the most beautiful females he had ever seen in his life. Only when his eyes finally came to rest upon her was there a suggestion of a slight thaw in those cool, strikingly blue depths a moment before he whipped off his hat to reveal a thick, healthy crop of perfectly arranged black locks.

'My name is Blackwood,' he announced in deeply rich cultured tones.

'Yes, I rather thought you must be,' Isabel returned candidly, as she felt Josh press against her. Instinctively she raised her left arm to place it reassuringly about the boy's shoulders, and surprisingly glimpsed what she felt sure was the faintest of twitches at the corner of the Viscount's thin-lipped mouth.

'Would I be correct in assuming that at last I have the felicity of making the acquaintance of Miss Isabel Mortimer, daughter of the late Dr John Mortimer?'

'Indeed you would, sir,' she answered, reaching for the hand that was extended to her. She felt it close briefly round her own, warm and comforting. Since his arrival she felt as if she had experienced the whole gamut of emotions. Foremost now was a sense of relief, and an overwhelming belief that this impressive aristocrat would offer assistance if she had the gall to request it of him on so slight an acquaintance. But dared she…?

'And your arrival, my lord, is most opportune,' she told him, before she experienced any second thoughts. 'Just prior to your own welcome appearance, my home was invaded by these two persons who are intent upon removing my cousin from under this roof… My cousin who just happens to be in your employ as governess to your wards, sir,' she finished artfully.

But would the gambit work? Study him though she did, she could detect no change in his expression, not so much as a suggestion of sympathy in his eyes before they turned from her to the boy still clasped against her, and then flickered briefly in the direction of his younger ward.

'Indeed?' he said at last in a tone that hovered so perilously close to boredom that Isabel was almost obliged to accept that her audacious attempt to attain his support must surely have failed, when assistance came from a most unexpected quarter.

'And I shall take leave to inform you, sir, that I have every right to do so!' Mrs Pentecost announced boldly.

Instantly his lordship's expression changed. He stared down his long aristocratic nose at the widow, a contemptuous curl to his lip. 'If I evince any desire to converse with you, madam, you will be under no illusions about it.'

Even the case-hardened widow was not proof against such a superb put-down, and automatically closed her unpleasant mouth as she retreated a pace or two.

His lordship's gaze again returned to Isabel. The contempt had vanished completely from his expression, though just what had replaced it was impossible to judge.

'You have no reason to doubt the authenticity of this person?'

'No, my lord,' she responded promptly, while dropping her arm from about Josh's shoulders, as though to convey to the boy that he need have no fear of the tall man standing before them. 'I have no doubt that she is indeed my cousin's stepmama. What I do challenge is her right to remove my relative from under this roof. Miss Pentecost was obliged to flee the family home because she was being coerced into marriage with this person.'

If Isabel's look of disdain was nowhere near as accomplished as his lordship's had been a short time earlier, Mr Sloane was left in no doubt about what she thought of him personally. 'Any man who resorts to coercion in order to attain a wife is beyond contempt. My cousin came here desperately seeking my help, not looking for charity, my lord,' she assured him, gazing earnestly up at him once more. 'She is more than prepared to earn her own living and make her own way in the world. Surely she should be allowed to do that?'

'Perhaps,' was all he said before turning to the widow and her companion, who had gone very red about the jowls since Isabel's condemnation of his conduct.

'I shall obtain your direction, madam, from Miss Pentecost, and you shall be hearing from my lawyers in due course. No, be silent!' he commanded, holding up one shapely hand against the protest the widow had been about to utter. 'If it should come to light that you are indeed legally responsible for Miss Pentecost, be assured she will be safely returned to your home at my expense. If, however, I discover that, for whatever reason, you have been attempting to exceed your authority, then you may be sure I shall take matters a good deal further should Miss Pentecost request me to do so. In the meantime, you have my assurance that your stepdaughter will receive my protection for as long as she remains in my employ.

'Now, if Miss Mortimer has nothing further she wishes to say to you, you may leave,' he continued curtly. 'I have matters I wish to discuss with her in private.'

After being so summarily dismissed, not even the hardened widow dared to utter anything further. Isabel watched them closely before they finally departed and thought she could detect a troubled look in Mr Sloane's eyes, even if the widow's remained hard and defiant.

Lord Blackwood waited only for the housekeeper to close the door behind them before turning once again to Isabel. 'Clearly I have not chosen the most auspicious of occasions to become acquainted with you, Miss Mortimer,' he announced, a ghost of a smile hanging about his mouth as he uttered this gross understatement. 'So I shall call again tomorrow, if I may—say, at eleven, when I shall hope to spend a little time with my wards and discuss certain matters with Miss Pentecost.'

'I assure you, my lord, that will be most convenient,' Isabel answered for her cousin, who seemed to have lost the power of speech since her stepmother's unexpected appearance. 'Please allow me to show you out.'

Isabel's final farewell was not protracted, as she too needed time to reflect on the unfortunate happenings of the morning. After closing the front door behind the distinguished visitor, she headed for the kitchen once more, pausing briefly as she did so before the large mirror in the passageway.

'Why on earth didn't you tell me I look such a fright, Bessie! she exclaimed the instant she had returned to the others. 'Not only is half my hair dangling about my ears, I'd flour on the end of my nose!'

Bessie almost found herself gaping. In all the dozen or so long years she had known her young mistress, not once had she ever heard her voice the slightest concern over her appearance. Furthermore, she very much doubted the first two callers were behind this surprising show of disquiet over grooming.

'Chances are he never noticed,' she returned above Josh and his sister's impish chuckles. For all the effect the assurance had, however, she might well have saved her breath.

'Not noticed…?' Isabel was momentarily lost for words. 'Lord, Bessie! Where have your wits gone begging? I've no notion where or what Lord Blackwood has been doing in recent years. But by the look of him I'll lay odds he hasn't been enjoying life's luxuries. What's more, I'd wager those blue eyes of his miss nothing!'

Isabel's assessment was remarkably accurate. As it happened his lordship hadn't enjoyed a comfortable existence during the past half-decade or so out in the Peninsula, spying for Wellington. Working mostly alone, he had needed his wits about him at all times, and had become intensely observant as a consequence.

Determined to discover the answers to several puzzling questions, Lord Blackwood returned directly to the Manor, and sent for his aged butler, the person he considered most able to satisfy his curiosity over certain matters.

He awaited his arrival in the library, which had been the first room in the house to be redecorated in readiness for his eventual return. Although age-old tomes still completely lined the shelves on two of the walls, everything else was new. His lordship had even ordered the painting of a hunting scene, which had graced the area above the hearth for many a long year, removed and replaced with one of his adored mother resting her arm about the shoulders of a handsome boy with jet-black locks and strikingly blue eyes. The pose instantly conjured up a much more recent memory, and his lordship smiled to himself as he poured a glass of wine.

The door behind him opened, and he turned to see his aged butler, who had now officially retired and was remaining at the Manor only until such time as his promised cottage on the estate was ready for habitation. Knowing Bunting was a rigid upholder of the old order, whereby a servant knew his place and never attempted to get on a more familiar footing with his master, his lordship neither offered him a glass of wine, nor the chance to rest his aching joints in the comfort of one of the easy chairs. Any such consideration, he felt sure, would have made the retired major-domo feel distinctly ill at ease, and therefore very likely less forthcoming with information.

Consequently, maintaining the status quo, Lord Blackwood took up a stance before the fire, and rested one arm along the mantelshelf. Outwardly he appeared completely at ease in his surroundings, every inch the relaxed, aristocratic master of the fine Restoration mansion, even though he had utterly loathed his ancestral home as a youth.

'I recall, Bunting, shortly after my long-awaited return here yesterday, you mentioning that you are acquainted with Miss Mortimer,' he said, getting straight to the point of the interview. 'Naturally, I'm curious about her. Not only was she instrumental in clearing my name, but also, as you may possibly be aware, she has been responsible for my wards these past months.'

'Although Miss Mortimer didn't make the children's true identities commonly known, sir, she did confide in me,' the aged butler confirmed, before frowning slightly. 'I believe the children have been happy enough living with her, sir,' he then added, having quickly decided that this must surely be what his master wished to know. 'At least I've not heard anything to the contrary. She brought them up to the house a few weeks back, and asked me to show them round, as it would be their home sooner or later. She wouldn't look round herself, sir. Not one to take liberties, Miss Mortimer isn't. Never known her attempt to venture any further than the kitchen and my rooms on the ground floor, sir, in all the times she came up to the Manor last winter, when I was poorly. If it hadn't been for Miss Isabel and that housekeeper of hers, I think the good Lord would have taken me. She's an angel, sir, that's what she is…an angel!'

His lordship could not forbear a smile as his mind's eye conjured up a clear image of the so-called angel brandishing a serviceable pistol in her right hand. And appearing as if she was more than capable of using it too!

'Evidently a lady of many contrasting talents,' he murmured, though loud enough for the butler to hear.

'Well, sir, the poor young lady was obliged to manage for herself from quite a young age. Seem to remember she lost her mother a year or so after the family moved into the house, sir,' he revealed, falling into a reminiscing mood. He cast his master an uncertain glance. 'Then, not long after the terrible happenings here, the good doctor took bad, and poor Miss Mortimer, little more than a slip of a girl herself at the time, was obliged to care for him.' He shook his head. 'She's not had an easy life, sir. Maybe if her mother had lived, she might have met and married some nice young gentleman by now. But as things turned out…'

His lordship had little difficulty in conjuring up an image of a face boasting more character than beauty; of a pair of large grey-green eyes whose direct gaze some might consider faintly immodest, of a determined little chin above which a perfectly shaped, if slightly overgenerous, mouth betrayed a lively sense of humour, even when confronted by adversity. When compared to her beautiful young cousin, she did perhaps pale into insignificance. Yet it was strange that it was the face framed in the disordered chestnut locks that should be more firmly imprinted in his memory.

And yet not so strange, he countered silently. After all, he owed that young woman a great deal, perhaps more than he might ever be able to repay. He felt a sudden stab of irritation. That didn't alter the fact, though, it had been grossly impertinent of her, not to say outrageous, to have embroiled him in an affair that had absolutely nothing whatsoever to do with him. Had it been anyone else he might well have just walked away and left her to her own devices. Yet he had found he could not withstand the look of entreaty in those large eyes of hers.

He shook his head, wondering at himself. 'I must be getting old,' he murmured.

'Beg pardon, sir?'

'Nothing, Bunting, merely thinking aloud.' He fortified himself from the contents of his glass whilst he gathered his thoughts and focused on what he wished to know. 'Now, the cousin who's living with Miss Mortimer has been acting as governess to my wards, so I understand. The girl, Alice, seems to have become quite attached to her.'

'That wouldn't surprise me, my lord, though I couldn't say for sure,' the aged servant responded, scrupulously truthful as always. 'I've only ever met the young lady once, and then only briefly. But she seemed a very gentle-mannered young woman. What I can tell you, sir, is the boy is very fond of Miss Isabel. Why, I've seen her time and again striding across the park towards the home wood, Master Joshua skipping happily alongside, and that great dog of hers not too far behind.

'Not that I think they were up to no good, my lord,' he hurriedly added, suddenly realising he may have revealed more than he should have done.

The Viscount, however, merely smiled to himself before dismissing the servant with a nod.

* * *

The following morning Isabel spent far more time over her appearance than she had ever been known to do before, a circumstance that certainly didn't escape the keen eye of the housekeeper, when her young mistress finally came down to the kitchen shortly before eleven.

The new gown her cousin had made for her suited her wonderfully well, emphasising the perfection of a slender, shapely figure, the colour enhancing the green flecks in her large eyes. Around her shoulders she had draped one of her late mother's fringed shawls, a stylish accessory she rarely donned, and her radiant, dark locks, although not artistically arranged, were for once neatly confined in a simple chignon.

Bessie almost found herself gaping at the transformation. Although it couldn't be denied that in looks she was a mere shadow of her beautiful cousin, few would deny that she was a fine-looking young woman in her own right, and one who never failed to make a lasting impression on more discerning souls.

Bessie might have been slightly concerned, though, about the obvious attempts to impress had she not been very sure her young mistress had a sensible head on her shoulders, and had made every effort for the most selfless reasons. Unless Bessie very much mistook the matter, there was no thought to attract the aristocratic gentleman's interest, merely a desire for all members of the household to appear in a more favourable light.

As the application of the door-knocker filtered through to the kitchen, Bessie made to break off from her task in order to answer the summons, but was forestalled by her young mistress who insisted on going herself.

'I'll give him one thing at least—he's punctual,' Isabel remarked as she headed for the door leading to the passageway. 'Let's hope he's also fair-minded.'

The housekeeper's silent judgement had been uncannily accurate. Isabel didn't wish Clara to be dismissed from her post, simply because of yesterday's unfortunate occurrence, if she could possibly do anything about it. Although she would have been the first to admit that her cousin was not very worldly, and could never be described as a blue-stocking, she was far from stupid, and was at the very least quite capable of teaching little Alice all the necessary female accomplishments.

After pausing only briefly before the passageway mirror, Isabel opened the front door, very well pleased with her appearance. Yet there was nothing, not even so much as a faint widening of blue eyes, to suggest that the Viscount noticed anything different about her from the day before. Had she been in the least conceited she might easily have taken umbrage at such a blatant display of indifference towards her as a woman. The truth of the matter was, though, she was more interested in whether she could persuade him to overlook yesterday's débâcle and retain her cousin's services as governess.

She invited him to step into the parlour, and could see at a glance that this at least met with his approval, even before he said, 'I've always considered this a most charming room, Miss Mortimer. I was a frequent visitor when my good friend Charles Bathurst resided here with his parents. You are to be congratulated. There is a

wonderful homely quality about it still. One senses it at
once. Would that the Manor could feel so welcoming!'

'It is mostly thanks to my cousin's efforts that the
room is now so pleasing, my lord,' she returned promptly, thereby not wasting any opportunity to point out
Clara's accomplishments, while at the same time wondering what had been at the root of his remark about the
Manor. Surely he was happy to be back in the ancestral
home? Or was the realisation of what had taken place
there just too harrowing to forget?

'Do sit down, my lord,' she invited, realising suddenly she was staring at him rather intently. What was
worse, she was receiving close scrutiny in return! 'May
I offer you some refreshment? I have a rather good
Madeira here I'm sure you'd enjoy.'

'Only if you join me, Miss Mortimer,' he returned
in that deeply rich velvety voice that was both oddly
reassuring and faintly disturbing at one and the same
time.

She had already decided that his years away hadn't
been altogether kind to him. He was still the same fine
figure of a man she well remembered, perhaps a little
more so now that sinewy muscle had replaced any slight
excess of flesh he might have been guilty of carrying in
his youth. Nevertheless, of those handsome, youthful
looks there was precious little sign now. His features
had grown markedly more severe. The hawk-like nose,
the thin-lipped mouth and the square line of his jaw
might not have seemed quite so harshly defined had
they been tempered by doe-like orbs of a softer hue.
Furthermore, the thin line that now ran from the corner
of his left eye down to his top lip gave his mouth a

slightly contemptuous curl. Yet, for all that, Isabel didn't consider him unattractive. In fact, the opposite was true. There was about him a sardonic quality that she found strangely alluring.

Although she refrained from imbibing in strong liquor as a rule, at least so early in the day, she decided in this instance that it might be wise to humour him, and so settled herself in the chair directly opposite before sampling the contents of her own glass.

'My lord, I am glad to have this opportunity to speak with you in private,' she announced, at last giving voice to the well-rehearsed speech she had been mentally practising since early morning. 'It offers me the opportunity to ask your forgiveness for my behaviour yesterday. I cannot apologise enough for the way I quite outrageously embroiled you in that fiasco. The truth of the matter is, though, sir, I was at a loss to know just how to proceed.'

Once again she thought she could detect the faint twitching of a muscle at the corner of his mouth, before he sampled the contents of his glass and then gave his assessment by a nod of approval. 'On the contrary, Miss Mortimer, you appeared to be in full control of the situation. I'm reliably informed you are no novice where the use of firearms is concerned.'

'Oh, pray don't remind me, sir!' she begged, her suddenly heightened colour proof of the mortification she still felt over her behaviour. 'I should never have threatened them in such an outrageous fashion had I known how to proceed. But the fact is, sir, I didn't know whether Mrs Pentecost could legally remove my cousin from this house, as Clara does not attain her majority until the middle of May. And I simply couldn't allow that to happen! Poor Clara has looked to me, quite five years her senior, to protect her since her arrival here.'

His lordship stared across at her in silence for several moments, his cool gaze revealing nothing except, perhaps, a flicker of sympathy. 'The widow may well be within her rights, ma'am,' he told her bluntly. 'But do not be too disheartened,' he didn't hesitate to assure, when she appeared slightly downcast. 'If she had proof of guardianship with her, I believe she would have been back with the authorities. As this quite obviously didn't occur, I rather fancy there's nothing official in writing. It may well be that the late Mr Pentecost merely expected his wife to take care of the child from his first union. However, it might be that he did make provision for his daughter in his will. I'll wager that female was concealing something. And her companion didn't appear altogether comfortable either!'

'Ah, so you noticed that too!' Isabel returned, feeling inordinately pleased that she hadn't imagined those wary expressions just prior to her unwelcome visitors' departure. 'Mrs Pentecost certainly seems determined Clara should marry Mr Sloane.'

'Well, she could do worse,' his lordship pointed out, ever the pragmatist. 'His dress alone would suggest he's a man of reasonable means. Your cousin would no longer be obliged to earn a living.'

Isabel was appalled at the suggestion, and it clearly showed. 'My beautiful young cousin married to that portly tailor's dummy…?' she returned in disbelief. 'Why, it's obscene! Not only is he more than twice her age, and therefore old enough to be her father, he also has a most unpleasant, wet mouth. Besides,' she continued, ignoring the odd choking sound emanating from the chair opposite her own, 'Clara and I might not have a great deal in common, but neither of us is avaricious, and would never consider marrying for financial gain.

'And speaking of my cousin,' she went on, when all he did was to stare thoughtfully down into his glass. 'I'm sure you wish to see her and your wards.' So saying, Isabel rose and went over to the bell-pull.

Soon afterwards Bessie was showing the children, followed by their governess, into the room. Isabel herself made to leave, but his lordship forestalled her by requesting her to remain. She was then able to observe his treatment of his wards.

Clearly he was more at ease with Josh who, after an initial hesitancy, began to ask numerous questions about his late father, a gentleman who had been one of his lordship's closest friends, and who had died almost three years before during the capture of Badajoz. Alice, of course, couldn't remember her father in the least, and it rather amused Isabel when his lordship, betraying a faint disquiet when innocent brown eyes stared fixedly up at him, attempted to converse with the little girl.

Yet, as had happened the day before, Isabel could detect nothing in his lordship's demeanour to suggest he was in the least impressed by Clara's loveliness. His tone was quite impassive when he questioned her about the various subjects she had been attempting to teach his wards during the time they had been in her care, and although he showed no reluctance in retaining her services, at least where Alice was concerned, he evinced no delight whatsoever when his offer was readily accepted.

'I do not think there is anything further we need discuss at this time, Miss Pentecost,' his lordship said, at last rising to his feet. 'If you would have the children's belongings packed, my carriage will be here to collect you in the morning, and will return you to the Manor later in the day.'

He then took his leave of his wards and their governess, before surprising Isabel somewhat by requesting she accompany him round to the stable to collect his horse.

'For the time being it would be best if your cousin remains under your roof.' The Viscount registered the look of mingled surprise and doubt in her eyes. 'I know what a censorious world we live in, Miss Mortimer. It wouldn't be too long before your cousin's hitherto spotless reputation suffered as a result of residing permanently under my roof. But that hopefully will be avoided by her returning to your protection each evening.'

Easily guessing the reason for the lingering concern she cast up at him, he added, 'And pray do not trouble yourself over any possible actions of the stepmother's. I think we can safely rely on the excellent Mr Goodbody's abilities to delay proceedings until such time as your cousin attains her majority, should it prove that Mrs Pentecost is within her rights to remove her stepdaughter from under your roof. I shall write to him on my return to the Manor, requesting his help in the matter. He hasn't failed me yet.'

This admission brought something else to the forefront of Isabel's mind. 'And the children, sir—are they now safe from any claims to guardianship their uncle might make?'

His lordship's smile was not pleasant. 'The last I heard of Danforth, he was making for the Channel in an attempt to flee the authorities. He was proved to be the very worst kind of scoundrel. What might have happened to the children had they been left in his care, I shudder to think. Suffice it to say, he'd be unwise to show his face again in this country for a considerable time.'

Having reached the yard, Isabel noticed his lordship surprisingly frowning at the lad whom she employed to do odd jobs about the place, as Toby emerged from the stable, leading his lordship's fine bay.

'Is there something amiss, my lord?'

'I seem to recognise this lad.'

A thought occurred to Isabel. 'Possibly a family resemblance. His brother worked up at the Manor for several years, so I understand. He disappeared around the time of the murders. Is that not so, Toby?'

The boy confirmed it with a nod of his head. 'Disappeared on that selfsame night, so Ma said. Went out for a tankard of ale, and never came 'ome again. Not a word been 'eard of 'im since, neither.'

After learning this his lordship raised his head and stared across the meadow into the far distance. 'Yes, I remember, now, my friend Charles Bathurst mentioning something about young Jem disappearing on the night of the murders. I suppose I thought he'd just upped and left and got himself another situation somewhere else. Couldn't have blamed him in the circumstances.' His frown deepened. 'But he would never have gone without a word to a soul.'

'That 'ee wouldn't,' Toby confirmed. 'Ma were expecting 'im back that night. She reckons 'ee must 'ave been set on by footpads, or such like. But I don't reckon that be right. 'Cepting for that watch you give 'im all them years back, m'lord, 'ee couldn't 'ave 'ad more than an odd penny in his pocket.'

'I'm sure you're right, Toby,' Isabel agreed. 'But it is strange, is it not, that no one has seen or heard anything of him since. Don't you agree, sir?'

His lordship, however, continued to stare silently at some distant spot, his mind locked in the past.

Chapter Three

It was only to be expected that the children's removal to the Manor would result in a return to normality at the farmhouse. Isabel was obliged to admit that it was much quieter for a start. A little too quiet sometimes, she increasingly began to feel as the days passed.

She couldn't deny that their departure had resulted in a much lighter workload for both Bessie and herself. They were no longer obliged to slave over a hot range for hours a day in order to satisfy the appetite of a rapidly growing boy, not to mention his healthy younger sister. There was far less laundry to deal with each week as well. Yet, for all that the children had been hard work, Isabel missed not having them about the place.

Of course she looked forward to her cousin's return to the house each evening. Over supper, Clara would regale them with all the latest gossip from up at the Manor, and keep them abreast of the improvements to the house that were, apparently, daily taking place.

None the less, even her cousin's continued presence at the farmhouse couldn't suppress the ever-increasing discontent Isabel was for some obscure reason experiencing.

As February gave way to March, even seeing evidence that spring was not too far away quite failed to lift her spirits. She was reminded of how she had felt during those first weeks after her dear father had passed away. Then, of course, there had been a good reason for the malcontent that had gripped her. What excuse was there now for her feeling totally dissatisfied with her lot? There was none, of course. Yet, try as she might, Isabel simply couldn't shake off the mood of despondency.

A week of heavy rain did little to improve her spirits. Nor, it had to be said, did waking up one morning to discover her vegetable patch under a considerable amount of water.

Her prized garden had produced sufficient quantities of root and green vegetables to feed the household throughout the previous year, not to mention sufficient soft fruits during the summer months to preserve for leaner times. She doubted very much that this would be the case for the present year, for she very much feared that her attempt to produce early crops had been completely washed away by the deluge.

'That is it!' she declared, reaching for her cloak and stout, serviceable boots. 'I'm not prepared to put up with this any longer! I'm mindful of the fact that his lordship has been most generous to this household already, especially where Clara is concerned. But that doesn't give him the right to neglect his duties as a landowner. So don't you dare try to stop me, Bessie!'

The thought never crossed the housekeeper's mind for an instant. She knew well enough that, when her mistress had reached the limits of her patience, only a forceful airing of views would restore calm, and return her to her normally sensible and controlled state. None the less, Bessie sensed that more lay behind this present show of fiery tension in her young mistress than the washing away of a few vegetable seedlings. All the same, she was at a loss to know quite what it might be.

From the kitchen window she followed her irate young employer's progress up the drove to the meadow. Then she watched her clamber, in a most unladylike fashion, over the boundary fence that divided his lordship's deer park from her own property, her faithful Beau padding along at her heels. Bessie smiled to herself as she recalled a story she'd heard many years before about an ancient warrior queen, fearless and determined, setting forth to do battle with her enemies. Which was exactly how Miss Isabel looked right now! And there wouldn't be too many souls brave enough to stand in her way, she mused.

Although Mr Tredwell, the new butler up at the Manor, did not view the rather ill-groomed young woman, demanding to see the aristocratic master of the house at once, in quite the same reverential way as did her own devoted servant, her overall demeanour, quite frankly, did puzzle him. Had he been in town he maybe wouldn't have thought twice about denying admittance. But this was not London. And unless his adroitness at assessing a person's station in life had deserted him entirely, this was no country bumpkin either. Nor, he felt sure, was she a female of a certain disreputable calling.

None the less, having been in his lordship's employ a few short weeks only, Tredwell had no intention of jeopardising his superior position in the household by not fulfilling his role as major-domo. He had a duty to deny admittance to all those who might importune his lordship. And this young woman, he strongly suspected, was more than capable of doing precisely that!

Consequently, he was on the point of demanding to know the caller's name and business, when a high-pitched squeal from behind captured his attention, and he turned to see his master's elder ward bounding down the main staircase.

The boy knew well enough that he was only ever supposed to use the back stairs, unless instructed to do otherwise, and Tredwell was on the point of reminding him of this fact, when he was almost thrust rudely aside by Josh in his enthusiasm to reach the caller.

'Miss Isabel! Miss Isabel!' he cried joyfully, almost launching himself into her outstretched arms. 'You've come to see us at last! Why has it taken you so long? Have you come to take me fishing?'

Josh's enthusiastic greeting and subsequent barrage of questions had contrasting effects on the two adults: a look of enlightenment immediately flickered over the high-ranking servant's long, thin face, for he was very well aware that the children's surrogate guardian during past months had been none other than a Miss Isabel Mortimer; whereas the lady herself, after a brief glowing smile down at Josh, cast a look of comical dismay above the boy's head in the general direction of the butler.

'The truth of the matter is, Josh, I'm here to see his lordship. There's something I need to discuss with him urgently. But I haven't forgotten my promise,' she assured him. 'I will take you fishing. But we'll need to seek his lordship's permission first, and wait for warmer weather, of course.'

Out of consideration for the servants, Isabel first removed her boots, which not surprisingly had become caked with mud after her brisk hike across the sodden park land, before accepting the butler's invitation to step inside the hall, and leaving her trusty hound to await her return in the shelter of the roomy, stone-built entrance-porch.

'Why are you not at your lessons, Josh?' she asked him, thinking it most strange that he should be wandering about the house by himself at this time of day.

'Oh, I just happened to leave my book in the kitchen,' he answered, raising wide, innocent eyes, which didn't fool Isabel for a second. 'I often do, you know.'

'Yes, I can imagine,' she responded, favouring him with a quizzical look. 'And what prompts these lapses in memory—plum cake or apple tart?'

He chuckled impishly. 'Plum cake. But it isn't as good as yours.'

'Artful little demon!' she admonished lovingly. 'You'd best run along then, and have your mid-morning treat, before Miss Pentecost wonders what's become of you...although I expect she's a pretty shrewd notion already of why you're so forgetful.'

This touching exchange was witnessed by more than one person, as Isabel quickly discovered, when the butler requested her to take a seat whilst he discovered whether his lordship was available to see her.

'Don't trouble yourself, Tredwell. I'm quite at leisure,' a smooth voice assured him, and Isabel swung round to see the master of the fine Restoration building leaning against a door jamb, his arms folded across his manly chest.

'This is an unexpected pleasure, Miss Mortimer,' he declared, after moving to one side in order that she might precede him into the room. He then looked at her intently, studying her from head to toe, and paying particular attention to the wild and shining windswept locks, the glowing colour in her cheeks and her unshod feet, whilst all the time she took stock of her surroundings, in blissful ignorance of his scrutiny.

'Had I not happened to witness that touching little reunion between you and Josh, I might have been forgiven for imagining some personal calamity had befallen you. I shall take leave to inform you, young woman, you look a positive fright! In fact, little better than any ill-groomed labouring wench!'

'And so would you, if you'd traipsed across the park in this wind,' she defended abruptly, clearly nettled by the criticism, though she did whip off the red ribbon that had earlier confined her locks at the nape of her neck and retied it as best she could without the aid of a mirror.

Secretly he had thought she looked stunningly attractive with her rich chestnut locks framing the healthy glow in her face. She was so different from so many of those high-born society ladies who made full use of any artificial aid to beauty. Miss Isabel Mortimer might never be considered by some to be a gem of loveliness, a pearl beyond price. But she was certainly out of the common way, he decided, and quite refreshingly natural.

'Do sit yourself down, Miss Mortimer, and tell me how I may serve you,' he invited, while pouring out two glasses of wine. 'Here, drink it,' he added, when she attempted to refuse the Madeira. 'It will calm your nerves.'

'There's absolutely nothing wrong with my nerves,' she assured him, reluctantly accepting the glass. 'I'm merely damnably annoyed.'

'About what, may I ask?' he enquired, not wholly approving the unladylike language, which was strange, considering that he never objected to plain speaking as a rule.

'For the past six years, my lord, the ditch on the western boundary of your property has repeatedly overflowed on to my land, after any prolonged spells of rain, to the detriment of my vegetable crops. Time and again I approached the last steward, Guy Fensham, to do something about it, but to no avail. Why your family ever employed such a lazy—' Isabel pulled herself up abruptly, realising suddenly that she was going beyond what was pleasing by voicing opinions on matters that were absolutely none of her concern.

Taking a moment to fortify herself from the contents of her glass, she peered up at him through her lashes. He didn't seem in the least annoyed by her outburst. But then it was sometimes very difficult to judge what was passing through the mind of this enigmatic aristocrat, she reminded herself. 'But you do not need me to tell you how he neglected his duties during your time away, sir.'

Without uttering a word, his lordship went over to his desk and proceeded to write a brief note. The silence in the room was punctuated by the scratching of the quill across the sheet of paper, the steady ticking of the mantel-clock and a distant low and eerie howling. Which Isabel did her best to ignore whilst taking further stock of her surroundings.

It really was a very masculine room, with its dark wooden furnishings, and heavy leather-bound tomes lining two of its walls. The claret-coloured curtains at the window matched almost perfectly the shade of the leather upholstery on the heavy chairs. Only the fine painting of the woman and the boy above the fireplace might have been considered by some to be out of keeping with the rest of the room. Yet the more Isabel peered up at the portrait of the striking dark-haired woman, with her arm lovingly placed round the shoulders of a handsome boy, the more she considered it provided a necessary relief to the library's ambience of rigid masculinity.

As his lordship rejoined her by the hearth, and Isabel watched him reach for the bell-pull, her eyes automatically returned to the portrait above his head. Then stark reality hit her like a physical blow, almost making her gasp.

'Good Lord! That's you, sir!'

He raised his eyes briefly to the likeness of himself as a boy. 'Yes, handsome young rogue, wasn't I?'

'Indeed you were,' she acknowledged. 'And that woman is your mother, I assume? You certainly favour her in looks... Well,' she amended, 'at least you did. I believe, like myself, you lost your mother when you were quite young?'

Just for an instant his eyes betrayed a flicker of sorrow before he tossed the contents of his glass down his throat, and placed the empty vessel on the mantelshelf behind him.

'Yes, I was fourteen, and away at school when I learned of her death from typhus. She had been visiting one of the families on the estate, and contracted the infection there.' He released his breath in an audible sigh. 'The house was never the same after she'd gone. I grew to hate the place.'

Isabel felt saddened to hear him say this. 'That's a great pity, sir,' she responded softly, echoing her thoughts. 'It's a fine old house, and this room is both elegant and comfortable.'

'I had it completely refurbished before my arrival,' he enlightened her. 'I knew I should be obliged to spend at least part of each year here, and I had no intention of suffering constant reminders of my late father.'

She had heard rumours, of course, of how much he had loathed his father and half-brother, and now she'd had confirmation of the fact from the man himself.

She couldn't help wondering from where the hatred had sprung. It would have been true to say that his father hadn't been universally liked, and there were plenty round these parts who certainly hadn't mourned his passing, she reminded herself. But to be disliked so intensely by one's own child...? It was all so very sad.

She raised her eyes to discover him staring intently down at her. There was a decidedly saturnine smile playing about his mouth, an indication, perhaps, that he had guessed precisely what had been passing through her mind. She felt acutely uncomfortable, and for the first time in his company felt unable to meet that knowing gaze. Fortunately the butler came to her rescue by entering the room a moment later, thereby instantly capturing the Viscount's attention.

'Get one of the footmen to take this note over to my new steward without delay, Tredwell,' his lordship instructed, handing over the folded sheet of paper. 'I want as many of the estate workers as can reasonably be spared taken off other duties and sent down to the western boundary to clear the ditches down there.'

The butler was on the point of departure, when his lordship forestalled him by demanding to know, 'What on earth is that confounded noise?'

Isabel acknowledged the butler's apologetic glance with a smile, before she said, 'I'm afraid I'm to blame. It's my dog, Beau. I'd better leave.'

'Nonsense, child! Sit down, and finish your wine,' his lordship countered, as she made to rise. 'Leave the library door ajar, Tredwell, and let the misbegotten creature in. I don't doubt he'll locate his mistress's whereabouts without causing too much mayhem.'

It was a matter of moments only after Isabel had detected the sound of the front door closing that Beau came bounding into the room. After satisfying himself that she had come to no harm, he did something that she had never known him do before. He stood on his long hind legs and placed his front paws high on his lordship's chest. A lesser man might well have staggered, or at the very least betrayed signs of alarm. His lordship did neither. He merely looked appalled when the hound appeared as though he was about to lick his face by way of an introduction.

'Oh, no, you don't, you abominable creature! Get down at once!'

Although the dog surprisingly enough obeyed the command, his immediate compliance didn't appear to impress the Viscount, who followed the hound's subsequent exploration of the fine library with a jaundiced eye.

'What did I hear you call him…? Beau, was it?' At her nod of assent, he rolled his eyes ceiling-wards. 'A singularly inappropriate name. A more ill-favoured brute I've yet to clap eyes on!'

More amused than anything else by this most unjustified criticism of her beloved hound, Isabel smiled up at him. 'Ah, but you see, my lord, you do not view him through my eyes.'

He regarded her in silence, his expression, as it so often was, totally unreadable. Then he said, 'What on earth possessed you to acquire such a breed? You know what it is, I suppose?'

'Yes, a wolfhound—er—mostly,' she responded. 'When a pup he was discovered scavenging for food round the cottages in the village by some urchins, who then considered it would be wonderful sport to tie a large stone about his neck and throw him in the millpond,' she explained. 'I happened along at the time, rescued him and took him back with me to the farmhouse. Naturally I made enquiries about the village, and in

Merryfield, too, to see if anyone had lost a wolfhound pup, but no one came forward to claim him. So he's been with me ever since.'

While she had been speaking Lord Blackwood had seated himself in the chair opposite. Not many moments afterwards Beau had returned to the hearth and had settled himself on the rug before the fire, making use of one of his lordship's muscular thighs to rest his head.

Isabel watched as his lordship raised one long-fingered hand and began to stroke the hound gently. He appeared perfectly relaxed, and she would have been too, strangely enough, had she not been convinced that striking blue orbs were avidly scrutinising her from behind those half-shuttered lids.

'Well, I'd better not waste any more of your time, my lord,' she said hurriedly, suddenly feeling embarrassingly aware that the hem of her skirts and cloak were caked in mud.

Although she had always remained particular in her personal habits, she would have been the first to admit she had never spent an inordinate amount of time before her mirror, simply because being perfectly groomed at all times had never ranked high on her list of priorities. Yet she couldn't deny that being likened to an ill-groomed country wench had touched a very sore spot indeed. Why suddenly should her appearance matter so much? Moreover, why should this aristocrat's approbation all at once be so important to her?

'It was good of you to see me,' she added, 'but now I'll be on my way.'

'Nonsense, child!' he countered, when she made to

rise. 'Sit and finish your wine. As I mentioned before, I'm quite at leisure.'

She was forced silently to admit that he looked it too. Sitting there, with his long, muscular legs stretched out before him, and his eyes fully closed now, he appeared totally relaxed, completely at ease with himself. Had she needed more proof that he could never have committed that terrible crime all those years ago, she was being given it now. Surely no man who had carried out such a dreadful deed could look so at peace with himself?

Yet the murders did take place, she reminded herself, once more taking stock of her surroundings. There was no refuting that fact. Could the grisly events have taken place here, in this very room? She couldn't help wondering.

'Something appears to be troubling you, Miss Mortimer,' he remarked, his eyes once again fully open and as acutely assessing as her own had been only a short time before. 'I trust you are not concerned about being in here alone with me. You are in no danger, I assure you. And if, for any reason, I should experience an overwhelming desire to lay violent hands upon you, I'm sure your trusty hound, here, would come to your rescue.'

'Ha! I'm not so very sure he would!' Isabel returned, quite without rancour. She was more amazed than anything else that Beau had taken such an instant liking to someone. It had never happened before. Which just went to substantiate her belief that his lordship was not the black-hearted demon he had sometimes been painted.

'So, what were you thinking about a few minutes ago that brought such a troubled expression to your face?'

Lord! Isabel mused. Was he always so observant? 'Well, since you ask, I was experiencing a surge of morbid curiosity,' she finally admitted. 'I was wondering whether your father and brother were killed in this room.'

'No, in the drawing room, as it happens. Should you like to visit the scene of the crime?'

Had she not witnessed it with her own eyes she would never have supposed for a moment that those icy-blue orbs could dance with wicked amusement. He really was a most attractive and engaging gentleman when he chose to be. And, she didn't doubt for a second, a damnably dangerous one, to boot, to any female weak enough not to resist his charm! Was she mad even to consider remaining with him a moment longer?

'Well, yes, I would, as it happens,' she answered, curiosity having rapidly overridden sound common sense.

Rising smoothly to his feet, Lord Blackwood escorted her and his new-found friend across the wood-panelled hall and into the large room situated at the back of the house. Of all the ground-floor rooms, the drawing room boasted the most commanding view of the formal gardens at the rear of the house, which could be reached by means of tall French windows leading out on to a wide, stone terrace.

His lordship recalled vividly the many large parties held in the drawing room when his mother had been alive. It had once been, without doubt, the most elegant salon in the entire house. Sadly this was no longer the case. It smelt musty through lack of use, the wallpaper and curtains were tired and faded, and what few bits of furniture remained scattered about the floor were sadly worn and heralding from an age long gone by.

As she moved about, noting the dark, intricately patterned carpet and the elegance of the marble fireplace, Isabel didn't experience, strangely enough, any sense of disquiet because of what had taken place in the room. If anything, she felt saddened by its neglect. Undoubtedly the carpet, the wallpaper and the curtains had been expensive. All the same, they were far too dark and oppressive, an ill choice for such a room as this in her opinion.

His lordship, easily detecting the tiny sigh of discontent, smiled ruefully. 'No, not the most pleasant of atmospheres, is it, Miss Mortimer? Such a dark, depressing place!'

'I couldn't agree more,' she returned at her most candid. 'But it has little to do with what took place here. I do not know who might have chosen the décor, my lord, but whoever it was betrayed a sad want of taste, if you'll forgive me saying so. The wall-coverings are far too dark, and totally at odds with the patterned carpet. And as for the crimson curtains…'

Isabel went over to the French windows, where the offending articles hung. Once it must have been a wonderful view. Now even the gardens were showing clear signs of neglect. As the windows were securely bolted, both top and bottom, denying access to the terrace, she wandered over to the windows in the east-facing wall, and was instantly reminded of how windy it was outside.

'Great heavens! Little wonder it strikes so cold in here. This window, here, is very ill fitting, my lord.'

He came to stand beside her, and tested the catch himself. 'That is something that must be put right without delay,' he remarked. 'The Lord only knows how long it has been like that. I've seldom set foot in here since my father had it redecorated some eighteen years ago.' He looked about him with distaste. 'You're quite right, the room is damnably depressing. I dislike it intensely!'

No one could have mistaken the disdain in his voice, which she felt was a great pity, because it could have been made into such a lovely bright and airy room without too much effort.

Conscious of his nearness, and the fact that he was staring at her in that intensely disturbing way once more, she put some distance between them by wandering about again, noting what items of furniture were left in the room and, perhaps, more importantly, those that were quite obviously missing. Maybe the furniture had not been to his taste either. Or perhaps certain items still bore the evidence of what had taken place. After all, the old butler had told her once that it had been nothing short of a bloodbath.

Something in her expression must have betrayed her train of thought, for when she happened to glance in his lordship's direction once more, she caught him staring back at her, that cynical curl to his lips very much in evidence.

'My father, by all accounts, was found over there in his favourite chair.' He pointed in the general direction of the impressive fireplace. 'My brother somewhere over here, so I understand, on one of the sofas.'

She frowned. 'So you never...?'

'Saw for myself?' he finished for her. 'No. As soon

as the bodies were discovered, Bunting, I believe, sent immediately for the local Justice of the Peace, Sir Montague Cameron, and the constable. I was still sound asleep when they arrived, covered in blood, with a bloodstained sabre on the floor by my bed.' The cynical smile was suddenly more pronounced. 'Pretty damning evidence, wouldn't you say? Had it not been for your intervention, and the help of some good friends, I might still be living in obscurity across the Channel. But when one has none other than Wellington as a staunch ally, other influential people begin to take notice.'

Isabel's ears pricked up at this. 'You know the Duke personally?'

'I was with him throughout most of the Peninsular Campaign,' he revealed so casually that one might have supposed he had found the whole experience quite uneventful and dull. 'I was on his staff, as it happens, one of his Exploring Officers. As you might already be aware, my mother was a Frenchwoman. She taught me to speak her native tongue so well that I could pass for one of her fellow countrymen. Which, as I'm sure you can appreciate, proved most useful when I was obliged to ride deep into enemy territory.'

It took Isabel a moment only to assimilate what she was being told. Then a feeling of bewilderment, not to mention irritation, gripped her. 'You were a spy, you mean. You spied for Wellington. You put your life at risk attempting to discover things he needed to know?'

His faintly ironic bow confirming this only served to irritate her further. 'Then why—for heaven's sake!—with all your experience, have you never attempted to discover who tried to frame you for the murder of your father and brother? Your name has been cleared, yes. But mud sticks,' she reminded him bluntly. 'There will always be those who will wonder.

'No, you might not care, my lord,' she continued when all he did was to raise his broad shoulders in a shrug of complete indifference. 'But your wife might, should you ever choose to marry. More importantly, so would any children you might one day be blessed to have. Do you suppose they would ever wish to hear their father called a murderer?'

He stared at her for so long in silence, his expression, yet again, totally unreadable, that she was convinced her words had fallen on deaf ears. Then he astonished her by asking, 'So, where do you suggest *we* begin? The events, may I remind you, took place almost nine years ago. All the old servants were discharged soon afterwards, and found new positions, I know not where.'

'With one exception,' she reminded him.

'Bunting was questioned at the time by Sir Montague. He neither saw nor heard anything,' he responded.

Isabel, knowing this to be true, acknowledged it before adding, 'I'm certain what he did reveal was the absolute truth. But I should still like to know how the murderer managed to get into the house without using force, and left it again, without anyone being any the wiser.'

'In that case, Miss Mortimer, we'd best go and ask him.' Leading the way back into the hall, his lordship gave orders for the carriage to be brought round to the door as soon as possible, before he turned to discover an expression of doubt flicker over a finely boned face.

He guessed at once the reason behind the troubled look. 'Had you come here alone, ma'am, I wouldn't have hesitated to consider the proprieties. However, as you have your own four-legged duenna to hand, I think we might dispense with the services of a maidservant for the short journey to Bunting's cottage, don't you?'

Chapter Four

The journey to the old butler's cottage on the edge of the estate was conducted almost in silence. His lordship couldn't quite make up his mind whether this was because his fellow passenger felt uneasy at being in the close confines of a carriage alone with him, or she was merely not garrulous by nature. Whatever the reason, he considered her a restful young woman for the most part. For instance, he could never envisage her getting into a state over trifles. Or ever succumbing to a fit of the vapours, come to that. None the less, he could well imagine she could be a managing little madam on occasions, if not sufficiently bridled.

He couldn't resist smiling to himself. Few in his life had ever exerted sufficient influence over him to bestir him into doing something he had no real desire to do, or to persuade him to look at something from a totally different viewpoint. Miss Isabel Mortimer had succeeded in doing just that, however. No mean feat!

he was silently obliged to concede. Whether he would thank her for it in the long run was another matter entirely. But he had embarked, now, on this quest to solve the mystery of who had killed his father and brother, and he had no intention of changing his mind.

'You may relax now, Miss Mortimer, we've arrived at our destination,' he teased gently, as the carriage drew up before a double-fronted cottage at the end of a row of newly limewashed dwellings. 'You'll not be obliged to suffer my baneful presence alone any longer.'

The implication was clear. 'I do not feel in the least ill at ease in your company, sir,' Isabel assured him. 'Why should I? You've never given me any reason to mistrust you. I apologise, though, if I seemed a little distant. It's merely that I've never travelled in such a comfortable carriage before, and I've been enjoying the experience hugely, not to mention travelling across part of the estate where I've never ventured before.'

As he threw wide the door to allow Beau to jump out, his lordship felt something within him stir. It wasn't pity, he felt sure. What she had revealed was the simple truth, not an attempt to arouse compassion. Yet it had moved him none the less.

He let down the steps himself, and as he helped her to alight, and she placed her hand briefly in his own, he could feel the calluses in the palm. His old butler had revealed that, for a gentleman's daughter, she hadn't enjoyed the most favourable existence. The elderly retainer clearly had not lied.

Yet again something within him stirred.

Making use of his silver-handled walking stick, the

Viscount made their presence known, and it wasn't long before Bunting answered the summons.

'Why, your lordship!' he declared, clearly astonished. 'This is a most unexpected pleasure! And Miss Isabel, too! Oh, do come in, please!'

'Don't wait for Beau,' Isabel advised the old man as she stepped over the threshold. 'He's obviously picked up the scent of a rat, or something or other. He'll come and find me when he's ready.'

'So long as he doesn't present any vermin he does happen to locate to me on his return,' his lordship remarked drily, which resulted in Isabel gurgling with mirth.

The Viscount's immediate smile in response held the old butler transfixed for a second or two before he turned to close the door. Not since his lordship had been a boy had he seen him smile so naturally or so warmly.

His astonishment was no less marked than Isabel's when she stepped into the low-ceilinged front parlour and first glimpsed the elegant furnishings. She had a fairly shrewd idea from where they had come. At least his lordship had put some of the old drawing-room furniture up at the Manor to good use, and no doubt Bunting had been most appreciative. Undeniably it was a deal more respectable than hers at the farmhouse, and she couldn't help feeling a twinge of envy.

After taking a seat, but refusing the offer of refreshment, his lordship didn't waste time in coming to the reason for the visit, which resulted in the old man's smile instantly disappearing.

If the truth were known, it was something the ex-butler would far rather forget. A lifetime in service, however, could not be so easily forgotten. He would never consider disobeying one of the Viscount's requests, even though, strictly speaking, he was no longer in his lordship's employ. None the less, the young master had been generous since his return by providing a comfortable little home, fully furnished. It was little enough to ask in return, Bunting decided.

'What precisely do you wish to know, my lord?'

'I'd like you to go through the events of the evening before, when my cousin Francis came to dine. That much I can remember, and storming out of the house in a rage just prior to his arrival, after a—er—slight altercation with my sire.' His lordship's teeth flashed in one of his saturnine smiles. 'Which I'm positive you must surely have overheard, or, at the very least, learned about later.'

'Quite so,' the old butler acknowledged apologetically.

Something occurred to Isabel as rather odd at this point in the discussion, but she decided to keep her own counsel for the present, and listened intently to what the old man had to say.

'Mr Francis Blackwood arrived around six. Dinner that evening was not what you might term an enjoyable affair, as I recall. His lordship was still angry with you, sir. And I have to say your brother didn't help the situation by reminding his father of certain of your past—er—misdemeanours, though Mr Francis came to your defence on more than one occasion, as I recall, suggesting a career in the army might be the best thing for you.'

'How very magnanimous of him!' his lordship put

in, still smiling faintly. 'I must remember to thank him when next we meet. And thank him, too, for taking some responsibility for the Manor during my absence.' His lordship ceased to contemplate the logs in the hearth, and looked across at his old servant once more. 'But I interrupted you, Bunting. Pray continue.'

'Your father, of course, wouldn't even consider it. Said something about, if you wished to join the army, you could work your way up the ranks, because he'd never purchase a commission for such an ingrate. In the next breath he threatened to disinherit you.' Bunting shrugged his thin shoulders. 'You must remember, though, sir, he'd worked himself up into a passion, and was drinking more than usual.

'Well, they eventually repaired to the drawing room, where Mr Francis and his lordship played cards,' he went on, after a moment's silence. 'Your father was wont to say, if you remember, sir, that Mr Francis was the only decent player in the family. He blamed you for not being there to make up a fourth at whist, but Mr Francis managed to console him with a few hands of French ruff.

'It was very late, well after eleven, nearer midnight, when Mr Francis finally rang for his carriage,' he continued, once again having taken a moment or two to gather his thoughts. 'Master Giles was already dozing on the sofa, and your cousin was pouring his lordship a final brandy, as I recall, but didn't have one himself. His lordship ordered me to show Mr Francis out, then bolt all the doors and retire. His lordship sounded weary, I seem to remember. At the time I assumed he must have dropped off to sleep, like Master Giles.'

'And you did check all the doors and windows before you retired?' Isabel asked him.

He confirmed it with a solemn nod. 'I always checked the windows before I drew the curtains earlier in the evenings, miss, never failed, and I always checked that all doors were locked at the same time. I only ever threw the bolts across them just before retiring. If I knew Master Sebastian was out of an evening, I wouldn't bolt the side entrance. He always entered that way on account of it being nearest to the stables. But on that particular night I went round and bolted them all.'

Isabel's ears pricked up at this. 'What, even the side door?'

'Yes, miss,' he confirmed, before casting Lord Blackwood an apologetic glance. 'It was his late lordship's own orders, sir. He muttered something about you could sleep in a hedgerow for all he cared.'

The Viscount's response to this was to smile that crooked smile of his. Isabel, on the other hand, thought it extremely callous, even though, with hindsight, she realised that it was a great pity her father and the others had somehow managed to sneak the present Lord Blackwood back into the house by way of the side entrance and up to his room, before the side door had been securely bolted for the night, and echoed her thoughts aloud.

'About what time was this feat accomplished?' his lordship asked her, having no memory of anything that had taken place after he had visited the local inn.

'I seem to recall Bessie telling me Papa was home just as the long-case clock in the kitchen chimed midnight. So I suppose it must have been some time around eleven. Papa mentioned, in his written account, about using the back stairs, and seeing no servants about.'

'He wouldn't have done, miss, not at that time,' Bunting confirmed. 'I'd sent them all to bed long before then. Neither his lordship nor Master Giles required their valets at that time of day. They always got themselves ready for bed, as indeed did you, my lord,' he continued. 'I could manage well enough on my own at that time.'

It was little wonder not one of the old servants at the Manor would ever say a word against Bunting. He had always been so considerate to them all, she mused, before asking him if he'd heard anything himself. After all, attempting to get an inebriated man, who was incapable of walking, up to his room must have caused some commotion, she reasoned, but he shook his head.

'I was keeping myself occupied at the other end of the house, miss, tidying the dining room, and setting the table in the breakfast parlour in readiness for the morning. I never went anywhere near the back stairs until I first checked the side entrance door was locked earlier in the evening. Then, of course, later, when I threw the bolts and retired to bed.'

'And you discovered the bodies at what time, Bunting?' his lordship asked.

'Oh, it wasn't I who first saw the terrible sight,' he enlightened his visitors. 'No, it was the poor young scullery maid, when she went into the drawing room to lay the fire. It might have been early May, sir, but it could still get quite chilly of an evening.'

'About what time would she have begun her work?'

his lordship asked, thereby betraying his complete ignorance of such household practices.

'About half past six, sir. That's what time she always began laying fires, and always started with the one in the breakfast parlour. Then she did the library, and then the drawing room. So I suppose it would have been about seven, or soon afterwards. I was then informed of the tragedy, and sent for Sir Montague Cameron at once. He wasn't best pleased, I seem to recall. Apparently he'd had little sleep the night before.'

'I'm not surprised. My father was there until quite late delivering his sixth child,' Isabel revealed. 'It had been a difficult confinement and he had been there since the afternoon. It was while he was making his way home, sir, that he came upon Jem Marsh and your old steward outside the village inn attempting to get you on to your horse. Without much success, I might add. In the end my father took you back to the Manor in his gig. You couldn't even stand on your own two feet, let alone wield a sabre, for heaven's sake!'

His lordship couldn't forbear a smile at the clear note of derision in her voice, and silently acknowledged that his behaviour that evening, what he could remember of it, didn't redound to his credit. None the less, he was obliged to point out that several hours might have elapsed before his father and brother were murdered. Time enough, surely, for him to have sobered up sufficiently to commit the deed?

Isabel, however, wasn't so sure. Her father had witnessed more than one man in a drunken stupor, and his lordship, according to her father's statement, had been as good as unconscious, and would have remained so for a good many hours. 'The murders could only have taken place after Bunting had retired, and before the servants rose the following morning,' she reminded them. 'My father was convinced that you would have been still sleeping off your excesses when the servants rose. But just let's suppose you did recover from your drunken stupor and went downstairs and murdered your relatives, would you then have gone back up to your room and calmly gone to sleep again? I hardly think so,' she told him, when he didn't attempt to respond. 'You'd have to be totally insane to do such a thing, and I do not imagine anyone would consider you a candidate for Bedlam.'

'Well, my lord, I remember quite well that it took me quite some time to rouse you that morning, as it so often did when you had been—er—imbibing quite freely,' Bunting disclosed, clearly thinking on the same lines as Isabel. 'And you didn't seem best pleased when I did. You swore at length, advising me to go stick my head in a bucket.'

'Ha! That's rich!' Isabel muttered. 'You'd have been well advised to have done that to yourself.'

Ignoring the aside, his lordship frowned, trying desperately to recall just what had occurred that morning. He remembered waking with the worst head he'd experienced in his life. The next thing he knew, Sir Montague and the constable were in the room, staring aghast at his clothing. 'When did you first realise I was in the house, Bunting?'

'Not until I entered your bedchamber, sir. It was Sir Montague who suggested I should check you weren't in your room. Of course, I thought you hadn't returned.'

'And there was no sign of a break-in, Bunting, you're sure of that?' Isabel asked him to confirm, knowing as she did that it had been this one fact, and the evidence of Guy Fensham, the former steward at the Manor, that had so incriminated the gentleman seated opposite her.

'Miss Isabel, I'd stake my life on it. I wasn't myself that morning, I'll admit, but I swear all the doors were still securely bolted when the servants rose. Cook assured me the kitchen door was as it should have been, a footman said the same about the side entrance. He unbolted it himself when he went for Sir Montague, and I unbolted the front entrance later that morning, when Sir Montague arrived. No, all the doors were secure and none of the windows had been broken or forced, except…'

'Except what?' Isabel prompted when all the old servant did was to frown heavily.

'It was something that struck me as odd at the time, although it might have been nothing. I noticed the key was still in the lock of the French windows, and yet I felt sure I returned it to the usual place in the top drawer of the bureau the evening before, when I closed the curtains.' He shrugged. 'Perhaps his lordship or Mr Francis wandered out on to the terrace for a breath of air. The door was certainly locked and securely bolted, so no one could have gained entry by that means.'

'Thank you for your time, Bunting,' his lordship said, when his delightful companion appeared to have fallen into a meditative mood. He rose to his feet, exchanging one or two more commonplaces with his old servant before he returned Isabel and her faithful hound to the carriage.

The return journey seemed as if it too would be undertaken in stony silence. Only this time his lordship sensed it was for an entirely different reason. The increasingly endearing Miss Mortimer wasn't so much interested in the passing countryside as attempting to solve a conundrum, if the deep furrow drawing her charmingly arching brows together was anything to go by.

'Something certainly appears to be troubling you this time, Miss Mortimer, even if it was not the case on the outward journey.'

'What…? Oh, I do beg your pardon, my lord.' She cast him an apologetic smile, which he secretly thought was lovely. 'I do have a habit of drifting into a world of my own when something is troubling me, and not sharing my thoughts. It comes from having been so self-reliant for so many years, I suppose.'

Again he found himself in the grip of that strange sensation, but ignored it as he said, 'Would I be correct in assuming your puzzlement stems from something discovered from the estimable Bunting?'

'Several things, as it happens,' she disclosed, staring at him fixedly, and without seeming in the least self-conscious about it either. 'You must have taken a key with you that night. Bunting said he made a point of locking the doors when he went about drawing the curtains and checking the windows in the evenings. He only ever threw the bolts across just prior to retiring, and then not those on the side entrance as a rule, if he knew you were out, except on that particular night.'

'Well, what of it? He was merely following my father's orders.'

'The door would already have been locked by the time Papa and the others returned you to the Manor. You must have had a key about your person, otherwise they couldn't have got you back into the house. The side door must have been re-locked by someone. Bunting said he checked it and it was locked,' she reminded him. 'So who relocked it? It wasn't Papa, that I do know.' She frowned. 'Could the person who retained the key have returned to the house shortly afterwards, before Bunting had thrown the bolts, and hidden somewhere?'

Lord Blackwood agreed it was certainly a possibility before adding, 'So we're looking at Jem Marsh, and the former steward, Guy Fensham, neither of whom is here to question.'

'True,' she acknowledged. 'I wasn't acquainted with Jem Marsh, but if he was anything like his young brother, I cannot imagine he'd hack someone to death with a sabre. What was the motive? Nothing was taken from the house, was it?'

'Not as far as I'm aware. And, as you surmise, Jem was a good lad, one of the best. My father liked him too, and was all for him becoming head groom one day. He had no reason to kill any member of my family. And neither did Guy Fensham.

'Yes, I'm well aware he's been lining his pockets from the estate these past years,' he added, when it looked as though she would disagree. 'And I'm also aware that his account of what took place that night differed considerably from your father's. But let's try to be fair and suggest he might not have been perfectly sober himself that night, and maybe became confused. Furthermore, he did his job well when my father was alive. I cannot see how it would have benefited him to murder his employer, and incriminate me. The next holder of the title just might have brought in his own people.'

Having no in-depth knowledge of his family, Isabel asked, 'And who is next in line, after you, my lord?'

'My dissolute and debauched Uncle Horace. I came across him in London a few weeks ago. He hasn't changed.'

Suppressing the strong urge to suggest deplorable behaviour must surely run in his family, Isabel concentrated her mind on something else that had puzzled her whilst in Bunting's cottage, and asked his lordship outright if it had been the norm for him to storm out of the house in a rage after a disagreement with his father.

Easily detecting the note of censure in her voice, Lord Blackwood smiled crookedly. 'I was a hot-headed youth who grew into an angry young man. I'm not proud of my past behaviour, but there's nought I can do about it now.' He turned to stare out of the window, but was oblivious to the pleasing landscape flashing past. 'Whenever I paid a visit home to the Manor during my years at Oxford and, indeed, after I'd left university, there was hardly an occasion when my father and I didn't argue about something. I was nothing like my older brother, who would agree with our father over everything in order to remain in his good books. Sometimes I would return to London after one of our rows; on other occasions I would find solace in Merryfield.'

Realising he had disclosed more than he had intended, he turned to look at his companion again, and easily detected the rising colour before she hurriedly turned her head away. How very revealing! he mused. An innocent she might be, but she was not naïvely stupid. She knew well enough what went on in the world, and the desires of the opposite sex, even if she didn't approve.

'But I digress,' he added, when she resolutely continued to stare out of the window on her side of the carriage. 'On that particular night, I chose not to stay away, but drown my sorrows at the local inn.'

This surprisingly caught her attention, and forced her to look across at him again. 'That is what I find so confoundedly puzzling,' she revealed. 'Why didn't the murderer kill you too that night?' She frowned deeply, at a loss to understand. 'Instead, he did his utmost to have you hanged for the murders. So was it his intention all along to make you suffer most of all? Or was he merely taking advantage of the fact that you had returned to the house to make doubly sure that the finger of guilt wasn't pointed in his direction? But if the latter is true...' she shook her head, totally perplexed '...how on earth did he know you'd returned to the house, and in such a condition that it was highly unlikely you would rouse even when your clothing was being smeared with your relatives' blood? Furthermore, unless the murderer knew the precise whereabouts of your room, my lord, he took an awful risk wandering about the house at the dead of night. He might so easily have woken one of the servants. Which suggests to me that the murderer knew the layout of the Manor, and also possessed a good knowledge of your character. Which also suggests to me that he is someone you know.'

'Well, haven't you given me a great deal to mull

over, Miss Mortimer?' he said lightly. 'How fortunate it is that I had already decided not to offer my support to Wellington again.'

Although disappointed because his tone had suggested he wasn't particularly concerned about the events of years ago, his latter remark did puzzle her. 'What do you mean, sir? The war with France is at an end.'

His brows rose. 'Evidently, my dear Miss Mortimer, you haven't heard. It was all over the newspapers a few days ago…Napoleon is once again in Paris, undoubtedly gathering more of the faithful about him as we speak.'

So stunned was she by the shocking revelation that she almost didn't notice when the carriage went past the turning to the Manor. 'Oh, but, sir, surely your coachman has missed the turning?'

'Clegg might be new to the area, but he's finding his way about remarkably well. No, Miss Mortimer, he is merely following instructions.' His crooked smile appeared. 'My, my, what a very poor opinion you must have of me, if you thought I'd expect you to walk home.'

Nothing could have been further from the truth. In fact, Isabel's regard for the Viscount was increasing every time she was in his company. He was undoubtedly intelligent, and a most charming companion when he chose to be. She just wished he would apply himself and use the fine brain with which the good Lord had seen fit to bless him, and uncover his father's murderer. She was not a pessimist by any means. All the same, she couldn't help feeling, as they arrived at the farmhouse, that unless the mystery was solved, there would always be a dark cloud hanging over Blackwood Manor and its occupants.

* * *

Little did Isabel realise that, far from taking a light-minded view of the whole business, the Viscount was determined to unravel the puzzling events of that eventful night all those years ago. Throughout the short journey back to the Manor he mulled over everything he had discovered that morning.

As soon as the carriage drew up before the front entrance, he made his way directly to the scene of the crime, pausing only to hand his outdoor garments to a waiting footman and to give orders for the butler to join him in the drawing room as soon as possible.

His expression of distaste as he entered the large room had little to do with the events that had taken place all those years before. It was simply that he clearly recalled how it had looked when his dear mother had been alive: an elegant salon, tastefully decorated in pale greens and cream. It was almost as if his father had wished to obliterate all memory of Louise Carré, his very pretty second wife. Not many weeks after her untimely death, he had either given away or sold most of her clothes and other personal belongings. He had replaced all the elegant couches and chairs in the drawing room with solid, heavy pieces. Dark blue and gold had replaced the pale green on the walls, tasselled crimson curtains had been chosen for the windows and a garish multicoloured carpet for the floor.

His lordship closed his eyes, thereby momentarily blocking out the offending décor. Dear God! He'd been in more tastefully decorated houses of pleasure! he decided, striding down the length of the room to the spot where the only piece of furniture his mother had brought with her from France all those years ago stood against the wall.

Pulling open the right-hand drawer he saw the key to the French windows; just where, according to the old butler, it had always been kept almost from the day his mother had become mistress of the house. The rose garden had been her pride and joy, and she would often throw wide the French windows enabling the fragrance to waft into the room on warm summer evenings. At least, during his lifetime, his father had never neglected the garden his second wife had so loved, his lordship was obliged to acknowledge. He shook his head. His mother would have hated to see it, now, looking so overgrown and neglected.

After making a mental note to interview the head gardener in the very near future, his lordship slipped the key in the lock of the French windows. That was where Bunting had found it on that fateful morning. Yet he swore it had been in the drawer, just where it should have been, when he had come into the room to draw the curtains the evening before. So what did that suggest?

He ceased his deliberations the instant his new butler entered the room, and wasted no time in discovering what he wished to know. 'And you're absolutely certain about that, Tredwell—there are only three keys to all the outside doors, including the French windows here?'

'Most definitely, my lord,' he confirmed. 'The keys are kept in the doors themselves, or close by. Then, I have a set, as does the housekeeper. The spare keys in my charge are kept on hooks just inside my rooms, should one of the other staff have need of them.' He glanced briefly at the French windows. 'That key is always kept in the bureau, according to what Mr Bunting told me. And I assumed you would not wish that changed,' he added, after noting the key was in the lock.

The Viscount assured him this was so, before adding, 'And you are sure you haven't come across a fourth key to the side entrance? I had an extra key made some years ago, but it seems to have disappeared.'

The butler appeared concerned. 'I shall instigate a search, my lord.'

'No...no, don't do that,' his lordship countered. 'But if you, or any other member of the staff, should come across it somewhere, perhaps you'll be good enough to let me know.'

'Of course, my lord. Will there be anything else?'

'Yes. When I was in here with Miss Mortimer, earlier, we noticed one of the windows here is very ill fitting and letting in the most confounded draught.'

'I shall have it attended to at once, my lord.'

'Very good, Tredwell, you may go. No, wait a moment,' his lordship corrected, when a thought suddenly occurred to him as he studied the offending window.

Reaching for the catch, he raised it, and then let it go. 'I wonder,' he murmured. Then, much to his butler's surprise, he threw the window wide and, raising one long leg, stepped over the sill on to the gravel path outside. For a tall man it was no difficult task. More importantly, neither was closing the window securely from the outside, as he discovered a moment later when he raised the catch until it was upright. Then he very carefully pushed the window closed, before giving the wood a hearty thump with his fist.

The bemused butler came to his rescue in a trice. 'Oh, my lord, you've shut yourself out,' he declared, throwing the window wide once more, thereby enabling his lordship to step back inside.

'Yes, didn't I just!' He studied the window from behind half-shuttered lids. 'A very tidy means of escape, and undetectable, wouldn't you say, Tredwell? But that still doesn't solve the conundrum of how he gained entry.'

'Does it not, my lord?' Tredwell ventured, appearing more bemused than ever.

'No, it does not,' his lordship confirmed, smiling to himself. 'I think it behoves me to consult with the estimable Miss Mortimer again before too long. Delay having the window repaired, Tredwell, for the time being at least.'

Chapter Five

Т he following morning, directly after breaking his fast, Lord Blackwood repaired to his library as usual to deal with those estate matters requiring his attention. It was a routine to which he had swiftly grown accustomed; moreover, one he thoroughly enjoyed.

The love of the land was in his blood, and it was to his credit that never once during his youth or early manhood had he felt any jealousy towards his older half-brother, who, in the normal course of events, would have inherited both title and land.

It would also have been true to say that, although he hadn't felt the least envious of his brother's more favourable position, he and his sibling had never been close. The twelve years' difference in their ages had been too great, he supposed. With one exception, they had had absolutely nothing in common, which had resulted in each pursuing his own interests without involving the other. Only the love of the land had been common to them both. Sadly, instead of binding them together on occasions, it had had the opposite effect. Giles had resented the interest his younger brother had taken in what he had considered was destined to be entirely his own domain, and numerous heated arguments had resulted.

His lordship sighed as these memories, quite unbidden, came back to haunt him, and he turned to stare out of the window at the many acres of deer park that Fate—capricious jade!—had decreed would be his.

There was no refuting the fact that he had disliked his father and elder brother. But had this antipathy induced him to murder…? No, he didn't believe so. In fact, he had never thought it was so, not even on that fateful morning when he had woken to find himself smeared in his relatives' blood. As he had revealed to the enterprising Miss Mortimer, his response to any heated family argument had always been to storm out of the house, either to return to London and his friends, or to find solace in the arms of a very understanding young widow residing in Merryfield. On the odd occasion he had been known to drown his sorrows at the village inn before returning to the Manor. He wished now he and his father had enjoyed a better understanding. He doubted they would ever have become close. All the same, he bitterly regretted much of what he had said and done in his hot-headed youth.

He shook his head as he was assailed by further bitter regrets. Sadly, it was impossible to undo what had happened. All he could do was ensure that he enjoyed a better understanding with his own son…with all his children, should he ever be blessed to have any.

He smiled wryly as a thought then occurred to him. But he had two already, of course. At least, he amended silently, two children to whom he stood in place of a father.

Their natural father had been one of his closest friends. Daniel Collier had been one of the first to come to his aid when he had been most in need of help. In fact, it had been none other than Daniel and his darling wife, Sarah, who had safely hidden him away in their home, until such time as others had managed to get him safely across to Ireland. The least he could do in return was honour his obligation and take the very best care of the Colliers' children, he decided, leaving his library to make his way up the stairs to the old nursery.

He had had little contact with his wards since their removal from the farmhouse to the Manor. Not only had he been extremely busy dealing with long-neglected estate matters, he had also wished to give the children time to settle to life at his ancestral home. He had felt, too, that Miss Pentecost's reputation would be less likely to suffer if he refrained from visiting the nursery too often. Added to which, he had never been given any reason to suppose his presence there was at all necessary, until the day before, when he had witnessed the touching little interlude between Miss Mortimer and Josh. It became quite obvious then, of course, that a lack of discipline was prevailing above stairs.

He couldn't deny that, ordinarily, he would never have dreamed of offering the position of governess to Miss Pentecost. He would have much preferred someone older, with a deal more experience. And someone far less pleasing on the eye, come to that! He didn't doubt that she was competent enough to teach little Alice most all she needed to know. Josh, on the other hand, was a different matter entirely. He clearly needed more control, a firmer grasp on the reins than the gentle Miss Pentecost was able to exert.

The lovely girl he employed to care for the children betrayed a moment's surprise when he entered her domain. She rose at once to her feet, thereby offering him an unfettered view of her charming figure. She was undeniably a rare specimen, certainly one of the most ravishing girls he'd ever clapped eyes on in his life. Yet it was strange, that, apart from a healthy masculine appreciation of her evident charms, he experienced no very real attraction. Unlike that managing little baggage of a cousin of hers, Miss Pentecost singularly lacked the power to retain his interest!

Briefly his eyes slid to his younger ward who, at her governess's prompting, had risen to her feet to execute an awkward little curtsy. 'Forgive the interruption,' he said, returning his attention to the ethereal being with the guinea-gold locks and limpid blue eyes. 'I'm here merely to satisfy myself that you have everything you need.'

'Everything is just perfect, my lord, I thank you.'

The Viscount moved forward to study the picture his younger ward had been creating. If little Alice did indeed possess any artistic ability, patently it hadn't manifested itself quite yet, and it was left to her kindly teacher to reveal the subject of the picture.

'And a most remarkable flower it is too!' his lordship declared, with only the merest trace of a tremor in his voice. 'I declare I have never seen one quite like it before! Perhaps, when the weather becomes a little warmer, you and your governess would care to explore the home wood and pick some wild flowers for the nursery. I know in the spring there are carpets of bluebells.'

Trusting brown eyes were raised to his. 'Would you like me to pick some for you too, sir?'

It pleased him to think that the little girl was gradually becoming less shy of him. 'I shall be honoured to accept them, Miss Collier,' he assured her, executing a graceful bow.

His response had clearly earned the governess's approval. Unfortunately her charming smile was, a moment later, replaced by a slightly concerned look when the door opened, and her other charge came striding boldly into the room, still bearing the evidence of the real reason for his absence around his mouth.

'Ah, so the truant finally returns!' his lordship quipped, instantly capturing the boy's attention and causing him to stop dead in his tracks.

'He's been away only a very short time, sir,' Clara Pentecost assured her employer, thereby instantly coming to her charge's aid. 'He just popped out to collect his book.'

'Via the kitchen, I do not doubt,' his lordship responded, favouring his elder ward with a stare of evident disapproval. 'These frequent absences from the schoolroom during lessons must cease, Master Collier, is that understood?'

His lordship then returned his attention to the teacher. 'If the children should require extra sustenance mid-morning, then send down to the kitchen for milk and shortbread, Miss Pentecost, or anything else Cook can supply. That is why I employ a nursery-maid—to cater for your needs. While Josh remains in your care, I expect you to maintain discipline.'

Although he had not spoken harshly, his wishes could not have been made more clear. 'However, I shall deal with the matter this time,' he added. 'Josh, come along with me.'

His lordship did not miss the look of alarm Josh exchanged with his governess before accompanying him out of the room. The fact that the boy dragged his feet as they walked down the long length of the picture gallery didn't escape his notice either, and eventually the Viscount relented.

'For heaven's sake, lad, stop looking so anxious!' he ordered. 'I've no intention of wielding a birch rod,' he assured him. 'I merely have things I wish to discuss and make clear to you.'

Reaching the door of the room that had once been his bedchamber, his lordship threw it wide to allow his ward to precede him. 'Would I be correct in assuming that it was none other than the estimable Miss Mortimer who maintained discipline whilst you resided at the farmhouse?'

The boy's impish grin was answer enough. 'I rather thought as much. Boxed your ears, did she?' He slanted his ward a warning look. 'Well, you just be aware of one thing—I can cuff a good deal harder. So, until such time as I can find a tutor to educate you, we'll have no more taking advantage of your governess's good nature. Is that understood?'

Josh appeared nonplussed for a moment. 'Am I to have my own tutor then, sir?'

'You are,' the Viscount confirmed, as he went across the room to a large chest, which stood at the foot of the bed. 'I rather think you would go along much better under a male's guiding hand. I would insist he involves you in more outdoor pursuits for a start. I hardly think you'll be vastly entertained going into the home wood to pick flowers.

'No, I thought not,' his lordship went on when his ward grimaced. 'But until I can find someone suitable, I shall take you out myself as often as I am able. I shall purchase a suitable mount for you within the next few weeks so that we might go out riding together. And we'll go fishing, too, if you would like?'

Josh instantly brightened. 'Can Miss Isabel come too?'

Smiling softly, his lordship favoured the boy with a searching stare. 'Do you really think she'd like to come?'

'Oh, yes, sir,' was the instant response. 'She's a great gun! She taught me how to shoot. Like Mama, she never gets into a grand fuss about things.'

This was the first time the Viscount had heard the boy mention either of his parents. 'I should tell you, Josh, that you and I have something in common,' he revealed. 'We both lost our mothers unexpectedly. Like yours, my mother too died of typhus. I was very fond of your mama. She was like a sister to me...just as your father was like a brother. I have some things of his here that I brought back with me from Spain.'

It was clear that he had captured the boy's full attention, and when he opened the trunk and handed Josh his father's sword, his lordship felt moved by the reverential expression on the child's face as he held it in his small hands.

For a few moments Josh appeared lost for words. 'Can I keep it, sir?' he managed finally to ask, whilst transferring his awestruck gaze to the Viscount.

'It is yours, Josh,' his lordship didn't hesitate to assure him. 'Just as all those other things in that chest are yours—the pistol, dress uniform, and your father's watch, among other items. But I should like to keep them here safely for you until you come of age. But you may come and look at them as often as you please, providing you do not attempt to do so during your lessons, and you do not attempt to take them from this room.'

Nodding dumbly, Josh placed the sword carefully back inside the trunk before reaching for the pistol. 'Miss Isabel has one of these, too. She keeps it on top of the dresser in the kitchen.'

'I'm very well aware of it,' his lordship responded, his disapproval all too evident. Unlike his ward, he had not been at all impressed to see a young lady wielding a serviceable firearm. Then, surprisingly, he found himself relenting when questioning brown eyes were raised to his. 'You're very fond of her, aren't you, boy?'

As Josh nodded, the Viscount had no difficulty recognising the shadow of sadness flitting over the boy's features. 'But she doesn't come to see me at all. Maybe she's too busy.'

His lordship placed a reassuring hand on one small shoulder. 'I well imagine she's most always busy. But that isn't why she doesn't come to see you. I suspect there are many reasons, and mostly to do with me. I'll see her again quite soon, perhaps even tomorrow, and try to persuade her to come and see you. Then you can arrange to go over to the farmhouse to visit her. Why not Saturday afternoon, weather permitting, of course?'

The following morning Isabel received a surprise visit from the young curate, Benjamin Johns. She had liked him from the first. He had been a regular visitor to the house when her father had been alive. The visits, understandably, had lessened after Dr Mortimer's demise, though there had been a noticeable increase in recent months. It was quite evident to Isabel just what the attraction had been.

'I'm sorry I've been unable to call round with these before,' he said, depositing the pile of newspapers he'd brought with him from the vicarage down on the kitchen table. 'I've been so busy since poor Mr Walters has taken to his bed with that terrible chill. He doesn't seem to be improving at all. In fact, I think he's a good deal worse. It's gone to his chest.'

Isabel couldn't resist casting a sceptical glance in her housekeeper's direction. Unlike his curate, the Reverend Mr Cedric Walters had never earned her approval. Whether his present malady was serious or not, she couldn't have said with any conviction. What she did know, however, was that the local vicar was a self-seeking, indolent man who cared only for his own creature comforts and little for the trials of his parishioners. It had been none other than Mr Johns who had done nearly all the good works in the parish since his arrival in the village some three years before.

'I suppose you've heard the dreadful news by now,' he remarked, after accepting the offer of a seat, but declining the offer of refreshment, declaring he couldn't stay very long.

'If you're referring to the events across the Channel, then, yes,' Isabel responded. 'It so happens Viscount Blackwood told me the other day.'

The handsome boyish face across the table looked thoughtfully back at her after learning this. 'Oh, did you visit the Manor? Did you, perchance, call to see Miss Pentecost? Is she well…happy in her post?'

Having always been quick-witted, Isabel required few things explained to her, and she guessed what truly lay at the root of the curate's questions in a trice.

'Mr Johns, let me assure you my cousin returns here to the farmhouse each evening, and seems remarkably content in her post. Not to put too fine a point on it, I do not believe Lord Blackwood has ever attempted to seduce her, or cause her the least discomfiture in any way, come to that.'

As so often happened, Isabel's plain-speaking had once again caused embarrassment, if the curate's expression was anything to go by. 'I'm sorry, Mr Johns, if I shock you, but I see little point in prevaricating. Personally, I truly believe that much of what is said about his lordship is totally untrue.' Ignoring her house-keeper's surprised glance, Isabel added, 'I have been alone with him, and he behaved like a perfect gentle-man, not attempting to take advantage of the situation.' She didn't add that she suspected this was because she was not in the least to his taste.

'I'm sure that is true,' he hurriedly concurred. 'Indeed, I have heard nothing but praise for him whilst I have been about my duties. I know already that he has improved the lot of his estate workers, ensuring that necessary repairs have been made to their cottages, and offered several local people employment, not to mention engaging the services of local tradespeople. I believe I'm right in thinking also that Toby Marsh's young sister is now employed up at the Manor as nursery-maid.'

Isabel was aware of this herself, just as she was very well aware that Mr Johns's regard for her cousin had grown over the months. He had always behaved with the utmost decorum towards her, and it was clear that Clara favoured his society. Isabel felt that her beautiful cousin could do a great deal better for herself than become attached to a penniless curate. But, then, what right had she to interfere? In less than two months Clara would attain her majority—old enough, surely, to make her own decisions?

'Why don't you visit Clara on Saturday afternoon? His lordship has been most generous where she is concerned. Not only does he allow her a half-day every Sunday, he allows her to leave early on Saturdays too, and she's usually home by mid-afternoon. I'm sure she'd be pleased to see you.'

'Well, you've certainly changed your tune, I must say!' Bessie declared, the instant she had closed the door behind the contented young man. 'I thought you said you'd try your best to discourage that attachment.'

'Did I?' Isabel was nonplussed for a moment. 'Well, if I did say that it was very presumptuous of me. Who am I to interfere in Clara's personal concerns? If she seeks my advice that's a different matter, because I cannot deny she could do rather better than to tie herself to an impoverished clergyman,' she readily revealed, echoing her thoughts. 'That said, I would far rather see her wed to a man like Mr Benjamin Johns than that ill-favoured roué her stepmama had selected for her!'

'Now, who's that, do you suppose?' Bessie said irritably, when a further knock on the kitchen door obliged her to interrupt her task yet again.

'Why, if it isn't Mr Clegg!' Isabel declared, recognising at once Lord Blackwood's bow-legged coachman.

'Aye, that's right. Tom Clegg be the name.' At Isabel's invitation, he took a step into the kitchen, casting an admiring glance over the housekeeper's well-rounded figure as he did so. 'His lordship's compliments, miss. And could you spare time to visit up at the Manor?'

Isabel was on her feet in a trice, instantly fearing the worst. 'Why, what's wrong?' she demanded. 'Has something happened to his lordship...the children...my cousin?'

The head groom shrugged. 'Not that I know to, miss. His lordship just strolled round to the stables earlier and said as 'ow I were to bring you back with me, if convenient. But I can come back later if you'd prefer, like?'

'No, no, that's all right,' Isabel assured him, more intrigued than anything else as to why her presence should be required up at the Manor. She was on the point of collecting her serviceable cloak, when a somewhat embarrassing recollection gave her pause for thought. She then changed direction and headed across the kitchen to the door leading to the passageway.

'As the matter doesn't appear to be at all urgent, perhaps you'd be good enough to wait a few minutes so that I might change into something more suitable?'

It wasn't so much Tom Clegg's immediate acquiescence to the request that captured her attention as the quizzical look the housekeeper instantly shot in her direction. Isabel, however, was determined not to be swayed by anything Bessie might foolishly suppose.

The truth of the matter was a certain someone's criticism of her appearance had continued to rankle. Yet, at the same time, innate honesty obliged her to admit that she had allowed her standards to fall over the years. Of course, it mattered not how she looked when she was hard at work, dealing with her poultry and other creatures she kept about the smallholding. There was no excuse, though, not to make an effort when she ventured beyond her own property.

Determined never to be found wanting again, she hurried upstairs to her bedchamber and changed into the pretty turquoise day dress her nimble-fingered cousin had created for her, whilst all the time studying the poor selection hanging in her bedchamber's most impressive piece of furniture.

There was no denying her wardrobe was sadly lacking even the basic commodities a gentleman's daughter ought to possess. Yet she was sensible enough to appreciate that it would be foolish to suppose that she could ever attempt to ape the elegance of the fashionable ladies of the *ton*. A light purse would always prove a bar to success. Furthermore, she had absolutely no desire to become a fashion plate either. Nor try to win his lordship's approbation, come to that, she told herself firmly. No, it was simply that it had been made clear by certain persons, Bessie included, that she had been woefully neglectful over her appearance in recent years, and she was determined to rectify the fault.

By the time she returned to the kitchen, her hair had been neatly confined beneath a charming straw bonnet trimmed with ribbon of the exact same shade as her dress. With the black-velvet pelisse that she kept for Sunday best neatly buttoned over her gown, and her work-roughened hands perfectly concealed in a pair of kidskin gloves, she knew her appearance this time could not be found wanting. Not only did Bessie's look of approval confirm this, but also Tredwell's glint of appreciation as he bowed her into the Manor a short time later.

'His lordship awaits you in the garden, Miss Mortimer,' he informed her, slightly to her chagrin.

Had his lordship been so sure she would instantly obey the summons? The mere idea that it might be so irked her, and a determination to make it clear at the earliest opportunity that she would not be at his beck and call in future quickly followed.

This firm resolve was instantly forgotten, however, when she first caught sight of the master of the house, standing in the centre of the sadly neglected rose garden, in earnest conversation with an older man.

His lordship's immaculate attire was in stark contrast to the estate worker's raiment. Highly polished top-boots emphasised the perfection of his straight, muscular legs, just as the immaculately tailored blue jacket highlighted the strength in his shoulders. His boyish good looks might have long since disappeared, but there was no refuting he was a fine figure of a man.

The smile of welcome he cast the instant he detected her footfall on the gravel path obliged her to revise her assessment of his looks—perhaps no longer handsome, but damnably attractive, none the less!

'Your arrival is most timely, my dear Miss Mortimer,' he assured her, after dismissing the butler with a nod. 'Monk, here, is my new head gardener, and I have instructed him to supply you with all the seedlings you need to replace your losses.'

Isabel made no attempt to hide her mortification at such a suggestion. 'Oh, my lord, no! No, I simply cannot accept… You…you have done more than enough already. Your people have worked solidly these past couple of days clearing the ditch.'

'In that case, this fresh supply should be in no danger of being washed away,' his lordship responded, before turning to the gardener and instructing him to have the selection placed in the carriage in readiness for Miss Mortimer's departure. Then, without further ado, he entwined Isabel's arm through his and walked away in the direction of the terrace.

Although secretly pleased that she made no attempt to release herself, Lord Blackwood couldn't help thinking that this was mostly due to the fact that her mind was definitely elsewhere.

'What's troubling you, child?' he finally asked, for some obscure reason not liking to see her looking so subdued.

'You make me feel so ashamed,' she revealed promptly. 'You have been generous to us already. That money you sent for Josh and Alice's keep was more than enough. I was able to save a goodly portion of it.'

She might have expected her honesty to please him. Instead, when she chanced to glance up, she discovered him frowning in evident disapproval.

'I am very well aware of it, young woman. And I shall take leave to inform you that I was not best pleased about it! Part of that extra money was to enable you to employ a maidservant, not to be at the beck and call of the children yourself.'

'You don't know the half of it, sir,' she freely admitted, hardly chastened by the reproof. 'We didn't buy them any clothes either. I went into Merryfield and bought all the necessary materials, and dear Clara made all the garments they required.'

He considered her apparel. 'Did she happen to make that dress for you?'

'Yes,'

'I thought it charming the first time I saw you wearing it,' he surprisingly revealed, before adding after a moment's consideration, 'But you'd look better in richer hues—dark green or blue, or perhaps a deep red would suit you best, with your colouring. Which reminds me...'

They had by this time arrived at the terrace. Mounting the stone steps, they entered the Manor by way of the French windows leading to the drawing room.

'I have decided to have this room redecorated next,' he told her, 'and would value your opinion on a possible colour scheme. I totally agree that it is dull and cheerless in here. It needs brightening. So, what would you suggest?'

Although somewhat surprised to have her opinion sought Isabel, none the less, gave the matter some thought. Disengaging herself at last from his gentle hold, she moved into the centre of the long room and looked about her, paying particular attention to the greenish tones in the marble fireplace. 'Well, I'm no expert, sir. But if this happened to be my drawing room I would choose pale green and cream.'

When he made no comment, she turned to find him staring strangely at her, the look in his ice-blue eyes intense. 'My God,' he muttered at last. 'My God…'

Taking this to mean he totally disapproved her choice, she said, 'Well, I did say I'm no expert. It was merely personal preference. You could do it in a shade of yellow, I suppose. That is supposed to be all the rage at the present time, is it not? I believe I read somewhere that the Regent himself is fond of it.'

'Nauseating colour!' his lordship declared, waving his hand in a dismissive gesture. 'I had one of the spare bedchambers done out in primrose.' His eyes glinted with a suspicion of malicious delight. 'I think I shall place my esteemed godmother in there when she pays a visit. It should prove amusing. I know precisely what she thinks of Prinny!'

All at once his expression changed and the look in his eyes became almost gentle as they rested upon Isabel. 'No,' he said softly. 'I think your suggestion perfect—green and cream it shall be.

'Now, before you disappear upstairs to see the children, there's something I want you to see.'

'Was I summoned here to see the children then, sir?'

'Why, yes, didn't I say?' He appeared nonplussed a moment before he turned and headed down the room to that certain window sited in the end wall. 'They both miss you, Josh especially. He wants to visit you at the farmhouse. I said he might. I hope you don't mind.'

'Not in the least,' she assured him. 'I look forward to it.'

'Why not stay and take luncheon with them? I'm sure they'll all enjoy that, your cousin included. In fact, I might well eat in the nursery for a change myself. Now, come over here and take a look at this,' he went on, with a complete change of tone, and then without further ado revealed what he had discovered about the window catch two days before.

'How interesting,' Isabel murmured, as she reopened the window and leaned out to stare down at the gravel path. 'Someone could certainly have got out that way without anyone knowing about it. But that still leaves us with having to solve just how the murderer gained entry.'

After clambering back inside, his lordship went over to the bell-pull before rejoining Isabel again at the end of the room. 'Tredwell informed me earlier today that he has been able to locate only three keys to the door leading to the stable-yard. I know for a fact there used to be a fourth.'

'So one is missing,' Isabel murmured. 'The one you had with you that night, I suppose?'

'Most likely. But until we are able to question either Jem Marsh or Fensham, we'll not discover what happened to it.'

'Neither of whom you believe committed the crime,' she reiterated. 'So that still leaves us with the mystery of how the murderer gained entry.'

His lordship's eyes strayed to the French windows.

'According to old Bunting there had been a fire in here that evening, and yet someone must have braved the chill evening air and gone out on to the terrace, otherwise why should the key have been in the lock, when it's normally kept in the drawer over there? Undoubtedly I shall run into my cousin Francis before too long. I shall mention it to him—see if he can recall wandering out on to the terrace that night. If my memory serves me correctly, he has always taken an interest in gardens, especially his own. His passion is for roses, I believe.'

The door leading to the hall opened and the butler entered, instantly capturing his employer's attention. 'Ah, Tredwell, be so good as to inform Cook that there will be a guest for luncheon. Also, Miss Mortimer and I shall be eating in the nursery.'

'Very good, my lord. Will there be anything else?'

'Yes, be good enough to show Miss Mortimer the way up to the nursery now.' His lordship accompanied her to the foot of the stairs. 'I shall look forward to rejoining you presently,' he assured Isabel, and then turned on his heels and went directly into his library, where he helped himself from the contents of one of the decanters.

Taking the filled glass with him, he went to stand before the hearth and stared up at the portrait taking pride of place above the mantelshelf. Smiling enigmatically, he raised the glass in a silent toast. 'Well, well… Who would have thought it, Mama? Who would have believed that I should return and discover the very one for me, here, in this unlikely place…'

Chapter Six

❦❦❦❦❦❦

As Isabel walked up the deer park's slight rise towards the Manor, her faithful Beau padding alongside, she spotted Josh awaiting her, at the prearranged spot, by the great oak that had been struck by lightning two years before, and had lost one of its huge branches as a result. The instant he saw her he ran down the slope to greet her, taking time to pet the huge dog, before capturing one of Isabel's hands and retaining it possessively in his own.

As they set off towards the home wood together, they little realised that the entire greeting had once again been witnessed by none other than the owner of the magnificent deer park himself, standing before his library window.

'Why didn't you bring your gun with you?' Josh asked, all at once noticing that it wasn't resting upon her shoulder. More often than not when they had ventured forth together in the past they had hunted for rabbits, and on one memorable occasion had even bagged a brace of pheasants.

'What, with the master of the house in residence!' Isabel stared down at the boy in mock horror. 'Are you trying to get me hauled before the local magistrate for poaching?'

'His lordship wouldn't do that…at least not to you,' Josh responded in all seriousness. 'He likes you, I can tell. I watched him when we all ate luncheon together in the nursery yesterday. He looks at you funny…different, somehow.'

'You're imagining things,' Isabel countered, wondering what on earth the boy could possibly mean. 'We rub along together surprisingly well, it's true. And I suppose his lordship feels grateful to me for helping him to overcome a—er—certain problem he was experiencing at one time. But that is all.'

There was a decidedly unhealthy gleam in the brown eyes that were raised now to hers. 'You mean about the murders, don't you? I hear the servants talking about it a lot. There was blood everywhere—all over the floor, and dripping down the—'

'For heaven's sake!' Isabel exclaimed, successfully bringing the lurid recital to an end. 'You shouldn't listen to servants' gossip, Josh! It's all a lot of nonsense, anyway! None of the servants employed up at the Manor now was there at the time, so how on earth would any one of them know?'

He seemed to consider this for a moment, before asking, 'Did you ever see what happened?'

'Naturally not. I was little more than a girl myself at the time. I doubt his lordship or the other members of his family even knew of my existence. They knew my father, of course. I believe I've mentioned before that, at the time, he was the only doctor for miles around. So the Blackwood family did call upon his services when required.

'Now, where shall we go?' she continued, as they reached the outskirts of the wood. 'Shall we walk towards the southern part? I've never been in that area before.'

Isabel suddenly received a very suspicious look. 'We're not going to pick flowers, are we?'

She couldn't stop herself chuckling at this. 'Not unless you want to, though I doubt we'll find too many about at this time of year. Remember it's still only March.'

'Thank goodness for that!' he declared with feeling. 'Lord Blackwood knew I wouldn't want to do such silly things with my sister. That's why he's getting a tutor for me.'

'Is that so?' This was news to Isabel, though not entirely unexpected. Had she been in his lordship's position, she would undoubtedly have done the same. 'When is he likely to arrive at the Manor?'

When Josh revealed that he didn't think the post had been filled, Isabel immediately recalled a conversation she'd had with the curate, not so very long ago, regarding Mr Johns's younger brother, and made a mental note to repeat the gist of the conversation to his lordship at the earliest opportunity.

'Well, as you've no desire to go hunting for wild flowers, Josh, shall we just go exploring, instead, and see what we can find?'

This seemed to please him, and he walked happily alongside, lashing out at the odd hapless piece of foliage with the sturdy stick that he had just happened to find lying conveniently on the main path.

As they continued in a southerly direction the wood grew markedly denser, and noticeably darker too. Isabel wasn't unduly troubled, though. They were both sensibly dressed in warm outdoor garments and the day was dry, with little prospect of rain. Her only slight concern occurred when Beau failed to return to her side after one of his explorations.

Pausing along the wide track, she whistled and then called his name, but surprisingly gained no response. Her concerns mounted when she repeated the exercise again to no effect. Beau rarely failed to respond to her bidding. Either something had succeeded in capturing his interest in a big way, or he was unable to return to her side. A rather disturbing possibility then occurred to her.

Only the day before she'd discovered from her housekeeper, always a mine of local gossip, that his lordship had recently employed a gamekeeper. Throughout Lord Blackwood's long absence from the estate a great deal of poaching had taken place. Why, she'd even indulged in the illegal practice herself on the odd occasion, especially when she'd become enraged over damage to her vegetables from floodwater. The difference between her and the average poacher, however, was that she'd taken quite openly, and usually from the trout stream. She had never attempted to lay traps in the woods. She didn't doubt for a moment that the practice had been drastically curtailed since his lordship's return; she didn't doubt either, though, that there were traps aplenty still littering the woodland floor. And if Beau had just happened to become entangled in one of those…?

'Josh, we'd best search for Beau. Something must have happened to him.' She looked down at the boy earnestly. 'Now, I want you to walk directly behind me, understand? And for heaven's sake look where you're putting your feet! We'll need to go off the main path and search. And we don't know what we might find lurking there.'

Josh had learned quickly not to disobey one of Isabel's orders, most especially when he knew she was in earnest, and dutifully remained a pace or two behind as they ventured along narrow pathways, covered inches deep in leaves. Every so often both she and Josh would call, but to no avail, and Isabel was just beginning to fear the worst had indeed happened, when her call was at last answered by a low howl.

Heading in the direction of the bloodcurdling noise, they soon discovered the dog, thankfully unharmed, just sitting in the middle of a glade. For once he never made any attempt to greet her, and she soon discovered the reason for the hound's disquiet. Scattered over a considerable area were human remains, possibly the result of animals scavenging in the undergrowth. Beau had stumbled upon a grave… But whose?

Unlike Isabel, who shivered involuntarily, Josh regarded the find with ghoulish enthusiasm, and began to poke around the general area of what remained of the torso with his stick. 'Oh, Josh, come away, do!' she implored him. 'You don't know what the poor fellow might have died from.'

'How do you know it's a man?'

'I'm no expert, Josh, but there is a way of finding out. A doctor would know, of course. I'm merely guessing, I suppose.' Isabel looked at the remains more closely, especially the skull. 'What I can tell you is that I don't imagine the person was very old. He still had many of his teeth when he died.'

'And what's this?' Josh said, having uncovered an object in the peaty soil with his stick.

Even before she knelt down to take the object from the boy's hand, and wipe it with her handkerchief, Isabel could see it was clearly a pocket-watch, and undoubtedly silver, even though sadly tarnished. Quickly locating the clasp, she soon had it opened, and could only stare dumbly as she read the inscription: *With my undying gratitude, S. Blackwood.*

'Oh, my God,' she murmured, suddenly fearing she knew whose remains had lain hidden in the glade for so many years; realised, too, as she once again stared intently at the skull, that it was unlikely his death had been due to natural causes.

'Josh, I want you to return to the Manor, and take this with you.' Carefully wrapping the watch in her handkerchief, Isabel slipped it inside the boy's jacket pocket. 'If his lordship is at home, I want you to seek him out at once, and give him the watch. He'll not be angry. Tell him where I am, and that I need to see him urgently. If his lordship isn't there then…then go round to the stables and see Tom Clegg.'

The Manor's head groom had already favourably impressed her by his sound common sense. He'd impressed her housekeeper a deal more, if Isabel was any judge, though whether for the same reason was debatable. All the same, she knew she could trust Tom Clegg to come to her aid.

'You're to stay on the main track and run all the way, and not stop for anything, or anyone, understand?' she impressed upon the boy. 'And you're to take Beau along with you. He'll stay with you if you keep throwing your stick for him, and he'll be able to lead whoever is able to come back to me.'

Heeding the advice, Josh ran as fast as his young legs would carry him back to the Manor, only pausing from time to time to catch his breath, and to encourage the large hound to stay with him.

Tredwell wasn't slow to respond to the pounding on the front door. Unfortunately he wasn't so eager to permit his lordship to be interrupted, as the master of the house was still ensconced in his library with the steward. Josh, on the other hand, experienced no such qualms and, easily dodging the butler's restraining hand, darted into the room, unannounced, Beau not far behind him.

'I'm sorry, my lord. I wasn't able to stop him,' the butler apologised, while favouring the miscreant with a baleful glance.

His lordship, as Isabel had predicted, was more surprised than annoyed over the interruption. 'Why the need to see me so urgently, young fellow?'

Still breathless after his hurried return, it took Josh a moment or two before he was able to explain, 'It's Miss Isabel, sir. She needs to see you now.'

No one observing the Viscount would have supposed for a moment that something within had suddenly lurched painfully, or that his heart rate had increased dramatically. He even sounded remarkably composed as he asked, 'Has she sustained some kind of injury, Josh?'

'No. But we did stumble upon a body, sir,' he revealed with youthful enthusiasm. 'Well, at least Beau found a skeleton in the wood.' He gave a start as he recalled something else. 'Oh, and Miss Isabel said I was to give you this.'

After removing the square of, now, soil-smeared linen from the boy's outstretched hand, his lordship unfolded it to discover the skilfully formed tarnished piece of silver and knew, even before he took a few moments to examine it more closely, to whom it had belonged.

Although she had little patience for childish superstition or, indeed, for those who allowed foolish imagination to influence their behaviour, Isabel couldn't deny that she didn't feel perfectly comfortable after Josh and Beau's departure. More than once she found herself peering between the trees, expecting to discover someone lurking, avidly watching her. Worse, still, she seemed unable to stop the hairs on the back of her neck standing on end every so often as she continued to study the burial sight, hoping to discover some other clue that might verify the identity of the corpse. And, if that wasn't bad enough, the surrounding area seemed resonant with eerie, unearthly sounds! She knew, of course, it was only the late March wind whistling through the trees. None the less, she couldn't suppress a sigh of relief when she first detected that all-too-familiar deep barking.

She wasn't certain what pleased her more—to have her faithful hound at her side again, or to see that tall figure on horseback fast approaching along the main track.

'Do have a care, my lord,' she urged him, as he securely tethered his fine bay hack and began to approach on foot. 'The Lord alone knows how many traps might be lurking beneath all these leaves!'

'My new gamekeeper has come across quite a number,' he revealed, not altogether pleased. 'I've already made my feelings clear on the matter in certain quarters. What went on during my absence I'm prepared to overlook. But woe betide anyone I find poaching now.'

He reached her without suffering mishap, and looked at her intently for a second or two. She was paler than he might have liked, but apart from this nothing in her demeanour suggested she was in the least perturbed by the gruesome discovery. But then, he reminded himself, she wasn't the type to fall into hysterics. All the same, he made a mental note to take her away as soon as his steward arrived with some of the estate workers.

Squatting down, he studied the remains more closely, noticing as Isabel had done the shattered portion at the back of the skull, a strong indication that the victim had been struck from behind with some violence. 'It looks very suspicious, wouldn't you say, *ma belle*?'

So concerned with the discovery was she that Isabel hardly registered the endearment. 'It's very worrying, certainly, because robbery couldn't possibly have been

the motive.' She transferred her gaze to the strong pro-
file that she was increasingly finding more appealing.
'Do you suppose it is Toby Marsh's brother?'

'The discovery of the pocket-watch I gave him many
years ago would suggest as much. But I'll need await
my new steward's arrival, with some men, before committing myself. They'll undertake a thorough search of
the area and see if they can discover anything else.'

He raised his head as he detected sounds in the
distance. 'Ah! And unless I much mistake the matter,
they're heading this way now. My ward—bless him!—
was able to reveal which area of the wood you'd been
visiting, as well as providing me with Beau's invaluable assistance. I'm beginning to view this great shaggy
brute of a dog of yours in an entirely different light,' he
surprised her by admitting.

Together they returned to the main track, thereby
enabling the steward, Perkins, who was tooling the cart
containing several estate workers, to see them quite
clearly. Their progress was of necessity fairly slow and
steady. Several days of heavy rain during the month
had left the woodland floor soft, not the ideal place to
manoeuvre a substantial cart laden with a wooden crate,
not to mention several burly men.

Thankfully the small cavalcade arrived without
mishap, and his lordship wasted no time in issuing
instructions to the small group who knew only too
well that they owed their livelihood now to the seventh
Viscount Blackwood. All the same, it didn't prevent
some slanting curious glances in Isabel's direction as
they received their orders. She knew most all of them,
of course, at least by sight, and could almost guess what

was passing through their minds. She didn't in the least blame them for wondering what she was doing alone in the middle of the home wood with only the Viscount to bear her company. It was hardly conventional behaviour, after all, for a young woman whose reputation had hitherto been spotless to be found fraternising with a member of the aristocracy in such a lonely spot!

His lordship didn't precisely enhance her standing in the locale, either, by grasping her by the waist a moment or so later, and tossing her effortlessly up on to the back of his handsome bay hack. So shocked was she by the totally unexpected manhandling that she inadvertently let out a squeal of alarm. Which naturally only made matters worse, because it instantly captured the attention of all the workmen once again. Her disconcertion increased fourfold when his lordship proceeded to settle himself on the saddle behind her, and it took quite some time before she could regain sufficient control to prise her tongue from the roof of her mouth in order to castigate him comprehensively for his actions.

His lordship regarded her in amused exasperation. 'What the deuce did you expect me to do…? Let you walk back along the track whilst I calmly rode alongside? A very poor opinion you must have of me if you thought that, my girl! Or is it that you suspect I might succumb to my baser instincts the instant we're out of sight, and throw you down on the woodland earth round the very next bend and attempt to seduce you?'

'Well, of course I don't think any such thing!' she countered weakly, all too painfully aware of his nearness, of her left leg resting alongside his and of her back pressed against his chest, not to mention the strong arms brushing against the sides of her waist. 'Nothing like that would ever occur to you,' she added in an attempt to concentrate her thoughts. 'I do realise I'm not to your taste.'

'Now that, I shall take leave to inform you, young woman, is a most provocative remark to make to any red-blooded fellow like me,' he returned in a flash. 'Furthermore, I cannot help wondering whether it was uttered in an attempt to have me prove you wrong. Or were you merely fishing for compliments?'

Suddenly uncaring that her every movement brought her into closer contact, Isabel swivelled round slightly so that she might look into his face, and instantly recognised the wicked amusement dancing in his eyes. He really was enjoying himself hugely at her expense. 'Oh, you're outrageous! You know I never meant any such thing!'

'That's better,' he approved, his smile full of the special warmth it so often contained these days. 'Missish behaviour doesn't suit you, Belle. Instead, turn your mind to something else, and satisfy my curiosity.'

She regarded him with misgiving, suspecting he might be in a deliberately provoking mood. 'About what, precisely?'

'About why it took you so long to reveal your father's written statement about the events of that night? Charles Bathurst mentioned something about it when I stayed with him last year, about your father having suffered a seizure and being unable to speak. But this, so I understand, sadly happened at least a month after the murders had taken place.'

'Oh, I see! Evidently you don't know all the details.'

Isabel took a moment to collect her thoughts. 'As I may have already mentioned, my father returned to the house late that night. I had long been in bed. I didn't see him the following morning either, because he'd already left for Hampshire to visit his ailing sister, Clara's mama. Although they had seen each other rarely since we left London, they did correspond often, and Papa knew his sister was dying of the wasting disease. That month-long visit was destined to be the last time they would see each other.'

'Did you not correspond with your father during the time he was away?'

Although his tone had been in no way accusatory, Isabel could understand his puzzlement over her and her father's failure to act on his behalf far sooner, and was more than happy to explain.

'Of course news of the tragedy at the Manor spread quite quickly, as indeed did rumours of your subsequent arrest. After a week or so accounts began to appear in the newspapers. Unbeknown to me Papa must have read one of these during his stay in Hampshire, but he didn't write to me concerning the matter, and I refrained from regaling him with local gossip on the one occasion I did write to him, because I assumed his only concerns at the time were for his sister. I believe I enquired merely about my aunt. You must remember also that, at the time, I was blissfully ignorant of the fact that he had witnessed your condition on that night.'

'Yes, of course,' he acknowledged softly, while surveying the woodland track ahead with narrowed assessing eyes. 'I seem to recall my good friend Charles

Bathurst telling me that your father suffered his first seizure on the very night he returned home.'

'Yes. We hardly exchanged more than a dozen words before he retired.' She shook her head sadly at the memory. 'It was a tragedy not only for him, but for you too, my lord. Had he not been so very weary, we would undoubtedly have caught up on each other's news, and he would have almost certainly informed me about what he knew concerning the happenings on the night of the murders.'

Although she shrugged, it wasn't a gesture of indifference, far from it. 'Because his speech was so impaired, he received few visitors during his last years. Which was so sad because there was nothing wrong with his understanding, and when in the mood he was able to play a decent game of chess. I shall always feel grateful to our local curate, Mr Johns. He was one of the few who took the trouble to visit my father regularly during the last year of Papa's life. He took the trouble also to attempt to communicate with Papa by regaling him with various happenings in the district. Indeed, it was none other than Mr Johns who first reminded my father about the events up at the Manor.

'I remember quite clearly,' she continued, after once again pausing to collect her thoughts, 'that I was in the kitchen at the time preparing dinner, when Mr Johns came rushing in, saying that Papa had become very agitated. I understood some of what Papa could manage to say, but not enough to comprehend just what had upset him so much about Mr Johns's disclosures about the murders at the Manor. He suffered a further seizure that very night, and never fully regained consciousness. He died a few days later.

'It was many, many months before I could bring myself to go through his belongings,' she continued, after a further moment's thought. 'It was then I stumbled upon what Papa had written about that night. The account was written in my father's hand, dated and signed by him. It had clearly been written during the visit to his sister in Hampshire. Perhaps he decided not to send it by post in case it got lost. It's my belief that he intended to present it in person to Sir Montague Cameron on his return here. But Fate, sadly, intervened. The rest you know.'

'I shall for ever be in your debt, *ma belle*,' he murmured softly.

'Nonsense!' she returned, dismissing his gratitude with an impatient wave of her hand. Then, 'Oh, what did you call me?'

His only response was to smile provocatively before bringing his mount to a halt at the edge of the home wood, where his carriage stood awaiting them. In his turn dismissing Isabel's assurances that she was more than capable of walking home, he lifted her gently to the ground, and then waited until she was safely inside the chaise before returning to that certain spot in the wood.

By the time the Viscount returned to the Manor, some two hours later, more evidence had been unearthed to confirm the remains were none other than those of Jem Marsh. His mother was able to identify the five pewter buttons found scattered about the body as the very ones she had stitched on to her eldest son's one and only waistcoat.

Having had to break the tragic news to the widowed mother, his lordship, understandably enough, wasn't feeling highly sociable. Consequently he wasn't in the least pleased to find a strange carriage in his stable-yard upon his return, suggesting he had a visitor. Upon learning the caller's identity, however, he didn't hesitate to join his visitor in the parlour.

'Why, Cousin Francis, this is a most unexpected pleasure!' his lordship declared convincingly enough upon entering the room. 'Can I offer you some refreshment…? Ah, no, I see the estimable Tredwell has already seen to your needs.'

The gentleman who immediately rose to his feet at the Viscount's entry was some few inches shorter than his titled cousin. None the less, he was a fine figure of a man, boasting regular features beneath a shock of expertly styled light brown hair, and a physique of such exquisite proportions that his London tailor openly bragged that he had the dressing of Mr Francis Blackwood. Not only that, the gentleman in question was renowned for his innate good taste, his polished manners and his love of the finer things in life.

'My dear Sebastian!' Francis moved languidly across the room to shake his cousin's hand warmly. 'How good it is to see you again. And, if you'll forgive my saying so, much changed,' he added, staring up slightly at the harshly defined features of his tall cousin.

Anyone who was ignorant of their respective ages could have been forgiven for supposing that Francis were the younger, when he was, in fact, the elder by some four years. His boyish countenance had changed little since their last encounter, a circumstance that his lordship was not slow to remark upon, before adding, 'A hard existence, however, leaves its mark, Cousin. Yes, indeed, I have changed. And in more ways than one. Come, let us make ourselves comfortable by the hearth, and you may tell me what brings you here.'

Light brows were instantly raised at this. 'Why, I have come for the pleasure of being reunited with you, Sebastian. Family is everything, dear boy, and I'm determined not to lose touch! There are precious few Blackwoods left nowadays. We have lost several family members since you have been away.'

'All through natural causes, I trust,' his lordship responded, before smiling that cynical smile for which he was now famed, when he received a nod in response. 'I cannot express the relief I feel having the fact confirmed, Cousin. Had it been otherwise, I might have begun to believe there was a vendetta against our family, given the way my father and brother met their end.'

'Yes, a bad business, a very bad business,' Francis solemnly agreed. 'And the devil of it was there was absolutely nothing I could do to help you at the time.' He shook his head. 'It might have been all so very different had I accepted your father's invitation to stay the night, but...' he shrugged '...it was a fine night, clear and bright, as I recall, if surprisingly chilly for the time of year. And I live only a matter of three miles from the Manor. No very great distance, after all. Besides which, I had intended travelling down to stay with some friends in Devonshire the following day. That, of course, was delayed, when I discovered what had occurred.'

'As well you didn't stay overnight. You might well have become the slayer's third victim,' his lordship pointed out.

'But you didn't,' his cousin returned directly.

'How very true… And it is a mystery just why not, wouldn't you say?' This time the Viscount's smile was distinctly warmer. 'As quite a remarkable person said to me only recently—was I the intended victim all along, or merely a very convenient scapegoat?'

His cousin appeared utterly bewildered. 'I'm sorry, Sebastian, that's far too deep for me, old fellow. You'll need to explain what you mean.'

'Oh, it's quite simple, Francis. Someone wanted me hanged for the murders. Was this the intention from the start? Or did the real killer, or killers, merely make full use of my unexpected presence upstairs, and implicate me in order to divert any suspicion away from him, or them? If this was the intention, then it was remarkably successful. Once I was taken into custody, no further enquiries were ever undertaken. Very convenient for the real killer, wouldn't you say?' His lordship peered grimly down into the contents of his glass. 'And a damnable pity in another way. Had a more thorough investigation been undertaken at the time, poor Jem Marsh's remains might not have been left to rot in a shallow, unmarked grave for almost nine long years.'

Francis frowned at this. 'Marsh…? Should I know him? Was he connected with the crime in some way?'

'Oh, not directly, I don't suppose for a moment. But

I'd lay odds he knew something the killer didn't wish spread abroad, and that is why he was murdered on that very same night, I suspect.'

His lordship took a moment to sample his wine and collect his thoughts. 'It was one of the few things my father and I had in common—we both thought highly of Jem Marsh. I would frequently invite him to ride out with me. He was good company. Jem was totally uneducated and yet very level-headed—in those days the exact opposite to me, in fact.' His shout of laughter held a distinctly self-mocking ring. 'It was none other than Jem who rescued me when I was foolish enough to attempt to swim across that river near your place, remember? The current was strong, and I had been imbibing too freely. You've always maintained an excellent stock of claret in your cellar. Had it not been for Jem diving in after me, who could say what might have happened?'

'Indeed, I remember the incident well,' Francis acknowledged. 'I tried to dissuade you from doing such a foolhardy thing.' He spread his hands in a helpless gesture. 'But you were foolishly headstrong in those days.'

'My dear Francis, I was not known for my sobriety, either, in my youth,' his lordship reminded him, smiling grimly. 'I was too intoxicated to remember much at all. But I do recall Jem diving in after me. I rewarded him for his courage by presenting him with a fine silver pocket-watch, inscribed. It was found with his remains. So we might safely rule out theft as a motive, wouldn't you agree?'

He did readily, before asking, 'But are you sure he

was murdered? Might he have had an accident on his way home? I assume he lived in one of the estate cottages?' he added when his lordship regarded him keenly.

'Yes, he still resided with his mother and siblings. The back of his skull was smashed in. He could, I suppose, have sustained a bad fall. But I strongly suspect he was murdered.'

Francis shook his head, appearing genuinely appalled. 'Well, unless the murderer is overcome by remorse and confesses to the crimes, I don't see there's much the authorities can do after all this time.'

'Perhaps not,' his lordship agreed. 'But there is something you can do for me.' It was clear he had his cousin's full attention. 'Be so good as to cast your mind back and recall, if you can, precisely what it was my father and I argued about before your arrival.' Once again his brief smile was faintly cynical. 'I have it upon the best authority that my beloved sire was consigning me to the devil throughout most of the evening, so you must have some idea.'

'Is it important?' Francis enquired, appearing bemused.

'It might be, yes,' the Viscount assured him.

'Oh, dear...well, let me see.' He frowned, evidently in an attempt to remember. 'It was clear that Uncle Henry was vexed about something, and when your name was mentioned it wasn't too difficult to work out precisely who had annoyed him. But then you were forever at loggerheads, weren't you, Sebastian? And I believe I inadvertently made matters much worse by suggesting it might be best for all concerned if he bought a commission for you, which enraged him even more, if my memory serves me correctly.'

Francis raised his eyes from their contemplation of the hearth to cast his cousin a considering look. 'By the by, Sebastian, is the little rumour I've heard true—that you have been out in the Peninsula during these past years?'

'Yes, perfectly true,' he confirmed. 'But I shan't be offering my services again to King and country should the need arise. Which I very much fear it will. I have far too much to occupy myself here.' He smiled grimly. 'I might have retained certain reservations before, but now, after what I've discovered today, I'm determined to do all I can to uncover the identity of my father's killer.'

Francis Blackwood appeared vaguely surprised. 'Well, I wish you well, Sebastian, old fellow. But I don't see that I can be of much help. What I really remember about that particular evening is that it wasn't one of the most convivial I've spent beneath this roof.'

'In that case, Francis, I shall endeavour to make the next occasion quite the opposite. Although I have every intention of visiting the metropolis in the near future, I have no desire to spend the Season in London this year, and so shall hold a party here in May, and trust you will attend?' His lordship rose to his feet. 'Unfortunately I'm unable to ask you to dine this evening. As I'm sure you can appreciate, I must inform the local magistrate, Sir Montague Cameron, about the unfortunate discovery in the home wood, and know not what time I shall return to dine myself.'

Francis, too, rose at once to his feet, appearing not in

the least put out that this their first encounter in many years was to be so short. 'Perfectly understandable, old fellow. And I shall very much look forward to returning to the ancestral pile in a few weeks.'

Chapter Seven

Jem Marsh's funeral took place three days later. Deputising for the vicar, Mr Johns conducted a most moving service. Bessie, who had known the Marsh family all her life, accompanied Isabel, and they, together with a large congregation, including his lordship, saw Jem finally laid to rest in a corner of the churchyard.

Isabel had already guessed that it had been none other than Lord Blackwood himself who had ensured that Jem had not been placed in a pauper's grave which, sadly, had been the fate of so many of the Marsh family's forebears. It wasn't until the following day, however, when she was informed by Mr Johns that his lordship had also provided much of the fare served after the funeral in the Marsh family's cottage, that she realised just how generous his lordship had been.

'The Viscount put in an appearance himself, briefly,' the curate went on to reveal. 'I was invited, and can truthfully say the food, undoubtedly prepared in the kitchens up at the Manor, was excellent. It is little wonder his people think so highly of him. It's a great pity so many of his class are not nearly so benevolent. One ought to consider oneself fortunate to work for such a man.'

This instantly struck a chord of memory with Isabel, and she didn't hesitate to ask the young clergyman if his brother had managed to find himself a position.

'Only temporarily, I'm afraid. For a few weeks only, so I understand. Poor Simon, he's such a capable young fellow too. Sadly our parents cannot possibly provide him with sufficient funds to enable him to study law. He'll come into a little money when he's five-and-twenty left to him by a generous godfather. But until then...' He shook his head. 'I wish I were in a position to help.'

'Well, you might be,' Isabel enlightened him. 'It just so happens that his lordship is looking for someone to tutor Josh until the boy goes away to school. Do you think your brother might be interested?'

'Oh, I'm sure he would!' Mr Johns enthused, but then appeared slightly perturbed. 'I hardly think, though, I'm in a position to put Simon's name forward as a possible candidate for the position.'

'Don't worry,' Isabel responded. 'Write to your brother, and if he is at all interested, I'll speak to Viscount Blackwood on his behalf.'

'Not for a while you won't,' Clara countered, having entered the kitchen in time to overhear the last threads of the conversation. 'His lordship left for London first thing this morning and doesn't expect to be back for at least three weeks. I think he's gone to the capital for some peace and quiet. The house is in a positive uproar.

He's having the large drawing room completely refurbished, and four of the larger bedchambers too. There's an army of workmen clumping through the house.'

Perversely, Isabel felt hurt because his lordship hadn't seen fit to apprise her of his plans. Without taking time to consider what the reaction might be, she echoed her thoughts aloud, and was immediately the recipient of several startled looks.

Bessie was the first to recover from the shock. 'Well, why for heaven's sake should he tell you that he's having his drawing room redecorated?'

Isabel dismissed this with an impatient wave of her hand. 'Oh, I knew all about that. But he might at least have mentioned, when we spoke in the churchyard after the funeral, that he was going jaunting off to the metropolis.'

Once again three pairs of eyes regarded her with varying degrees of speculation. 'Well, I shan't be able to approach him now about your brother, shall I?' she added inspirationally, fervently hoping that this would satisfy her listeners' evident curiosity over her show of mild pique.

At least it seemed to satisfy her cousin, who turned to Mr Johns to declare her delighted surprise at finding him at the farmhouse. As the curate had more often than not made a point of calling when he knew full well Clara would be there, Isabel considered the remark the most ingenuous piece of nonsense she'd heard in some considerable time, and was rather relieved when there was a knock on the front door, enabling her to leave the room before she uttered something else she might later regret.

Although she made a point nowadays of always changing her attire after working out of doors, it had also become second nature to check for imperfections in the passageway mirror before answering the door to callers. Consequently, although she was slightly taken aback to discover none other than the ample frame of the august local magistrate filling the small porch, she had no need to feel any qualms about her overall appearance as she cordially invited Sir Montague Cameron to step into the parlour.

Even though her father had been invited to dine numerous times at Sir Montague's fine Georgian mansion, Isabel could recall only one occasion when the Baronet and his wife had taken the trouble to call to see how her father went on during the six long years of his illness.

Yet her father had been more than their physician, he had quickly become a family friend since moving into the area and setting up his practice. Before today the only occasion Sir Montague had graced the farmhouse since her father's demise had been after she'd stirred up something of a hornets' nest by placing into a certain very safe pair of hands her father's written account of what he had known about the happenings on that dreadful night the murders had taken place. The Baronet had been aggrieved, perhaps understandably so, because she hadn't seen fit to pass the information directly on to him; and she very much suspected that resentment because she had apprised the Viscount, and not himself, about her grisly find in the wood was what lay behind his visit now.

'No doubt, Miss Mortimer, you are surprised by my

visit,' he began, after accepting a glass of Madeira and seating himself in one of the comfortable chairs.

'Not at all, sir,' she swiftly disabused him in her forthright way. 'I imagine you're here to discuss the skeletal remains of Jem Marsh, which I had the misfortune to come across a week ago.'

Although it would have been true to say that few members of her mother's family had had any contact with her, there was no refuting the fact that her maternal grandmother had been the daughter of an earl. It was perhaps for this reason that Isabel had never felt particularly in awe of such persons as the Baronet. When he had called on that memorable previous occasion to take issue with her for not presenting him with her father's written account, she hadn't been afraid to point out that his initial handling of the enquiry could not withstand close scrutiny. As he had on that occasion turned an alarming shade of puce, she rather thought she would be well advised to exert a little diplomacy this time, if only because she had no desire to cause ill feeling between him and the Viscount.

'When I spoke with Lord Blackwood yesterday, after the funeral, he mentioned he'd apprised you of what had been found. I do not believe there's anything more I can add.'

Within the space of a very short time Isabel once again found herself the recipient of a considering stare. Although she didn't hold the Baronet in particularly high regard, and might deplore the fact that he had possibly allowed past grievances with the present Lord Blackwood's father to cloud his judgement all those years ago when the murders had taken place, she would never have considered him a dullard. Therefore she could only speculate on what was passing through his mind. She wasn't left wondering for long.

'I didn't realise, my dear Miss Mortimer, that you were so well acquainted with Viscount Blackwood.' When she deliberately refrained from comment, he added, 'Because I respected your father very much, I shall take the liberty of proffering a piece of advice— the present Lord Blackwood might indeed have been completely innocent of the sin of murder, and I am inclined now to believe this is so, even though it has yet to be proved beyond question. None the less, Sebastian Blackwood in his youth was guilty of many indiscretions, and earned himself something of an unsavoury reputation. I should guard against too much familiarity in that quarter lest your reputation should suffer as a result.'

Only the belief that the advice had been kindly meant stopped Isabel from telling him outright to mind his own business and not interfere in her concerns. After all, not once since her father's demise had he taken the trouble to call to see how the only daughter of his good friend went on. Notwithstanding, her resolve to maintain her composure remained firm.

'I believe your advice, sir, was kindly meant,' she responded, after fortifying herself from the contents of her glass, 'if totally unnecessary. Lord Blackwood's interest in me is purely in the spirit of good-fellowship, and is based, in my opinion, on misplaced gratitude. I've already told him that he owes me nothing for making my father's account known.'

The Baronet, however, wasn't wholly convinced, as

his next words proved. 'What you say might be true.
And I must admit when he came to consult with me
over the discovery of young Marsh's remains, I was
favourably impressed. He is undoubtedly, now, a man of
strong character and sound judgement. So I cannot help
wondering why he should have entrusted you, someone
he'd never met until he returned to the Manor earlier this
year, with the temporary guardianship of his wards.'

Isabel at last began to appreciate why the Baronet
should believe her association with the Viscount was
much closer than, in fact, it was. During the period Josh
and Alice had resided at the farmhouse she had made it
generally known that they were the children of a close
friend. Somehow the Baronet must have got wind of this
information. Servants' gossip, she could only suppose.

'You must ask him for an explanation as to why,
precisely, he entrusted the children into my care. I can
only speculate. But I believe, first and foremost, he
desired to keep the children's whereabouts secret. At
the time his lordship and I had never met. Therefore no
one would have been likely to seek the children here
at the farmhouse. I imagine also, because of my past
actions, he believed I might be relied upon to care for
his wards, if I promised to do so.' She returned the Baronet's steady gaze without so much as a blink, before
adding, 'And you must remember, he does now need to
be extra careful. Someone intended he should be framed
for murder,' she reminded him, 'and that person has yet
to be identified.'

Even though he acknowledged this with a nod, he
didn't seem altogether satisfied with the explanation,

and Isabel was left wondering, as she showed the Baronet out, what had really prompted the unexpected visit.

Her thoughts were momentarily diverted when she returned to the kitchen to discover only Bessie there. 'Has Clara gone upstairs to her room?'

'No, she accepted Mr Johns's invitation to accompany him on a visit to the old lady who lives next to the mill house. Seemingly she's been struck down with the same ailment that has kept the vicar in his bed these past few weeks, though I don't believe her case to be quite so severe.'

Winning no response, Bessie joined her mistress at the table. 'Your visitor didn't bring bad news, I trust?'

'Truth to tell, I'm not quite sure why Sir Montague Cameron called,' Isabel revealed, finally withdrawing her eyes from her frowning contemplation of the plates on the dresser. 'You know I've never held him in the highest regard. Not only did he virtually ignore Papa during his last years, but his handling of the murders up at the Manor left much to be desired.'

She shook her head, unsure what to think. 'Although his long-standing feud with the late Viscount was common knowledge, I don't for a moment suspect he was in any way involved in the crimes himself. Nor do I imagine he achieved any kind of satisfaction from taking the present Lord Blackwood into custody years ago... But I do mistrust Sir Montague, and his motives.'

By the time the Viscount returned to the manor, five weeks later, Isabel had long since thrust the local magistrate's odd visit to the back of her mind. Comfortably settled in one of the chairs in the front parlour, repairing a slight rent in a gown, she was apprised of the news of his return by her cousin, who came into the room, armed with two large packages.

'The children were so pleased to see him, especially Josh,' she went on to reveal, her eyes suddenly lit by a spark of excitement. 'And whilst he was visiting the nursery he revealed his intention of holding a large party in two weeks, a few days after my birthday, in fact. Oh, and he wants me to attend!'

Unlike her cousin, Isabel was faintly troubled by the tidings. After all, it wasn't the norm for employees to be invited to such grand affairs, and she echoed her worrying thoughts aloud.

'Perhaps not,' Clara conceded. 'But he wants me to bring the children down early in the evening, just for a brief period. But he said I might remain, if I so wished.'

Abandoning the sewing, Isabel gave her cousin her full attention. 'And is that what you want? Aside from his lordship, it's unlikely you'll know anyone else present,' she pointed out gently.

'Oh, yes, I shall…you,' Clara countered, and before Isabel could recover from the shock, she had thrust an invitation card into her hand.

For several moments it was as much as Isabel could do to gape down at her name written in the finest copperplate. 'But I cannot possibly attend,' she announced, when she had finally recovered from the shock. A score of reasons for refusing crossed her mind in quick succession, the foremost among them being, 'For a start I've absolutely nothing suitable to wear for such an occasion.'

'Yes, his lordship said you'd say that.' For the first

time Clara betrayed an element of doubt. 'He suspected I might too, and as it is his expressed wish I attend he... he took the liberty of buying me a length of material. Oh, and it's so beautiful, Isabel!' she declared, stroking the brown paper package reverently. 'It's white, with a silver thread running through it. His lordship said that he'd discovered what an excellent seamstress I am, and felt sure I was more than capable of creating a suitable gown.' Raising her blue eyes, she cast an imploring glance. 'Oh, do please say I may accept it, Cousin!'

'It has absolutely nothing whatsoever to do with me,' Isabel returned bluntly. 'Your own conscience must decide. Though, I suppose,' she added, when Clara appeared slightly crestfallen, 'as it is at his lordship's expressed wish you be there, then there's some justification for accepting the gift.'

'Indeed, yes,' Clara agreed, brightening briefly before appearing decidedly troubled again. 'And he also said, as you were nowhere near as competent with a needle, you'd better have this.'

Clara almost tossed the larger package on to her cousin's lap. If the truth were known, Isabel wasn't altogether pleased to receive it either. She eyed it for several moments with misgivings before reaching for her scissors and snipping the twine that kept it securely bound.

Several items dropped to the floor in quick succession as Isabel reached for the parcel's major content and, rising to her feet, held it at arm's length. Unlike Clara, who gazed wonderingly at the beautifully made gown, Isabel was anything but impressed.

Only partially successful in stifling a squeal of vexation, she let the garment fall to the floor before fleeing the room, her feelings of wounded pride not precisely lessening when she discovered none other than his lordship's head groom sitting beside her housekeeper at the kitchen table, and working his way through a generous portion of apple tart.

'What the deuce are you doing here?' she demanded to know ungraciously.

Although not one to suffer fools gladly, Isabel could never have been accused of the sin of talking down to those less fortunately circumstanced than herself. Strangely enough, though, neither of the pair seated very companionably at the table appeared in the least surprised by her unusual outburst. In fact, if anything, the opposite was true. After a conspiratorial wink at Bessie, Clegg revealed that his master had instructed him to bring Miss Pentecost back to the farmhouse as she had parcels to carry.

''Ee also said as 'ow I wasn't to 'urry back, on account of 'ee rather thought you'd appreciate a ride in the carriage back to the Manor.'

'Oh, he said that, did he!' Isabel was almost beside herself with rage. She took a few deep steadying breaths before she informed the little coachman that she would require a few minutes only in order to fetch her bonnet.

The sound of that certain pleasantly melodic female voice filtering through from the hall brought a ghost of a smile to his lordship's lips. Setting aside his quill, he rose to his feet and was halfway across to the door when Isabel swept into the room, the clear light of battle flashing in her large grey-green eyes.

'How are you, Belle?' Unperturbed by the lack of response, he added, 'Looking extremely well, I'm pleased to say, if flying a trifle more colour than I like to see.'

He watched the slender hands ball themselves into fists. He felt sure she would derive much satisfaction from administering a sound box to his ears, and could only admire her self-control for resisting temptation.

'Why the heat, child?' he added, deciding not to goad her further. 'Didn't you approve my choice of gown? I chose it with particular care.'

'You shouldn't be buying gowns for me at all!' Isabel admonished, striving to maintain control, and not sound like some belligerent fishwife. 'People will suppose I've become your latest doxy, if ever word gets out!'

'My dear girl, I should never consider buying such a gown for a mistress,' he assured her, with only the faintest betraying sparkle in his eyes. 'It is far too demure.'

'Demure…?' she echoed, nowhere near appeased. 'It's red!'

'On the contrary, the modiste assured me the colour was claret—refined and the Season's must-have shade for any discerning young matron. Of course, I wouldn't have considered choosing such a colour for your cousin, but you will carry it very well.'

Successfully capturing her hand while she was fully occupied in formulating some stinging retort, he led her across to a chair by the hearth, and left her to grapple with her temper and compose herself while he poured out two glasses of wine.

After handing her one of the filled vessels, he took up a stance before the hearth, determined to persuade her to overcome her misgivings. 'The dress apart, tell me what's really troubling you, child?'

'I cannot possibly attend your party, sir,' Isabel finally admitted, suspecting he would eventually get to the truth, anyway. 'I'm not of your world. You're asking me out of kindness...out of gratitude. And I do wish you would not. You've given me so much already.'

When she attained no response whatsoever, curiosity got the better of her, and Isabel raised her eyes to his face. Then promptly wished she had not. His lordship's reputation in his youth, it had to be said, had not been without blemish. He had been hot-headed, unpredictable and an unconscionable womaniser. Yet his behaviour towards her had always been beyond reproach, save for the occasional provocative remark. Now, though, he was revealing that darker side. It was now wholly controlled, and all the more frightening because of it.

Every vestige of warmth had faded from his eyes, leaving them icy-cold and calculating. 'Don't you ever spout such flummery at me again, do you understand!' The threat was all the more disturbing because it had been delivered so softly. 'And before you attempt to say anything further, I should warn you that I had a fairly lengthy conversation with my godmother, Lady Augusta Pimm, during my recent sojourn in the capital, and she knew your grandmother, on the distaff side, extremely well.'

Isabel shrugged, determined to make light of it. 'So, what if I am distantly related to the present Earl of Trowbridge, and members of other notable families? My maternal grandmother had little contact with the other members of her immediate family after her marriage. And now the connections are too distant for me to remark upon.'

'Perhaps,' his lordship agreed, his gaze still assessing. 'But one cannot mistake breeding. I recognised it in you from the first. Furthermore, I'd wager your mother didn't come to the marriage penniless.'

A grey-eyed gaze flew upwards to meet his. Then his lordship watched as she set her glass aside, her hand not perfectly steady, and rose to her feet. He continued to watch her avidly as she went over to the window, moving with a natural grace from the hips. She stood there, merely staring out across the park, much as he had done when he had witnessed her meeting with his ward, on that eventful afternoon when Jem Marsh's remains had been found.

Then at last she broke the silence by admitting, 'You're right. Mama did have a dowry. Perhaps not substantial by your standards, my lord, but certainly not to be sniffed at. Yet it meant nothing to Papa. Unlike so many of your own class, who marry merely for money, my parents' marriage was that idealistic union that sometimes happens—a love match. Papa was the son of a gentleman, and although he was obliged to earn a living, he was what I believe is termed reasonably circumstanced.

'None the less,' she continued, after a further silent contemplation of the view beyond the window, 'he knew well enough that he couldn't afford those luxuries to which Mama had grown accustomed throughout her early life. He could provide her with a roof over her head, and a comfortable home, but not carriages and

jewels and the lifestyle enjoyed by members of the *ton*.
Those things Mama acquired from her dowry.

'Papa had a thriving practice in London. Unfortunately living there all year round did not suit Mama's
delicate constitution, and after several years her health
began to suffer. So Papa decided to set up a practice
in the country, and eventually got to hear about Mr
Bathurst's home. He fell in love with the farmhouse
and the area. It seemed ideal. There was room enough
to invite family and friends to stay in the house. Indeed
there was room enough to keep a carriage and horses.
Even I used to ride in those early days, after the move
from London.'

A sigh escaped her. 'But everything changed after
Mama died. We lived well enough, but those luxuries
I'd enjoyed throughout my early life slowly began to
disappear one by one. Mama's carriage and the horses
were the first things to go. Papa just kept the one animal
to pull his gig. I've since learned that the money Mama
brought to the marriage, at least what was left of it, was
placed in trust for me. Unfortunately I cannot touch so
much as a penny until I attain the age of thirty, or marry.
Papa, of course, left me well enough provided for until
then. Unfortunately during his long illness his savings
became sadly depleted.'

Turning to face him, she shrugged again. 'But I'm
no pauper. He did leave money in trust for me. We go
along very well at the farmhouse, and shall continue to
do so, I'm sure, until I come into my inheritance.'

'You'd go along a deal better if you didn't squander
money on wages that are unnecessary,' he returned
abruptly, thereby successfully concealing his feelings

of admiration and compassion for the stoic outlook she continued to maintain. 'You might easily dispense with young Toby Marsh's services for a start. Do so and I shall offer him employment here. Seemingly Clegg has spoken to him on several occasions during his visits to your home, and has taken a liking to the lad.'

Isabel wasn't prepared to dismiss the offer out of hand, simply because what his lordship had said was true: she could easily dispense with Toby's services. All the same, she was slightly suspicious about his lordship's motives. No matter what the world at large said about him, she knew him to be a most thoughtful and generous man.

'You require extra help in your stables, my lord?'

He nodded as he moved across to his desk. 'Clegg has just one lad under him at present. The boy works well enough, but is far too young to attempt to tool a carriage-and-four. Marsh would be ideal. He's strong and could deputise for Clegg whenever the need arises. Besides which, extra help will almost certainly be needed when guests begin to arrive for the party. And speaking of which…'

He came slowly towards her, stopping so close that she had to resist the urge to take a hasty step away. 'Now that I have successfully dispensed with your nonsensical notions for not attending, I shall assume I may count on your presence.'

'I have given no such assurances,' she returned, the light of battle once again in her eyes.

Which were so unlike his own that only contained the gentle warmth she so often glimpsed there. 'Come, Belle, your cousin will need your support, if only to protect her from the young bucks that will moon over such a beauty. You wouldn't wish to see her fall victim to any such foolish blade?'

'Ha! Not much chance of that,' she assured him. 'Although Clara might never be considered long-headed, she isn't fickle. She's well on the way to falling in love with the local curate, Mr Johns, if I'm any judge.'

'Really?' This was news to his lordship, and he didn't attempt to hide the fact. Secretly he had been very impressed by the moving way the curate had conducted Jem Marsh's funeral service. Whether the young woman before him regarded the clergyman in a favourable light was difficult to judge. She could be quite remarkably circumspect when she chose, and so he decided to ask her outright.

She shrugged. 'It isn't up to me to approve or disapprove. I'm not my cousin's keeper. Sadly, though, unless Mr Johns manages to acquire a living of his own in the near future, I cannot see how they could afford to marry, unless Clara herself does come into some money upon marriage.'

Mention of the curate had jogged Isabel's memory, and she mentioned Mr Johns's brother as a possible tutor for Josh, if one hadn't already been found. His lordship merely said he would bear it in mind, before returning the conversation to his forthcoming party, and giving the impression that he now took it for granted that she would fall in with his wishes.

'I haven't agreed to attend yet,' she reminded him, not hesitating to set him straight on the matter, and just as swiftly discovered that he could be equally determined, if not a deal more so.

'Of course you'll attend. There's absolutely no reason for you not to do so, Belle.'

'My name is Isabel,' she corrected, very much fearing that against her better judgement she would end by acquiescing. Yet, alongside this, she couldn't deny that it would enable her to satisfy a secret and long-standing desire to attend just such a prestigious event as her mother had enjoyed on numerous occasions in her youth. 'And I haven't given you permission to use even that yet,' she added, striving to remain firm.

'Then do so now,' he returned. 'Formality is quite unnecessary between…friends.' He reached for her hand, easily holding it captive in his own as he contemplated the finely tapering fingers. 'Little did I realise when in Spain that my future well-being would one day rest in these hard-working little hands.' He raised his eyes in time to catch the flicker of uncertainty in her own, and released her at once. 'My name is Sebastian, by the way. Sebastian, Arthur, Darcy, George, to be precise.'

'I do know that, sir,' she assured him, hurriedly moving away and inadvertently brushing against the corner of his desk with her cloak, knocking some papers on to the floor. She bent to retrieve them, and in so doing gave herself a moment or two to recover from his lordship's brief and gentle physical contact. Sir Montague Cameron was oh, so right! Lord Blackwood was still a dangerous man, and far too fascinating for someone of her limited experience of the opposite sex. She must be mad even to consider attending his party!

After making a great play of tidying the papers, Isabel finally became aware of what had been written on the topmost sheet, and frowned in puzzlement. It appeared his lordship had been practising his signature just prior to her arrival. It seemed rather an odd thing for him to do, and she echoed her thoughts aloud.

'Look closely, *ma belle*,' he urged her, and watched as she studied the signatures closely. 'Do you see any differences between them?'

'Yes, the formation of several of the *B*s is different. On some you finish the letter with a distinct loop.'

'Clever girl! And that, my dear, was a warning to Wellington and his staff that the contents of any letter received from me must be regarded with great suspicion, because in all probability I had been captured and had been forced to pass on erroneous information regarding French movements.

'Naturally, I was obliged to adopt an assumed name…well, almost assumed…when I was out in the Peninsula. Wellington, of course, and a few others, knew of my true identity. Whenever I sent in written reports, I always initialled them *S.B.* and it was the letter *B* that was of interest to Wellington. Fortunately I was never captured, so I shall never know now if the little ruse would have alerted the Duke to possible dangers.

'And it is so important to have people around you that you can trust, *ma belle*,' he added, after a moment's silence. 'That is why I do so want you, above all others, to attend my party.'

She looked up at him, uncertain. 'I do not perfectly understand, sir. You do not suppose an attempt might be made on your life, do you?'

'I should be most surprised,' he assured her. 'But, also, I must be prepared for every eventuality. There's always the possibility that the murderer of my father and brother might be among the guests or, at the very least, that among them lurks someone with a greater knowledge of what precisely took place that night than has hitherto been revealed. Having given the matter much thought in recent weeks, I'm now convinced the perpetrator of the crimes is someone I know very well. And I need you, *ma belle*, someone I trust implicitly, to be my eyes and ears, and help me bring the culprit to book.'

All Isabel's reservations about attending disappeared in an instant. 'Of course I shall attend your party, sir,' she assured him, and then as a reward had her hand raised and kissed in very much the grand manner.

Chapter Eight

During the following two weeks Isabel saw nothing of her friend the Viscount, though she continued to receive an almost daily recital of the comings and goings at the Manor from her cousin, and from Josh too when he paid his regular Saturday afternoon visit to the farmhouse.

It was in the middle of May when Isabel finally fulfilled her promise to take Josh fishing in his lordship's well-stocked trout stream. The day was so fine that she didn't feel the need to wear even a lightweight shawl, though she wisely took the precaution of donning a broad-rimmed straw bonnet to ward off the danger of freckles.

Considering she had spent so much time out of doors, most especially during the past half-decade or so, her skin had remained remarkably unblemished, save for a liberal covering of freckles on both arms. Her mother had always maintained the prized fairness of her daughter's skin was the result of having been blessed with a substantial amount of natural red highlights in her chestnut hair. Whether this was true or not, Isabel couldn't have said with any real conviction, though she was eternally grateful that the freckles she had carried over her nose as a child had blessedly disappeared with the passage of time.

She glanced down at her young companion. Hatless and coatless, he was happy to leave his skin at the mercy of the elements. Like so many blessed with dark brown hair, the boy's skin acquired a healthy golden tan when exposed to sunlight.

'You look as though you've been spending a deal of time in the fresh air of late, Josh,' she remarked, as they settled themselves on a shaded portion of bank by the stream, and prepared their fishing rods. 'Has Miss Pentecost been taking advantage of the fine weather by spending time out of doors?'

By his grimace she strongly suspected that his periods in the fresh air had not altogether met with his approval. Then he brightened suddenly. 'His lordship has bought me my very own pony. He's my godfather as well, did you know?'

'No, I didn't,' Isabel admitted, though she wasn't in the least surprised. From things Josh had told her over the past months, she knew that his father and his guardian had been very close.

'He said it was to make up for all the birthdays he'd missed not buying me presents while I was growing up.'

Isabel smiled softly at this. How any one could stigmatise his lordship now as being in the least selfish or heartless she quite failed to understand. 'And have you ridden him already?'

Josh nodded. 'His lordship has taken me out twice. He said I may ride every day, if the weather is fine. And he said if he cannot accompany me either Cleggy or Toby will come along.'

'Ah, yes! And how is Master Marsh settling in at the Manor?' In truth, although she had accepted it had been the sensible thing to do, Isabel had been reluctant to dispense with young Toby's services, simply because she had liked him from the first, and he had proved a good and willing worker. When she had approached him he had appeared slightly taken aback, not to say crestfallen; until, that is, she had explained there was a position awaiting him up at the Manor, which she sincerely believed would offer him far more opportunities to better himself.

'All right, I think. He goes about whistling a lot,' Josh revealed innocently. 'Just as he did at the farmhouse. And I think he and Cleggy like each other. They're always laughing and joking, at any rate.'

This was a relief to hear and, contented, Isabel leaned back against a conveniently positioned tree trunk directly behind her, and closed her eyes, whilst attending to her young companion's lively discourse about life at the Manor. Eventually, though, disgruntled by the lack of success, Josh announced that it had been shockingly poor sport that afternoon, and suggested they do something else.

Isabel slanted her young companion a mocking glance. 'And are you really surprised we've not had so much as a bite? You haven't stopped talking since you settled yourself down on the bank,' she reminded him. 'Fish can hear, you know. Especially Big Jake, although I expect he's keeping to the deeper water on the far bank.'

Young eyes, full of wonder, were raised to hers. 'How big is he?'

'Massive!' Isabel spread her arms wide. 'Almost as big as a whale. I very nearly had him once, and almost broke my rod in the attempt.'

Josh regarded the stream with renewed interest. 'See if you can catch him now,' he urged her, but Isabel shook her head.

'As I've said before he keeps to the deeper water on the far bank. But I'll wade in midstream and see if I have better luck there at catching a couple.'

Although Isabel as a rule never bared her lower limbs before members of the opposite sex, she experienced no qualms about doing so in front of Josh who, apart from a cursory glance, paid no heed to a lady peeling off her stockings and tucking her skirts into her waistband so that she might wade into the water, almost up to her knees, without getting her clothes wet. She might not have been quite so unconcerned about her immodest state had she realised that her slender straight legs were being favourably surveyed by someone successfully concealed in the small copse a few yards away.

It took Isabel minutes only before her skill and patience were rewarded, and she tossed a fine specimen on to the bank, much to Josh's delight.

'I want to look for Big Jake.' He began to jump up and down, and was voicing his determination to catch the monster trout, when a much deeper voice echoed a similar sentiment, and Isabel turned to discover none other than the owner of the trout stream sauntering across the grass towards them.

'Wait a moment, Josh,' the Viscount ordered, as his ward, having already divested himself of shoes and stockings, was on the point of joining Isabel in the water. 'Help me off with these confounded boots first.'

Isabel found herself unashamedly admiring his lordship's muscular calves as he peeled off his stockings. Although nowhere near as white as her own, the skin on his legs was several shades lighter than that on his face, and had a liberal covering of fine black hair, as did his arms.

Oddly enough, as he waded into the water towards her, she experienced not a single moment's disquiet at having a gentleman in a state of undress standing so close. In fact, the opposite was true, for she gurgled with mirth when he proceeded to take her to task for spinning Josh such a yarn about the gigantic trout.

'Whale, indeed! If I'd a shiny sovereign for every fishy tale I'd heard…'

'You'd be twice as wealthy as you are now,' she finished for him, grinning wickedly up at him, and receiving the full warmth of his own smile in return. 'I dare say. But it won't do him any harm. Look at him now,' she added, after watching Josh searching the depths on the far side of the stream for the monster trout, 'as contented as can be. He might never find the elusive Big Jake, but there's plenty of prize specimens lurking in these shallows. I can attest to that.'

'Yes, I'm sure you can, you baggage!' he returned and, although not sounding altogether pleased, not fooling her for a moment by the mock show of disapproval.

'I know how you've been making free with my game over these past years.'

'Ah, but only when my garden produce was damaged by your poor drainage,' she reminded him, totally unabashed. 'And never once since your return, until today.' She turned her head on one side, looking, he decided, most adorable. 'I considered it recompense.'

'You did, did you? Well, let us see if we can catch a couple more for your supper.'

Borrowing Isabel's rod, his lordship was more than equal to the challenge, and very soon caught three fine specimens before abandoning the sport in order to join Isabel on the bank. Unlike his companion, who had instantly readjusted her attire on leaving the water, he made no attempt to don any of his, and settled himself on the grass beside her, allowing the sun to dry his legs and bared portion of his arms.

By belatedly thanking him for the fish, Isabel broke the companionable silence, but his lordship, at first dismissing the gratitude with a wave of his hand, considered her for a moment.

'You can repay me by dancing with me at the party next week. You can dance, I trust?'

Isabel had not missed the wickedly mocking rise of those arching black brows. 'I'm not a complete country bumpkin,' she assured him. 'Of course I can dance! Well, most all the country dances, at any rate.'

'I thought as much.' He tutted. 'So you cannot waltz.'

'Of course not!' she returned primly. 'It has never been danced at the assemblies in Merryfield. Even I know it's frowned upon in polite circles.'

'Not so much now,' he enlightened her. 'It is at last

beginning to win approval at private functions. I discovered a good dancing master when in London recently. It just so happens he's agreed to break his journey to Nottinghamshire on Monday, so you can come over to the Manor in the afternoon, and receive expert tuition, if you'd like. In fact, I insist upon it,' he went on, adopting a very dictatorial stance. 'It's the least you can do to reimburse me for all the poaching you've done during my many years away. Besides which, dancing together will afford a golden opportunity to discuss what, if anything, we've been able to uncover at the party, without arousing suspicion.'

As he was lying beside her, with his head resting on his hands, and his eyes closed, Isabel wasn't able to judge whether he was being serious or not. All the same, she had the feeling that more lay behind his wanting her to dance with him than he was willing to reveal.

Decidedly suspicious though she might have been, Isabel, nonetheless, allowed herself to be conveyed to the Manor in his lordship's carriage directly after luncheon on Monday afternoon. Tredwell escorted her up the imposing wooden staircase to the long gallery, where she discovered not only his lordship talking with a dapper little man dressed formally in satin knee breeches, white stockings and pumps, but also her cousin, seated at a pianoforte.

'Ha! Miss Mortimer.' His lordship, instantly breaking off his conversation, came forward. 'May I make you known to Mr Petersham, the owner of the famous Petersham School of Dancing.'

'Enchanted, *mademoiselle*,' the little man greeted

her, bowing low over her hand. 'Already I have observed you move with ease and grace, and have a lightness of step. It should be no problem to teach you. Just as I had little difficulty instructing your fair cousin, who has kindly agreed to remain and provide us with music.'

'Aren't we bold?' Clara whispered, as Isabel placed her bonnet on the table beside the instrument.

She refrained from comment, though she couldn't help feeling that her cousin's employment at the Manor had not been wholly advantageous. One would hesitate to call her unbecomingly forward, exactly. All the same, her association with the Viscount over the weeks had definitely boosted Clara's self-confidence.

The little dancing-master's prediction turned out to be correct. Within the space of half an hour, Isabel had mastered the steps, and was confident enough to hold her head up, and not stare down at her feet. In fact, she found the dance exhilarating, and wasn't in the least self-conscious having a man's hand resting lightly on her waist, until, that is, his lordship ceased to turn the pages of music for Clara, and took the dancing-master's place. Then it was as much as Isabel could do to stop herself from treading on his feet, while she kept her gaze riveted to the intricate folds of his snowy-white cravat.

'Come, *ma belle*,' he chided gently. 'People will suspect I've coerced you into dancing with me at the party, if you look so terrified.'

Although she wasn't perfectly certain she knew quite what his touch was doing to her, of one thing she was certain, it had nothing whatsoever to do with fear. It took a monumental effort, but she managed to raise her eyes to his, then promptly lowered them again when she perceived the satisfied glint lurking in those blue depths. The wretch knew—knew full well that his touch was having an adverse effect on her equilibrium, sending her pulse rate soaring, not to mention increasing her bodily temperature to such an extent that the palms of her hands felt sticky, and she was sure she had gone quite red in the face.

Consequently she wasn't altogether sorry when the dance came to an end, and his lordship's attention was immediately afterwards claimed by the unexpected appearance of a very imposing elderly matron, dressed from head to toe in purple, making her way down the length of the gallery towards him.

'Good gad! Lady Pimm!' He placed a dutiful salute on the lined cheek presented to him. 'Didn't expect to see you until Wednesday at the earliest.'

'I cannot recall mentioning precisely when I should be arriving when you visited me in London recently. I trust there are rooms ready for me and my maid,' she added, casting a brief glance in the direction of the dancing-master, before favouring the two females present with her full attention.

Although Lady Pimm had been painfully well aware of her godson's rakish behaviour in his youth, she had never heard it said that he had ever attempted to seduce innocence. Nor could she recall that he had ever been guilty of bringing a light-skirt back to the ancestral pile. She could fully appreciate what might have attracted him to the golden-haired chit. The girl was quite stunningly lovely, and his name, of course, had been linked with several accredited beauties in the past. And not all of them unmarried, she reflected. But just what the attraction might be to the other female escaped her. The young woman was maybe here for propriety, a relative or some such, she finally decided.

'Won't you introduce me to your young companions, Sebastian? Petersham, I know, of course,' she revealed, acknowledging the dancing-master's bow with a slight nod. 'A year or so ago he successfully instructed my flat-footed niece to acquire at least a modicum of grace on the dance floor, for which the family remains eternally grateful.'

His lordship complied with the request with his customary aplomb, introducing Isabel first to his godmother before turning to Isabel's cousin and revealing, much to her ladyship's evident surprise, that Clara was in his employ as governess to his wards.

An awkward silence then followed, during which her ladyship cast such a withering look in the direction of the pianoforte that Clara blushed to the roots of her hair. His lordship didn't appear entirely pleased, either, by his godmother's quite obvious misconceptions, and so Isabel, with great presence of mind, filled the breach before any further needless unpleasantness arose.

'And no doubt, Clara, you are eager to return to your charges. Thank you for playing so beautifully. I could not have managed half so well without you. Nor, indeed, without you, Mr Petersham. I believe now I shall go on very well at the party,' she added, offering her hand in farewell to the dapper little man, before finally taking leave of his lordship's autocratic godmother.

'I shall see you to the carriage,' his lordship said, an offer Isabel hurriedly declined.

'Please do not trouble, sir. I know my way out. And I think, in truth, I should much prefer to walk back home. The fresh air will do me good.'

It wasn't so much Isabel's charming smile of farewell that captured her ladyship's attention as a certain look that just for one moment sprang into her godson's eyes as he followed the cousins' progress along the gallery. But precisely which of the young women had engendered a look of such tenderness her ladyship was far from certain now.

It was not until early that evening, when she joined her godson in the parlour before dinner, that she received her first opportunity to satisfy her curiosity regarding the two young women. Notwithstanding, she thought it might be prudent to begin by apologising for her earlier, possibly, erroneous misconceptions.

'Even so, in my defence, Sebastian, I have to say it was a mistake anyone might have made,' she continued, accepting the glass of wine he held out to her. 'In my day governesses were never so favourably packaged. And you always did have an eye for a pretty face.'

He smiled secretively down into his glass. 'I still do, ma'am. But you'll never hear it said that I attempted to compromise an employee in this, or any other household. Miss Pentecost relies on me for her livelihood. I would never betray her trust.'

She regarded him through narrowed eyes. 'You've changed, Sebastian. You've grown. It would seem your years in the army were the making of you.'

Once again he smiled down into his glass. 'No, ma'am, you err. It wasn't my years in the Peninsula that

persuaded me to view certain matters rather differently. Oh, no... It was...something entirely different.'

He raised his eyes to discover himself the recipient of a very penetrating look. 'Tell me, ma'am, are your rooms to your liking? Have you everything you need?'

'Everything is most comfortable, Sebastian,' she assured him. 'I must say the Manor is looking very fine. You've clearly transformed the place since your return. And the drawing room is splendid. Just as wonderful as it looked in your dear mama's day! It is the same colour scheme, is it not?'

'Why, yes, I do believe it is,' he replied, once again smiling that same infuriatingly enigmatic smile.

She would dearly have loved to know what he was thinking about, but as she was fairly certain he would not satisfy her curiosity she decided to steer the conversation back to the other topic that had intrigued her since her arrival.

'And I assume you will be holding the party in there?'

'Yes, indeed, as there is no ballroom here at the Manor, as you well know.'

'And am I right in believing you've invited none other than your governess's cousin?'

He shrugged, maintaining quite beautifully a display of indifference. 'I could hardly do otherwise, ma'am, now could I? Among my guests will be several friends of Daniel and Sarah Collier, who shall be putting up at several different locations in the area. I believe they would wish to see the children. So naturally I shall require the governess to present them. And she could

hardly attend the party without the support of the older cousin, Miss Mortimer, now could she?'

Far from satisfied, her ladyship peered owlishly up at her godson, who, save for a glint of amusement still lurking in those strikingly blue eyes, maintained an annoyingly expressionless stance before the hearth.

'Mortimer…? Mortimer?' she repeated. 'Now where have I heard that name before recently?'

'From me, I dare say. You knew her grandmother, Lady Mary Brent,' he reminded her.

'Ah, yes! A spirited minx in her youth, and not altogether wise, but I liked her. She eloped with a handsome young rogue, an inveterate gamester, and bore him a child, a daughter, before he got himself shot in a duel over some gambling dispute. The family never welcomed her back into the fold after her scandalous marriage. Her father, the sixth Earl of Trowbridge, was very high in the instep, and his successors equally so. But I believe Mary went on quite well, mainly due to the generosity of her wealthy godmother, with whom she resided when not visiting the capital. She had a wide circle of friends, and not all the members of the *ton* snubbed her, so she continued to socialise frequently, as did her daughter, I believe. What eventually became of the child, I cannot for the life of me now recall.'

'She married a Dr John Mortimer, and bore him one child. After several years in the capital, he set up a practice here in the local community.'

She regarded her godson in silence for a moment. 'So Miss Mortimer is Mary Brent's granddaughter, is she? I wonder if she possesses her grandmother's spirit?'

'You must judge for yourself, ma'am,' he told her,

almost conveying the impression the subject held no special interest for him. But then he said, oh, so very gently, 'She does, however, possess many fine qualities. Had it not been for the selfless actions of that young woman, I might even now still have been wanted for murder. I owe her more than I could ever hope to repay.'

Was it simple gratitude he felt towards Lady Mary's granddaughter? she couldn't help wondering. And what of the other girl, the cousin? Surely he wasn't so indifferent to her? Had she, too, some notable family connections?

'She is the daughter of a gentleman and undeniably a genteel young woman,' he responded in answer to her questions. 'Who her antecedents might have been, I have never troubled to enquire. She is employed as governess in my household, and carries out her duties to my satisfaction. That is all that concerns me.'

Lady Pimm wasn't entirely convinced by the assurance. How could such a red-blooded male like Blackwood be indifferent to such a beauty? Either his character had changed completely during the past nine years, or he was doing his level best to conceal something. She would need to do a little investigating of her own, if only to satisfy her curiosity. Something had happened to her godson. That much was certain! Maybe his experiences in Spain had influenced his behaviour, changing him from a wild and occasionally thoughtless young man into a person of sound judgement and discretion. Or had there been other beneficial influences in his life? Who could say? The only thing she was certain of was that never before had she seen him looking so relaxed, so at ease with himself.

* * *

Two days later, however, Lady Pimm was no closer to solving the conundrum of her godson's behaviour, save that she was certain in her own mind that Lord Blackwood's manner was not feigned. He seemed truly contented with his lot.

She paid a daily visit to the nursery, and by the time she had left on the second occasion she was firmly convinced that the beautiful cousin, amazingly enough, held no particular attraction for him. When she had happened to enter a short time earlier, and had discovered him there, she had glimpsed nothing in his expression to suggest he was even remotely captivated by the girl with the gentle blue eyes, golden locks and enviably flawless complexion. In fact, if anything, he had betrayed a deal more enthusiasm at the prospect of taking his elder ward out riding later that morning.

But what of the other cousin? she wondered, making her way back along the gallery to her allotted bedchamber. Did his interest in her stem only from a feeling of gratitude? Or was there, perhaps, something far more meaningful lurking beneath the surface, just waiting to be uncovered? There was only one way she would satisfy her ever-increasing curiosity.

'Dimmock, we are going out,' she revealed, discovering her personal maid of many years standing tidying the yellow bedchamber. 'Arrange for my carriage to be brought round to the door, and get ready yourself. I shall need you to accompany me. Your judgement is second to none!'

Isabel was unable to hide her surprise when Bessie showed her visitors into the parlour shortly before

midday. 'Why, Lady Pimm, this is an unexpected pleasure! Won't you sit down?' Her eyes slid briefly to the thin little woman who had seated herself near the door, before turning again to the imposing matron and offering refreshment.

'A glass of port would be most appreciated. My godson is most disapproving of my chosen tipple. But then I do not believe he likes to see females imbibing too freely.'

'I find that hard to believe, ma'am,' Isabel didn't hesitate to confess. 'He's always forcing a filled glass into my hand whenever I go to see him. Which fortunately is not so very often that I stand the risk of becoming a toper.'

For several seconds Lady Pimm studied the young woman who had seated herself opposite, noting the evenness of her features. There was a confident directness in her gaze, which her cousin's sadly lacked. Not only that, there was no mistaking the intelligence in the greyish-green eyes. She too had been blessed with a flawless complexion, and a healthy sheen to her chestnut locks, which today were merely adequately confined by a ribbon at the nape of her neck. 'Now I come to study you more closely, my dear, I see you have a great look of your grandmother about you.'

'Sadly she died when I was very young, ma'am. I do not remember her at all.'

Once again Isabel found herself the recipient of a long, assessing look. She wished she knew just why she had been honoured with this visit. However, not wishing to appear rude, she refrained from asking outright. Instead, she brought the uncomfortable little silence

to an end by enquiring whether other guests had now arrived at the Manor.

'Sebastian said one or two would be arriving this evening, but no family members. I believe they are all arriving tomorrow. Not that I should imagine they'll cause the staff at the Manor too much extra work. There are so few close members of the Blackwood family still living.'

Once again Lady Pimm stared long and hard over the rim of her glass, before sampling its contents and smiling approval. 'And you and your charming young cousin are to grace the event, so I understand?'

Isabel's grimace in response was most intriguing, and Lady Pimm's curiosity was instantly aroused. She immediately sought an explanation for the evident reluctance, and quickly discovered that the young woman who was rising in her estimation with every passing minute was quite capable of keeping her own counsel.

'Oh, there are several reasons, my lady,' was all Isabel would reveal, only to discover that her visitor was not to be so easily discouraged.

'Oh, come, my dear! Young women of your age love parties and dancing.' She looked thoughtfully at the neat, but clearly provincial day dress Isabel was wearing. 'Forgive my asking, child, but your reluctance doesn't stem from not having a suitable gown to wear for the occasion, I trust?'

If anything Isabel's expression betrayed even more disquiet. 'Oh, no, my lady. I have a gown, right enough!'

Lady Pimm could not mistake the disgruntled tone and, more curious than ever, requested to see the garment. The instant she detected Isabel's light tread

mounting a staircase, she addressed the other occupant of the room, who had sat in her chair throughout, quietly observing the young mistress of the house. 'What say you, Dimmock? Not too difficult a task to bring the chit up to scratch?'

The middle-aged abigail didn't pretend to misunderstand. 'She has good features, my lady, and an excellent figure.'

'Yes, and far more character than that cousin of hers. I wonder…? Yes, I'm truly beginning to believe it's possible. I shall rely on you, Dimmock, to bring to bear all your skills.' She raised a warning finger. 'Quiet now, I believe she is returning.'

Lady Pimm, never having been one to conceal her emotions, made not the least attempt to hide her astonishment when Isabel held the gown against her, the better for her visitor to pass judgement.

'I know, ma'am, you do not need to tell me,' Isabel assured her, having interpreted the astonished expression for disapproval. 'But it's too late now for me to have another made. Besides which, I don't wish to offend his lordship. The gesture was kindly meant, I know. But I have made it quite clear that I shall accept nothing else from him.'

It took Lady Pimm a moment or two to assimilate precisely what she was being told. 'Do I infer correctly from that, that it was none other than my godson who purchased the garment for you?'

Looking plainly guilt-stricken, Isabel nodded. 'And I do wish he had not. The gesture was well meant. But really there was no need. It was my father, not I, who wrote an account of what took place on that eventful

night, when his lordship's father and brother lost their lives. All I did was to ensure the information was passed on to the right people.'

Although Lady Pimm had listened to every word, her eyes had remained fixed on the beautiful gown. That her godson had gone to the trouble of choosing the garment himself told her all she needed to know. The dress was beautifully made, and clearly the creation of one of the capital's leading modistes. What a demon he was! she mused. Unless she was much mistaken, he had chosen the colour with particular care. And it suited the chit admirably!

'Well, my dear, it is hardly a suitable garment for a girl embarking on her first Season to wear. But, without wishing to give offence, a young woman in her mid-twenties can scarcely be looked upon in such a light. You will carry the colour extremely well. What say you, Dimmock?'

'Indeed, yes, ma'am,' the maid dutifully agreed, before adding, 'providing it is worn with the correct accessories.'

Feeling decidedly uncomfortable under the two females' continued scrutiny, Isabel informed them that his lordship had seen fit to provide her with silk shawl, evening gloves and slippers, all of which had been dyed the exact shade as the dress. 'And everything fits perfectly. Though the Lord only knows how he managed to judge my size so accurately!'

Her ladyship tactfully refrained from pointing out that her godson was no stranger to the female form. Instead, she asked what, if any, jewellery would be worn to the party.

'Well, I haven't quite made up my mind yet, ma'am,' Isabel admitted. 'I have a fine gold locket, or there's a single string of pearls, which belonged to my mother. Also, I have a garnet necklace.' She smiled reminiscently. 'Papa never objected to Mama buying jewellery. He was no expert, and so when she told him they were rubies, he believed her. She felt so guilty about spending so much money, you see, on a ruby set.'

'I consider any of those would be admirable,' Lady Pimm responded, adding, as she rose to her feet, 'And, my child, if you would not be offended, I should like to offer my maid's services to dress you for the evening. She has quite a remarkable way with hair. Mine, of course, being grey and wispy, can never do justice to her skills. Yours, on the other hand, most definitely shall. So may I send her over to you on Friday afternoon?'

In view of such kind generosity, Isabel considered it would be ungracious to refuse.

Chapter Nine

Throughout her adult life thus far, the nearest Isabel had ever come to having a personal maid had been Bessie, who had helped her to dress for the odd social evening Isabel had enjoyed since attaining the age of sixteen. Before her father had become ill, she had accompanied him from time to time when he had been invited to dine in the more affluent households in the locale. She had also enjoyed the rare evening's entertainment since her father's demise, and felt she had left the house on all these occasions always looking presentable enough, and without suffering the least qualms over her appearance.

None the less, Bessie herself would have been the first to admit that she lacked those special skills inherent in every professional lady's maid. Consequently, she was only too happy to place her young mistress into the hands of the birdlike little woman who arrived at the farmhouse at the prearranged time on Friday afternoon.

Because her cousin had decided not to return to the

farmhouse, and to dress for the evening at the Manor, with the young nursery-maid's assistance, Isabel was able to luxuriate for quite some time in the rose-scented water of the hipbath, placed next to the kitchen range, without fear of interruption. Having her hair carefully washed, and then relaxing outside, whilst all the time her locks were drying in the late afternoon sun, was a luxury she had never before experienced. So it was hardly surprising that, long before her long tresses had been piled high on the back of her head, the majority of which fell in a softly waving ponytail, and her lips and cheeks had been touched with colour, she had already begun to feel extremely special indeed.

As she gazed into her late mother's dressing-table mirror, she barely recognised herself. She had allowed the abigail to do precisely as she wished. With a few judicious snips of the scissors the lady's maid had fashioned several wispy curls to cascade on to Isabel's cheeks, and had strategically positioned a beautiful pearl comb into the glowing chestnut locks.

'I hardly know what to say, Dimmock. I would never have attempted such a style myself. There is almost a Grecian quality about it. Thank you so much.'

'Your hair is beautiful, Miss Mortimer, a real pleasure to dress,' the maid responded, looking rather satisfied with the results of her efforts herself. 'And the comb just adds that extra special touch, do you not think?'

'It certainly does, but... Who does it belong to?'

The maid's expression all at once seemed guarded. 'My mistress brought it with her from London,' she finally revealed.

'Then it is most kind of her to lend it to me for the evening,' Isabel responded, touched by the gesture, for she had nothing in her jewellery box to equal it. 'But I rather fancy it has settled on my choice of necklace—Mama's pearls, I think.'

'If I might suggest putting on your gown first, miss, and then decide,' the abigail suggested, going across to the good quality, if slightly old-fashioned, wardrobe where the dress had been safely stored since its arrival in the house.

With one expert movement the maid had the dress over Isabel's head, without so much as disturbing a single lock of hair. Once she had each fastening secured, she invited Isabel to sit again in front of the mirror, before she reached again for the velvet-covered flat box, which she had brought with her from the Manor.

Inside, resting on a bed of purple silk, were two pearl-drop earrings and the most beautiful matching necklace Isabel had ever seen. Two individual strands of pearls came together in a beautifully fashioned knot and then divided again to cascade over the wearer's chest.

'But surely Lady Pimm wishes to wear them herself?' Isabel suggested, after gazing in awe at the beautiful set.

'On the contrary, miss. Her ladyship would be only too happy if you agreed to wear them. She has always maintained that jewels always look much better when displayed against young skin.'

By the time the necklace had been fastened about her neck, and she had donned the earrings, Isabel was too astounded by the change in her appearance to voice

adequately enough her thanks to the little woman who had wrought such a miracle.

Her amazement, however, was as nothing when compared to Bessie's reaction on first catching sight of her mistress descending the stairs. Whipping out her handkerchief, she did no more than burst into tears.

'Oh, Miss Isabel, you look like a princess, so you do!'

With perhaps one exception only, there was no one's approbation that she valued more. Even so, Isabel was nothing if not a realist. She possibly looked the best she'd ever looked in her entire life, but she had not turned into a ravishing beauty in the space of a few hours, and she had sense enough to realise it.

'Pull yourself together, woman!' she scolded lovingly. 'And don't you dare to wait up for my return, understand! Clara and I are more than capable of helping each other to disrobe. Just leave the lamp burning on the hall table.'

Then, after hurriedly placing a kiss on Bessie's cheek, she whisked herself outside to where his lordship's carriage awaited her, before she was infected by her housekeeper's sentimentality and gave way to a weakness she despised.

The journey to the Manor, of course, took no time at all, and as there were no carriages waiting to disgorge their passengers she was able to enter the Manor without further ado. Tredwell, a prince among butlers, betrayed no sign whatsoever that he had observed the slightest change in her appearance, and merely turned to lead the way across the hall to the drawing room.

Isabel automatically followed, until, that is, she detected an impish chuckle filtering down from high above her head.

After mounting half-a-dozen stairs, she easily located the source of amusement. Two small faces were peering down at her through the banister rails. 'What on earth are you two doing about at this time?' she demanded to know.

'Our guardian said we might stay to watch the guests arriving, at least those invited for dinner,' Josh enlightened her. 'But we only really wanted to see you.' His expression revealed that he wasn't entirely impressed with what he saw, even before he added, 'You do look funny, Miss Isabel.'

'No, she doesn't,' Alice countered, casting her older sibling a disapproving look. 'She looks as beautiful as Miss Pentecost. She's been invited to dine as well, Miss Isabel.'

'In that case I'd best present myself to our host, and not keep the other guests waiting for their meal.'

'Indeed you had,' a velvety voice behind her softly agreed, and Isabel turned to discover his lordship at the foot of the stairs.

Never before had she seen him dressed in formal evening attire, and thought he looked magnificent. Secretly she might have preferred to see him in his less formal riding garb, but even so he looked so distinguished in his long-tailed black coat and buff-coloured knee-breeches. What he thought of her appearance was impossible to judge, for apart from a lingering look at the adornment hanging about her neck, his expression revealed little, before he bade the children goodnight,

instructing the little nursery-maid, who had remained hovering in the shadows, to take his wards to bed.

'Come, *ma belle*.' He held out his left hand. 'There are several people eager to make your acquaintance, and one other very eager to renew it.'

Once she had reached his side, he did not hesitate to wrap her arm round his so that they might enter the drawing room together. 'Tell me, *ma belle*, from where did you obtain that pearl set?' he asked casually, as they approached the beautifully redecorated room. 'Were they your mother's, perhaps?'

'Oh, no, my lord. They are your godmother's. It was so very kind of her to allow me to wear them for the evening, do you not think?'

'Kindness, I strongly suspect, had precious little to do with it, *ma belle*. And my name is Sebastian.'

'Yes, I know that, my lord.'

'Baggage!' he muttered, but to little effect, for Isabel was too intent on scrutinising the new décor to pay much heed.

'Oh, sir, how different it all looks! It's magnificent! You must be very well pleased.'

'Yes, very much to my taste. I could not have chosen better,' he declared, staring intently down at her. 'And now, *ma belle*, I wish to reacquaint you with an old friend of mine.' And without further ado he led her towards the only man in the room who was fractionally taller than himself.

'You remember Miss Mortimer, do you not, Charles?'

'How could I forget her?' the big man responded gallantly, while taking the proffered slender hand and bowing over it. 'Though, I'm forced to add, I would

have been hard put to it, my dear Miss Mortimer, to have picked you out in a crowded ballroom.'

He favoured the Viscount with a surprised look. 'And what are you still lingering for, Blackwood? I do believe Lady Pimm is trying to attract your attention. You may safely leave Miss Mortimer in my care. Go away, do, and see what the formidable matron wants, whilst I look out our friend Staveley and make him known to this charming young lady.'

The Viscount had a fairly shrewd notion why his godmother was so eager for a word, and sauntered over to where she was seated by the wall. 'And how long have you been in possession of Mama's pearls?'

'Since that wretch of a father of yours gave them to me shortly after her death. He said he thought I might like them, as your mother and I were particular friends. Wicked, it was! Just because he never purchased them for her. They should have been added to the family jewels. The Lord alone knows what became of the other fine pieces she brought with her to the marriage! But I always intended to return the set to you. That is why I brought it with me.'

When he continued to stare down at her with lazy affection, uttering not a word, she peered up at him wickedly. 'It has been some years since they have been seen in public, Sebastian... I trust the neck on which they are now being displayed is the right one?'

'Why my mama, who was so sensible as a rule, chose such a devious and wicked woman for my godmother, I fail to understand,' he responded, thereby igniting Lady Pimm's wicked sense of humour.

'I shall tell you why, you young rogue. It is because

she knew I was not easily shocked, and therefore would never be scandalised by your future behaviour. Although you have surprised me on this occasion,' she went on to admit. 'Pleasantly surprised me, I might add. That young woman is quite out of the common way. And, unless I much mistake the matter, like myself, not easily shocked. Not that you would ever seek my approval, Sebastian. All the same, I shall take leave to inform you that I think you have chosen wisely.'

For answer all he did was to offer his arm in order to assist her to her feet, a moment after the estimable Tredwell had announced dinner. He had already secured his good friend Charles Bathurst's services to escort Isabel in to dinner, and had been equally successful in persuading the very gentlemanly Sir Philip Staveley to offer his support to Isabel's much shyer younger cousin. Sebastian had also ensured that the position on his governess's left was filled by someone who would undoubtedly put the young woman very much at her ease, a fact that didn't escape Isabel's notice as she took her place between the two very personable gentlemen who had kept her very well entertained soon after her arrival.

She took a moment to stare round the table at her fellow dinner guests, twenty in all. Some she knew well enough, or at least by sight—the curate, Mr Johns, for instance, and Sir Montague Cameron and his wife and eldest son; others were complete strangers. Yet not one among the unknown female guests could she have said with any degree of conviction was likely to be married to either of the very personable gentlemen sitting either side of her.

'Did your wife not choose to accompany you, Mr Bathurst?' she finally asked, curiosity having got the better of her.

'No, unfortunately not. My wife is in, what you might say is, a delicate condition, as is Sir Philip's, I might add.'

'Oh, many congratulations, sir! When do you expect the happy events to take place?'

'Not until the autumn. Both ladies were disappointed not to be here, most especially Lady Staveley, who's a good friend of the Viscount. Sense, however, prevailed, and she, too, considered her unborn child.'

The instant Mr Bathurst's attention was claimed by the lady on his right, Isabel congratulated Sir Philip on his recent marriage, and happy future event. 'I understand your wife knows Lord Blackwood well.'

Not all gentlemen, she felt sure, would have been too pleased to discover that their wives had enjoyed a close association with the Viscount. Surprisingly enough, though, the charming Baronet seemed completely unperturbed.

'Yes, they were both out in Spain together,' he explained, once again displaying the ease of manner that Isabel found most winning. 'My wife was with her father throughout most of the Peninsular Campaign. Beth's father and Lord Blackwood were involved in similar work.'

'I see. And you, sir…? Were you also out in Spain?'

He shook his head. 'But I did know Sebastian slightly many years ago, but I didn't really get to know him well until he stayed in Somerset with my good friend Bathurst last autumn.' He leaned towards her, adding

in a conspiratorial whisper, 'It was during that period he had the impudence to propose marriage to the lady who I now have the honour to call my wife.'

Even though Isabel couldn't mistake the wicked twinkle in a pair of attractive grey eyes, something akin to an icy bolt tore through her at the mere thought of the Viscount being in love. It took a monumental effort to rally her disordered thoughts sufficiently to say, 'Well, sir, at least she had the sense to refuse and marry you instead. Clearly a lady of discernment.'

Sir Philip's spontaneous bark of laughter drew the attention of several of those at the table, including the host himself, who favoured Isabel with a half-reproachful, half-quizzical glance.

Thankfully the moment's madness, undoubtedly engendered by an unexpected surge of searing jealousy, was blessedly over. She now had herself well in hand again, and could only wonder at herself for experiencing such an emotion in the first place. After all, wasn't it more than likely the Viscount had been in love with a score of women and more during his incident-filled adult life? Of course it was! And it shouldn't matter a whit to her anyway, she told herself, determined to maintain a practical outlook and concentrate on why she had been invited to the party in the first place.

Consequently, as soon as the delicious dinner was over, and everyone had returned to the drawing room before the majority of guests began to arrive for the party, Isabel requested Charles Bathurst to take a stroll with her about the garden. He was only too willing to comply, and together they slipped out of the French

windows on to the terrace, and then down the steps
to the rose garden, which had truly been transformed
since the last time Isabel had strolled through it with
the Viscount himself.

'I do not wish to importune you, sir,' she began, not
wasting precious moments alone with him if she could
avoid doing so, 'but I could think of no one else here
tonight in whom I could happily confide.'

Quickly recognising the concern in her eyes, Charles
Bathurst suggested they sit on one of the benches sited
at intervals along the gravel path, before asking how
he might serve her.

'Sir, you know as much as I do about the events that
took place here nine long years ago, now,' she began.
'His lordship has asked me here tonight in order to help
him discover something…anything that just might shed
some light on the identity of the murderer.'

Masculine brows rose sharply at this disclosure.
'Indeed…? Said that, did he?' There was a suspicion
of an amused glint in his dark eyes. 'It would appear
my good friend is being remarkably cautious for once.
Well, well, well!'

'With good reason, sir,' Isabel pointed out, thinking
his reaction strange, 'if among his guests tonight is,
indeed, the murderer of his father and brother.'

It was clear she had captured his full attention now.
'And does he suppose this is so?'

She shrugged. 'That I couldn't say. All I do know is
that we're both convinced the crime was not perpetrated
by a stranger. And I was just hoping for your views on
the matter. You know his lordship well, sir, perhaps
better than anyone else here tonight knows him. You

know far more about his past misdemeanours. You must surely have a better idea of who would wish him harm.'

After an initial show of surprise at her plain speaking, he sighed. 'It would indeed be less than honest for me to pretend Sebastian was any kind of a saint in his youth, Miss Mortimer, for he was not. That said, he wasn't as black as he was sometimes painted, either. The truth lies somewhere between.'

'You misunderstand, sir,' she told him. 'It isn't so much his past that concerns me as his future. You see, I do not perfectly understand why his lordship was spared that night.'

She took a moment to stare down at the painted figures on her fan; yet another present from the gentleman who had come to mean so much to her that if she could in some way help to prove his innocence beyond doubt she would move heaven and earth to do so.

'If the grievance was against the Blackwood family as a whole, why then wasn't Sebastian killed that night too? Instead, the murderer merely tried to frame him. Why? Was Sebastian the main target? Was the intention that he should suffer more by being imprisoned and then hanged for something he didn't do? It's the motive, sir, that continues to elude me. Was it revenge for one of his lordship's past misdeeds, or a grievance against the family as a whole? If the latter, then why didn't the murderer take advantage of the fact that Sebastian was also in the house? After all, there was always the possibility he might be proved innocent. As, indeed, has turned out to be the case.' She shook her head, at a loss, still, to be sure of what the true answer might be.

'If we could only uncover the motive, I'm certain the identity of the murderer must surely follow.'

Charles Bathurst sighed. 'Believe me, my dear young lady, I too have pondered long and hard over those very same questions, and have come up with no conclusive answers.' He raised his eyes as he detected someone's approach. 'Ah, Staveley, the very man! See if that great brain of yours can aid our cause. Our friend Sebastian, it would seem, is at last determined to uncover the identity of the murderer of his father and brother, and has invited Miss Mortimer here tonight—er—ostensibly in order to help him in this task.'

Although she witnessed the two men exchange a look, Isabel was far too concerned about the Viscount's predicament to ponder over what lay behind the personable gentlemen's wry expressions.

'Really?' Sir Philip's brows rose markedly as he accepted Isabel's invitation to seat himself. 'At the risk of appearing obtuse, I do not immediately perceive how I can be of assistance to you, my dear Miss Mortimer, given that until quite recently his lordship and I were, at best, acquaintances only.'

'And given that he attempted to win the woman who is now your wife,' she parried, 'begs the question, does it not, of whether you'd wish to help.'

Once again the gentlemanly Baronet showed his appreciation of her ready wit by a bark of laughter. 'Charles, old fellow, I think we can both appreciate just why our mutual friend chose Miss Mortimer as his—er—accomplice. A keen intellect, coupled with outstanding physical attributes, is a combination gentlemen of discernment find most appealing.

'But let me assure you, my dear young woman,' Sir Philip continued on a more serious note, 'that I bear Blackwood no ill will. In fact, had it not been for him, I might never have been the thoroughly contented man you see before you today. I owe him a debt of gratitude that if I could repay by being of any assistance I wouldn't hesitate. The only thing I can tell you is that when business took me to London quite recently, I never heard an ill word concerning our mutual friend. In fact, the opposite was true. Talk in the clubs was all about his exploits in Spain, which now have become common knowledge. And how dignified he has become during his years away.'

'But not so dignified that I won't attempt to kick you into the nearest midden if you continue to betray your darling wife's trust by flirting with other women the moment you're away from Staveley Court,' the Viscount jokingly threatened, as he arrived at the bench without being noticed.

'Come, Belle.' Reaching for her hand, he assisted her to rise to her feet. 'Let me remove you from these rogues' pernicious influence,' he added, above the appreciative masculine laughter, 'and return you to the safety of the drawing room, where my esteemed godmother can offer you her protection.'

Although she accompanied him willingly enough, Isabel couldn't resist saying, 'Do you think I need protecting from your friends? They seem very personable gentlemen to me. What's more, they're both very happily married.'

When she failed to elicit a response, she asked, 'Did you really ask Lady Staveley to marry you?'

'Told you that, did he…?' He smiled crookedly. 'Yes, I did, as it happens,' he freely admitted, little realising that he had caused a further searing pain to grip her, only to vanquish it completely a moment later by adding, 'Thank God she had the sense to refuse! She was no more in love with me than I was with her.'

It took a monumental effort to stop herself from gaping up at him. 'You were not in love with her…? Then why on earth did you ask her to marry you?' she demanded to know, not unreasonably.

'I'm not quite sure. But I do believe I was overwhelmed by a surge of chivalry,' he said matter-of-factly. 'Without going into details, we were obliged to spend the most confoundedly uncomfortable night in a barn, sheltering from a snowstorm. Afterwards I felt honour-bound to offer her the protection of my name, of course. But, as I've already mentioned, the darling girl refused. She was in love with Staveley, you see, and had been for a considerable time. And now,' he went on, as they crossed the drawing room, which had been gradually becoming more crowded with the steady arrival of new guests invited to the party, 'I'm going to leave you with Lady Pimm, who has expressly wished to speak with you, whilst I repair to the adjoining parlour and organise the commencement of the dancing.'

Isabel wasn't in the least unhappy to be left with the imposing matron, simply because it offered her the opportunity to thank her sincerely for the loan of the pearls.

Lady Pimm swiftly set her straight on the matter. 'But, my dear, it isn't I who you should thank. I merely brought them back to the Manor in order to restore them

to the person I consider the rightful owner. The pearls belonged to Blackwood's mother. They were not from the family jewels, and so when she died Sebastian's father gave most all her personal belongings away to close friends and other members of the family.'

She shook her head. 'I cannot even begin to understand what possessed him to do such a thing! Cruel it was, an unfeeling thing to do. And all the more surprising because he was not innately a cruel person. But it was all of a piece with the rest where his attitude to his younger son was concerned.'

'Do you mean that he did not care for him at all, ma'am?' Isabel prompted when the font of knowledge beside her fell silent.

'I wouldn't go as far as to say that, my dear, no,' Lady Pimm responded, after staring thoughtfully at an imaginary spot on the carpet. 'The sixth Viscount Blackwood's first marriage had been, as so many are, an arranged affair. His wife Matilda was not a member of the aristocracy. None the less she came from good yeoman stock. And, more importantly, her wealthy father ensured that she came to the marriage with a generous dowry, a much-needed increment to the Blackwood family coffers. In return Matilda had her title. But, for all that, I believe it was a successful union, and of course the first Viscountess did her duty and presented her husband with an heir before she died.

'The Viscount's second marriage was somewhat different, however. Louise Carré was a member of the French aristocracy, accomplished and spirited, some might even say slightly haughty. Just like that son of hers can be on occasions when the mood takes him,'

she went on, easily picking out the tall figure of the present holder of the title as he emerged from the adjoining parlour, from where strains of a favourite country dance could now be heard. 'When Louise's father died, her mother brought her over to England, where she caused no small interest during her first Season. Why she chose Blackwood among all the eligible gentlemen vying for her hand, the Lord alone knows! He was certainly infatuated with her, and she, young as she was, certainly graced the Manor, improving both the house and gardens.'

Lady Pimm stared about her in evident appreciation. 'And there's no denying Louise showed excellent taste. I'm so pleased Sebastian has restored this beautiful room to its former glory, selecting the very same colour scheme his beloved mother chose soon after she became mistress of the house.'

It took Isabel a moment or two to assimilate what she had been told, then it was as much as she could do to stop herself from gaping yet again that evening. 'So it was once green and cream?' she asked, wanting to be sure she had not misunderstood, and the dowager confirmed it with a nod.

'The wall covering might be a shade or two lighter than it once was, but no less tasteful for that.'

Wishing to know more about his lordship's mother, Isabel once again steered the conversation back to the late Viscountess by asking Lady Pimm how she had come to know her.

'When she and her mother came to London they rented the house next door to my late husband's town house. Although I was a few years older than Louise, we

quickly became firm friends, and spent a deal of time in each other's company.' She sighed. 'I didn't whole-heartedly approve her choice of husband, and made my feelings known. But I am forced to admit that, at first, Louise seemed happy enough.'

'Evidently something happened to change that, ma'am,' Isabel prompted, when the dowager once again fell silent.

'Sebastian's birth, I should say,' Lady Pimm respond-ed, surprising Isabel somewhat. 'Oh, I wouldn't go as far as to say the marriage crumpled. But there was no denying that Henry Blackwood was a possessive man, and very much resented the affection and time Louise lavished on their baby son. She and Sebastian became inseparable, and Henry understandably, I suppose, resented that bond of affection. Matters didn't improve when Louise's mother came to live permanently in Eng-land. After her daughter's marriage, she returned to her native France for a while. She was an extremely astute woman, and had the sense to flee the land of her birth before the Terror began in earnest. More importantly, I suppose, she managed to leave with her fortune intact... a fortune that she left to her grandson. He came into the inheritance when he attained the age of five-and-twenty. But, of course, he was in hiding at the time, and never touched so much as a penny. During the intervening years the legacy has been amassing quite some interest, I do not doubt. Sebastian is now a very wealthy man, a very desirable matrimonial prize. And thankfully he has the sense to know it, and remains wary.'

Isabel wasn't so much concerned about fortune-hunt-ing débutantes and match-making mamas as she was

about wealth being a motive for murder. If his lordship died without issue, who would benefit by his demise? she couldn't help wondering, and turned to the lady who had done so much to satisfy her curiosity thus far.

'Concerning my godson's private fortune, I couldn't say. But the title and the estate would go to his uncle, Horace Blackwood.' She gestured towards the sofa nearest the impressive fireplace. 'He's that great bloated lump sprawled over there. If his over-indulgence doesn't kill him, his indolence will,' she predicted, betraying no sympathy whatsoever. 'The poor, insipid creature beside him is his long-suffering wife. The twiddle-poop on the end of the sofa is their son. Although I suppose I shouldn't say that,' she went on, looking faintly conscience-stricken. 'He was a sickly child, never strong, and it's clear to me he isn't well now—so thin and pasty. He was in Italy until a few weeks ago, until Napoleon's escape became common knowledge. A warmer climate suits Clement better. He's not long for this world, I fear. Consumption,' she revealed in an undertone. 'The best thing he could do for the Blackwood clan as a whole would be to marry and produce a male child or two before it's too late.'

Sensible advice, if slightly callous, Isabel mused, increasingly warming to the outspoken matron beside her. 'And has his lordship no other close relatives present tonight?'

'Let me see.' Lady Pimm cast a look about the room, her short-sighted eyes managing finally to pick out an impeccably attired young man of medium height, with a faintly haughty bearing. 'Yes, there's Francis Blackwood, over there,' she revealed, drawing Isabel's

attention to the gentleman in question. 'He's the only son of the youngest brother, Hubert. Well, I say only son...' She gave vent to a wicked cackle. 'Who knows how many of Hubert's by-blows might litter the land? A rake-helly young fellow he was in his day. But, like his two elder brothers, he married well. In fact, he did rather better than both Henry and Horace, at least financially. He married a wealthy cit's daughter and acquired a fine property quite near here. Francis and Sebastian saw each other frequently as children, though I rather fancy Francis was closer to Giles, Sebastian's half-brother.'

'And is he married, ma'am?'

'No, surprisingly not,' Lady Pimm revealed. 'And I cannot for the life of me understand why not. He's an extremely personable gentleman, in my opinion. His features are good, his bearing is even better, and his manners are most polished. I do not believe he's averse to female company, although I've never heard his name seriously linked with any lady's.' She shrugged. 'Perhaps, like Sebastian, he's choosy.

'Unlike George Blackwood, over there,' she added, once again indicating a certain spot in the room where a tall gentleman with dark hair was conversing with none other than Isabel's cousin. 'He's a more distant cousin. Against his family's advice he married that flighty piece who, you may or may not have noticed, was sitting on Sebastian's right at dinner. I seem to remember my godson's name being linked with hers at some point or other in the dim and distant past, but I believe it was only rumour. Sebastian's fond of his

cousin George. They're good friends. So he's hardly likely to snub George's wife, now is he?'

Indeed not, Isabel mused. All the same, given his lordship's past reputation where the fair sex was concerned, it was more than likely he'd made cuckolds of several men, and if George happened to number among them, he might still bear a grudge. Yes, revenge was certainly a strong motive for murder, as was the pursuit of wealth. But if either of those had been the inducement, then why had Sebastian's father and brother been slain and he had been effectively spared? No, there had to be something else behind it all; something that infuriatingly continued to elude her still.

Isabel was obliged to abandon her puzzling reflections when she and her companion were approached by a certain member of the Blackwood family, and she was introduced to Sebastian's cousin Francis who, she was silently forced to concede, lost none of his attractiveness when viewed from close quarters.

'Mortimer...?' he echoed, briefly retaining the hold he had on her hand. 'Now, where have I heard that name before, I wonder? Not one of the Devonshire Mortimers, by any chance?'

'It is more than likely, Francis, that you heard the name in connection with the tragic events that took place here some years ago. It was none other than Miss Mortimer's father who eventually made it possible for Sebastian to clear his name.'

Although his expression remained totally impassive, there was just for a moment a certain something about the intelligent grey eyes, when once again they rested upon her, that Isabel found hard to define, and which

vaguely reminded her of someone else; only for the life of her she couldn't bring to mind who it might be.

'Yes, of course—the doctor's daughter, if I mistake not. I did hear all about it. I can only suppose it must have been Sebastian who told me when I called to see him a few weeks ago. He will undoubtedly remain eternally in your debt.'

'Very likely,' Lady Pimm agreed, before changing the subject entirely by demanding to know why she hadn't seen him in the capital that year.

As it quickly became clear the two had many acquaintances in common, and therefore a quantity of gossip to exchange, Isabel excused herself the instant it was polite enough for her to do so, and made her way to the far side of the room in order to spend a little time with her cousin who was still being ably supported by the devoted Mr Johns. None the less, he remained only for the time it took to exchange a few pleasantries with Isabel, before tactfully moving away so that the cousins might converse in private.

'What an absolutely delightful party!' Clara enthused, fanning herself with the delicate ivory-and-chicken-skin present Isabel had given her for her birthday a few days before. 'Everyone has been so very kind to me, most especially his lordship, and Mr Johns too, of course. He has remained close by to support me throughout, should I become overawed by it all.'

Isabel rolled her eyes at this piece of naïve nonsense. Her cousin looked absolutely divine in the simple white-and-silver-thread gown she'd made. There couldn't possibly be a red-blooded male present who wasn't very

well aware that she was by far the most lovely female in the room. His lordship's show of attention towards her might well have stemmed from purely altruistic motives. The same, however, could not be said for Mr Johns! She had seen him scowling heavily on two or three occasions, when one or two of the young blades present had made themselves known to Clara.

'Even though I am employed here as a governess, several gentlemen have secured a dance with me. Is that not kind?'

Resisting the temptation to tease her, Isabel merely nodded, before revealing that no gentlemen had requested her to dance. 'Well, except his lordship, that is,' she amended.

Clara frowned slightly. 'Yes, I think he has been keeping an eye on you, Isabel. I noticed him staring at you on several occasions during dinner, and a short time ago when you were conversing with Lady Pimm, though I can perfectly understand why. I hardly recognised you when you arrived, and walked into the room with his lordship. You look splendid in that dress. Mr Johns said that he had never seen you looking so well... And those pearls!'

'Why, yes, they are beautiful, aren't they,' Isabel responded, her mind working furiously. 'Lady Pimm brought them with her from London,' she revealed artfully, for some reason not wanting to disclose that they really belonged to the Viscount. 'And as for his lordship's behaviour...' She shrugged. 'I expect he's merely making sure I'm fulfilling my promise, that is all. I've

pledged to behave with the utmost decorum throughout the evening and offend no one.'

'And also to dance with him,' a now very familiar, smooth velvety voice unexpectedly reminded her.

Chapter Ten

Although her cousin appeared slightly taken aback by the unexpected appearance of her employer, Isabel felt all at once so very gratified to be reminded of the promise she had made by none other than the host himself. For days she had experienced grave doubts about standing up and performing the *risqué* dance in public, and yet now, suddenly, she was spurred by a surge of heady recklessness. It mattered not a whit that her reputation might suffer. She'd never had any real standing in the community to lose, anyway. So why not enjoy to the full this one very special occasion to indulge in a little heady gaiety? After all, it was unlikely she would ever experience such intoxicating delights again, she told herself, as she willingly accompanied the Viscount into the adjoining room, where the master of ceremonies was announcing the commencement of the waltz.

Vaguely Isabel was aware of a few others taking to the floor. She thought she glimpsed Francis, accom-

panied by the wife of the distant Blackwood cousin, George, and Sir Philip Staveley too, partnering some lively young matron. Then she was conscious only of her partner, of the sensual warmth of his touch on her waist and hand as they took up their positions for the dance, of the warmth that instantly softened his eyes when they stared down into hers as they commenced to swirl about the room at the first strains of music.

'I do not need to ask whether you are enjoying yourself, *ma belle*,' he said, thereby revealing that he had no intention of performing the dance in stony silence. 'The radiance of your smile tells me all I need to know.'

Isabel was more than happy to follow his lead, and not only in the movements of the dance. 'Oh, sir, it's a wonderful party! You have some truly charming friends.'

'Yes, your outrageous flirting with Bathurst and Staveley didn't go unnoticed,' he returned, his dark brows snapping together. 'Lady Pimm was quite shocked to glimpse you holding two gentlemen whom you hardly know in conversation in the garden for such a long time. And two gentlemen who, might I remind you, are both happily married.'

'And I doubt I could do anything to alter that situation, even if I wished to try. Which I do not,' she parried, not fooled by this display of mock disapproval. 'I was merely endeavouring to fulfil the commission you placed upon me by speaking to as many guests as I can throughout the evening in the hope that one, at least, might be able to shed some light on those dreadful past happenings here at the Manor.'

This time when his brows snapped together his disap-

proval was not feigned. 'Then cease to do so forthwith. By all means continue circulating, and meeting as many of my friends and relations as you can. That is why you're here. And I shall certainly be interested to hear your views some time in the near future on several persons here present. But avoid asking direct questions about past events. You risk arousing suspicion if you do. Whoever murdered my father and brother is no fool, and he might well be among the guests here tonight, remember that.'

Although his lordship had no way of knowing for sure whether she heeded his advice, he kept a close watch on her throughout the remainder of the evening. She spent a deal of time on the dance floor with a number of different partners, as did her young cousin. This didn't surprise him in the least. They were without doubt in both face and form the two most well-favoured females present. Even so, whereas Clara Pentecost was possibly sought for her physical attributes alone, Isabel, judging by remarks made to him throughout the remainder of the evening, left a more favourable impression on her various partners.

He himself revealed a clear partiality for her company by selecting only her to dance with twice, besides escorting her in to supper. It had been his intention to show the more influential members of the local community that he looked upon her with complete approval, and by the time the evening had drawn to an end, he knew he had succeeded better than he could have hoped. It was only when he had seen the last of his guests safely away in their carriages that he began to doubt the

wisdom of his action, and decided in the end to confide in the two of his houseguests in whom he had absolute trust.

Repairing to the comfort of his library, he dismissed the butler, ordering him to retire, before dispensing three large brandies himself. 'I hope you enjoyed the evening, gentlemen?'

'Wouldn't have missed it for the world,' Charles Bathurst assured him. 'I'm sure I speak for Staveley, too, when I say the only circumstance that would have improved the occasion is if we'd been able to bring our wives along.' He cast a conspiratorial wink in Sir Philip's direction. 'I'm sure they'd have wholeheartedly approved of the belle of the ball.'

The Viscount checked in the act of raising his glass to his lips. 'Yes, I must agree, the young woman I employ as governess is something quite out of the common way, is she not?'

Although both listeners uttered a shout of derisive laughter in unison, it was left to Sir Philip to prove that neither of them was fooled. 'Indeed she is. But is totally lacking her cousin's natural charm and captivating personality. It is your Belle who will long be remembered for attending the occasion.'

'That was my intention,' his lordship confessed, his sombre tone revealing he was not altogether pleased by his success. 'I wanted to make it clear to local society that Miss Isabel Mortimer had my full approval. But I cannot help feeling I made a terrible mistake in singling her out for particular attention. Evidently I revealed more than I had intended to do.'

Once again the two gentlemen seated in the comfort-

able chairs exchanged glances, only this time they were both clearly puzzled. 'I do not perfectly understand, Sebastian,' Bathurst admitted. 'If, for some reason, you wish to delay before declaring yourself, I cannot foresee a problem arising. I spoke to Miss Mortimer on several occasions throughout the evening, and not once did she give me any reason to suppose that she has the least notion of how deep your regard is for her.'

'No, Charles,' his lordship acknowledged, after giving vent to a strangely bitter laugh. 'I've taken very good care to ensure she doesn't know. She believes it is only gratitude I feel towards her. If you knew the trouble I had persuading her to come here tonight...' He shook his head, smiling as certain recent memories assailed him. 'But if you two were able to judge my true state of mind where Isabel is concerned, then it is reasonable to suppose that others might have succeeded in doing so too.'

'Evidently this troubles you, but I do not immediately perceive why it should,' Sir Philip admitted. 'I do not believe Miss Mortimer is indifferent towards you, Sebastian. In fact, I would go as far as to say I believe she holds you in high regard.'

'I can only hope she will continue to do so after what I must now do in order, if I can, to rectify matters,' his lordship revealed. All at once there was an unpleasant taste in his mouth, which he attempted to remove by swallowing a mouthful of brandy. 'I knew hers would be no ordinary wooing,' he added softly, staring down at what remained in his glass. 'I knew I would need to be patient and win her gently, and by degrees. Now, it

seems, I must forgo even that pleasure for a while in order to ensure her continued safety.'

This time when his lordship's two friends exchanged glances there was an element of disquiet in both their expressions, a fact that was not overlooked by the Viscount, who continued to maintain his stance before the hearth. 'What would you do, gentlemen, to protect the women you love?'

'There is nothing we wouldn't do,' Sir Philip responded for them both. 'Do I infer correctly from that, that you believe Miss Mortimer might seriously be in some danger?'

'I can only pray not. In truth, though, I suspect much depends on what lay behind the murder of my father and brother. And that, gentlemen, I'm afraid, continues to elude me still.'

Charles Bathurst nodded. 'Yes, Miss Mortimer said much the same thing—uncover the motive, and one will discover the murderer.'

His lordship smiled softly, thereby erasing, in part, the troubled lines that continued to crease his high forehead. 'Yes, the perceptive little madam guided me down that path from the first, encouraging me to recall things that seemed totally unimportant at the time.'

'Such as what?' Sir Philip prompted, when the Viscount fell silent, after at last making himself comfortable in the chair nearest the hearth.

'Such as what led to the row that resulted in me storming out of the house that evening.'

Bathurst regarded the contents of his glass through narrowed eyes. 'Yes, I recall you mentioning that to me, after I had travelled from London to defend you

all those years ago.' He smiled suddenly. 'When Sir Montague Cameron arrived tonight, I couldn't help thinking how relieved he must now feel that he didn't have you immediately clapped in irons and thrown into the local lock-up, after taking you into custody. At least he paid you the courtesy of confining you in reasonable comfort in those rooms overlooking the courthouse... under heavy guard, of course.'

'Patently not heavy enough,' Sir Philip countered sardonically, 'as you managed to effect his escape and spirit him away to the safety of the Colliers' home in Hampshire, without too much trouble, and without throwing any suspicion upon yourself.'

'It took some careful planning, especially getting him away to Ireland soon afterwards,' Bathurst admitted, looking very well pleased with himself it had to be said. 'And, of course, when I arrived the next day to discover the man I was to defend in court had escaped, I affected as much shocked dismay as would anyone in my respected profession. I even went so far as to assist Sir Montague in the search for the runaway by quite openly revealing those many haunts we frequented in our misspent youth—all to no avail, of course.

'But we digress,' Bathurst reminded his companions. 'If my memory serves me correctly, I believe you told me back then that the row with your father had something to do with a suggestion you made to improve the running of the estate.'

The Viscount was on his feet in an instant, and began to pace the floor, his mind racing back over the years. 'By heaven, Charles, I believe you're right! I'd been talking with the steward, Guy Fensham, all that after-

noon, and he suggested it might be profitable to experiment with a different breed of sheep. I mentioned it to my father on my return. Initially he showed interest. Then Giles arrived home and, as usual, accused me of interfering in matters that were none of my concern. Father then took his part, and the inevitable row ensued.'

'Although it cannot be denied your previous steward's account of the events of that night did a deal to incriminate you, Sebastian,' Charles Bathurst reminded him, 'and the fact that he conveniently disappeared before your eventual return here is, undeniably, extremely suspicious. I cannot immediately perceive how Fensham could possibly have known for sure that a row would ensue between you and your father because of a suggestion he had made to you about sheep.'

'No, he couldn't be one hundred per cent certain, I'll concede,' his lordship readily agreed. 'But it would have been a fair bet. He would have been well aware that there was precious little sibling affection prevailing at the Manor. He would also have been aware of Giles's almost obsessive jealousy about the land he believed would one day be his, and that my brother bitterly resented any interest I showed in the running of the estate.'

'In which case, if his intention had been to cause disharmony, then you fell straight into the steward's hands by repeating what he said,' Sir Philip opined. 'But I do not immediately perceive how the death of your father and brother could benefit him... Unless, of course, he was working for two masters.'

'That possibility had occurred to me,' the Viscount

admitted. 'It has also occurred to me that the person who would immediately benefit from my father and brother's deaths, and myself being hanged for the crime, is my uncle Horace. And I can also reveal that my father and his two brothers were not particularly close. That said, I have never once been given any reason to suppose that Horace Blackwood coveted the title, or disliked my father so intensely as to wish to plot his death. I have spoken with him at some length since his arrival here at the Manor, and nothing he has said has roused my suspicion. He is an indolent and self-indulgent individual who cares for nothing so much as his creature comforts, which he gets in abundance in his London home. He wouldn't wish to burden himself with the cares of maintaining a large estate at his age.'

'No, indeed,' Sir Philip readily concurred, having experienced for some years the grave responsibility it could be. 'Even if he did secretly have designs on the title at one time, he doesn't give the impression of having so now. And, if you'll forgive me saying so, Sebastian, your uncle's over-indulgence in many vices over the years has well and truly caught up with him. I do not believe he's destined to live to a very great age, or hold the title for very long should—God forbid!—it ever come to him now.'

'I couldn't agree more,' Bathurst announced. 'And neither would that son of his. Consumptive, unless I much mistake the matter.'

'You don't,' his lordship assured him. 'He spent some time in Italy recently and his condition improved. Perhaps he'll return if Wellington and the allies can deal successfully with Napoleon this time.' He shrugged.

'Who can say. One thing I do know, though, is that my youngest cousin, Clement Blackwood, has even less ambition to inherit the title than his father. The only member of the family, according to Lady Pimm, who ever coveted the Viscountcy was Francis's father, Hubert Blackwood.

'He was the youngest of the three Blackwood brothers, and without doubt the most ambitious,' his lordship went on to reveal. 'In his youth he was purported to have been a little wild.' He threw back his head and barked with laughter. 'Must be a family failing! None the less, my uncle Hubert married a wealthy London merchant's daughter, and had a fine house built, some three or so miles east of here, and remained up until his death a frequent visitor to the ancestral home. He may well have been envious of my father's superior position in the family, but even so they rubbed along together reasonably well. Although, as I've already mentioned, the three brothers were not particularly close, my father did much prefer his youngest brother, Hubert.'

'Which all suggests, does it not,' Bathurst remarked, after digesting everything his friend the Viscount had revealed, 'that if it wasn't a member of the immediate family, then the murderer must surely be someone who had a grievance against your father, and possibly your brother too, and used you as a means to avoid suspicion falling upon him.'

'That seems the most logical alternative,' his lordship agreed. 'All I need to do is discover who, if anyone, hated my father so much as to murder him.' He sighed as he ran his fingers through his slightly waving black

hair. 'Sadly, though, unless something unexpected comes to light, gentlemen, I believe my task will be nigh impossible.'

Unlike the Viscount, who retired in something of a sombre mood, Isabel felt elated by her undoubted success at the party, and woke the following morning experiencing a complete change of outlook, and a desire to do everything she could to maintain her unexpected and meteoric rise in local society.

For years she had been determined not to live beyond her means. When her father had become ill, and unable to work, she had been obliged to run the house on money he had saved throughout his life. He had not been a poor man by any means. Isabel clearly remembered how successful her father had been when he had had his practice in London. Unfortunately, financially he had not fared so well since moving to the country. It wasn't that his popularity had suddenly waned. Quite the opposite, in fact! His services had been sought by many, and he had given of his time equally between those who were quite able to pay, and those who could not.

None the less, they had lived well enough throughout the last years of her father's life, even if they had not enjoyed every creature comfort. In truth, though, Isabel had not known the full extent of her father's financial state until after his demise, when it had come to light that he had owned shares in several ventures. She had never so much as attempted to touch the interest that had been accumulating over the years. Knowing that she could not touch so much as a penny of the money

left to her by her mother until she had attained the age of thirty, or married, Isabel had veered on the side of caution, and had continued to leave her father's little nest egg intact should some calamity arise where she had need of extra money at a moment's notice.

Viscount Blackwood's emergence into her life, or, rather, that of his wards, and the financial benefits she had managed to accrue from becoming a temporary guardian had ensured that she could well afford many things she had considered beyond her means. She couldn't deny she had enjoyed these extra luxuries during past months. Nevertheless, the enjoyment she had experienced was as nothing when compared to the pleasure she had attained from attending her very first significant social event.

Now Isabel could well understand why her father had always insisted that her mother continued to enjoy those privileges to which she had become accustomed before marriage. Fortunately Agnes Mortimer had been neither frivolous nor avaricious. Yes, she had enjoyed many of life's luxuries, such as owning her own carriage and attending social events. None the less, she had not squandered vast amounts on jewellery or very expensive clothes. Although she had experienced most every creature comfort before marriage, she had never selfishly attempted to persuade her husband to live beyond his means.

For perhaps the first time ever Isabel could appreciate just how much her mother had given up in order to marry the man she loved, and could only admire her for having done so. She would like to think she would have done precisely the same. Yet, at the same time, she

could appreciate too why her mother had been determined to maintain certain standards, and still enjoy the finer things in life. She herself had sampled just that the evening before. She had experienced for the very first time what it was like to be socially acceptable, and she had no intention of relinquishing this new-found status if she could possibly avoid doing so.

Consequently she paid a visit to the notary in Merryfield who had dealt with her father's business arrangements for so many years in order to discover precisely how much she was worth.

Well pleased with the outcome of the visit, she then dragged Bessie along to the town's most fashionable dressmaker's and placed an order for several new gowns, including a riding habit, as well as certain other necessities, which immediately won her the personal attention of the owner of the establishment.

Even more delighted with the outcome of that visit, she then returned to the inn where she had left her one-horse gig, and ordered a light luncheon to celebrate what she privately considered was the beginning of a new era in her life.

'Well, I must say this is a rare treat,' Bessie declared, when the fare was brought to them in a private parlour by a young serving-wench.

'Yes, and one I hope we'll be experiencing a little more often from now on,' Isabel revealed, having already decided she'd need to travel to the local market town more often in the near future if her plans for herself were ever to be realised. 'Dear Papa's reliable cob is very capable, still, of pulling the gig. He was quite young when Papa acquired him, as you know. But I

rather fancy taking up riding again. It's been too long since I enjoyed that form of exercise.'

Bessie was only partially successful in suppressing a little knowing smile. 'My, my, his lordship's return to the Manor has been no bad thing, I must say! At least not where you're concerned, at any rate.'

'Stop looking so smug!' Isabel ordered, not in the least amused by the assumption. 'I'll have you know, Bessie Wilmot, that my desire to take up riding again has nothing whatsoever to do with Lord Blackwood. If you must know there was a certain Major Radcliff and his wife at the party last night. They've recently moved into that large house on the outskirts of the village. I'd never met them before. Emily Radcliff and I rubbed along together remarkably well. It was she who suggested we might ride out together from time to time. Her husband is to rejoin his regiment almost immediately, and she said she'll need to find plenty to occupy herself whilst he's away. Not only that, I should very much like to accompany Josh from time to time, when he goes out... Satisfied?'

'If you say so,' Bessie responded, not looking wholeheartedly convinced.

'Well, if we're to talk about influences, Miss Wilmot,' Isabel returned in a flash, 'then I'd like to know who persuaded you to order that new bonnet. Scarlet feathers indeed!'

Although no response was forthcoming, Isabel was not deterred. 'Red wouldn't be the favourite colour of a certain bow-legged little coachman who finds any excuse to call in at the farmhouse when he's passing, by any chance?'

Bessie went quite pink with pleasure as she giggled like a schoolgirl. 'Oh, he's a downy one and no mistake, Miss Isabel! He's been getting me to teach him his letters a bit more. His wife started to teach him to read and write some years ago, before he joined the army. Right sad it was, miss. He came home from Spain to find his wife and son had died in poverty. Thrown out of their cottage they were. Poor Tom. Said he behaved badly for a time. Luckily the Viscount crossed his path, and offered him a position. Said it were the making of him.' She smiled smugly. 'The Viscount seems to have a good influence on a number of people, I'm thinking.'

Isabel wisely refrained from comment. So Bessie, seemingly realising her baiting would have no effect, turned to stare out of the window, and then gave a sudden start.

'Well, I'll be damned! I do believe that's the steward that used to be up at the Manor—the one you never cared for, miss. I always did wonder what became of him.'

'I believe you're right, Bessie. It is Guy Fensham,' Isabel agreed. Although she couldn't be absolutely sure, she strongly suspected he had emerged from the tavern across the street. She always avoided that particular hostelry, as it was often rowdy and frequented by drunkards.

'I wonder what he's doing here,' she went on, gathering her things together, and rising to her feet. 'Must have found employment locally, I can only suppose. I'll mention it to his lordship when next I see him. He might be interested.'

After paying their shot, Isabel turned, and was about

to emerge from the inn, when she almost collided with none other than Francis Blackwood, who was on the point of entry.

Although he politely doffed his hat, Isabel had the feeling that he was slightly put out by the chance encounter for some reason, and yet he had been urbanity itself the evening before at the party. They had even danced together. 'I never expected to see you again so soon, sir,' she admitted, when he didn't attempt to speak. 'Do you often come to Merryfield? I can never recall seeing you here before.'

'Not so very frequently,' he admitted, all at once seeming to collect himself. 'A little matter of business brought me here today.'

'You too. What a coincidence! Fortunately I've finished mine, and am about to return home.'

He appeared disappointed. 'Can I not persuade you to remain a while longer and join me in some refreshment?'

Although she had no desire to be rude to one of the Viscount's relations, Isabel had no hesitation in declining, especially as she strongly believed the invitation had stemmed merely from politeness, and no real desire for her company.

'In that case, Miss Mortimer, I shall very much look forward to seeing you again at the Camerons' dinner party the week after next.'

'I haven't received an invitation, sir,' she didn't hesitate to reveal, before detecting a strangely calculating look in his eyes.

The smile he bestowed upon her before bowing over her hand contained not an atom of warmth either. 'I,

for one, do not doubt for a moment that you shall, Miss Mortimer. Until then…'

The encounter left her feeling distinctly uneasy for some reason. 'I do not think I can be quite normal, Bessie,' she remarked, heading towards the inn's stables in order to collect the gig. 'The Viscount earned himself the reputation of being a wild, unruly womaniser. His cousin Francis, according to Lady Pimm, has never had even so much as a breath of scandal attached to his name. Yet it is his lordship in whom I would place my trust.'

Chapter Eleven

❧⎯⎯⎯⎯⎯⎯❧

Although Isabel made a mental note to mention the unexpected encounter with Francis Blackwood to his lordship when next they spoke, it was thrust very much to the back of her mind even before she had reached home.

As she rounded the sharp bend leading to the village, she happened to catch sight of a tall, unmistakable figure on horseback, cantering across a meadow. Riding alongside his lordship was his ward Josh, and none other than the vivacious wife of his distant cousin.

All at once she experienced a rush of searing resentment, and no matter how hard she tried to tell herself that he was merely fulfilling his duties as host by entertaining his guests for the duration of their stay at the Manor, she was unable to suppress the swell of bitter disappointment at not having been invited to join the little riding party. After all, hadn't she and the Viscount spent quite some time in each other's company

the evening before? Hadn't he shown his preference for her society by dancing with her twice, not to mention escorting her in to supper? He'd been granted ample opportunity to invite her out riding today. It was quite obvious, therefore, that he hadn't wished to do so. And that hurt.

Consequently, she didn't arrive back at her home in the happiest frame of mind, and her sombre mood didn't improve at all on finding her cousin, surprisingly, bent over the kitchen table, sobbing into a handkerchief.

'Why, whatever's wrong, Miss Clara?' Bessie asked before her mistress could do so. 'Has something happened up at the Manor?'

Clara shook her head. 'No, nothing like that. It's the Reverend Mr Walters. He passed away last night in his sleep.'

At this, Isabel exchanged a puzzled glance with Bessie. She knew well enough that her cousin possessed one of the kindest of hearts, but even so this show of grief seemed a trifle excessive, given that Clara had been barely acquainted with the elderly clergyman.

Having been blessed with a more down-to-earth approach to life, Isabel was quick to point out that, sad though it was, his death hadn't been unexpected. 'He's been ill for many weeks now, Clara,' she reminded her. 'Besides, I cannot help but feel the parish might benefit from the appointment of a much younger man. Mr Walters, as far back as I can remember, had always been sadly lax in his duties, even when he enjoyed reasonable health.'

If anything, Clara became more distraught by this common-sense approach. 'But that's just it!' she

exclaimed between renewed sobs. 'If a new vicar arrives, he might wish to appoint his own curate. Then what shall I do? If Mr Johns is sent away, I might never see him again!'

Over her cousin's head Isabel exchanged yet another glance with the housekeeper. Clara might have admitted the true state of her heart at last, which was perhaps no bad thing. None the less, Isabel didn't immediately perceive what she could do to influence future events, and voiced her reservations aloud.

'Oh, but you can!' her cousin countered. 'You can approach Lord Blackwood. He'll listen to you, if you suggest Mr Johns should remain.'

An image of his lordship, the very last time she had seen him, flashed before her eyes. 'I'm not so very sure that's true,' Isabel returned dully, still rankled over being excluded from the little riding party. 'I believe his lordship has—er—other things on his mind at present.'

'Yes, yes, of course he has. I understand that,' Clara responded, a glimmer of hope glinting behind the unshed tears. 'But once all the guests have left the Manor, will you speak with him then? I'm sure Mr Johns mentioned once that his lordship's father had something to do with the living being offered to Mr Walters. So I'm sure Lord Blackwood has influence enough to ensure Mr Johns remains in the parish, if you persuaded him to.'

In truth, Isabel didn't wish to involve herself in matters that were none of her concern. All the same, she discovered she wasn't proof against the look of entreaty in her cousin's eyes and found herself relenting, at least

up to a point. 'If an opportunity arises, then, yes, I'll put in a good word for Mr Johns. But I have no intention of approaching his lordship directly on the subject. It would do more harm than good if he was to view it as crass interference on my part.'

Although his lordship was not among the congregation on Sunday, he did attend the late vicar's funeral service held later that same week. He was accompanied by the Bishop who conducted the service, and who, according to Clara, had been staying at the Manor for several days. Although Lord Blackwood made not the least attempt to approach her, Sir Montague and Lady Cameron did make a point of doing so, and Isabel duly received that invitation to dine the following week foretold by Francis Blackwood.

For several days she remained in two minds, not knowing whether to accept or not. Her cousin's name had not been included on the invitation, which annoyed Isabel, but didn't seem to trouble Clara in the least. More irksome still was glimpsing the Viscount on two separate occasions riding through the village with none other than the Camerons' eldest daughter, Charlotte, who, for some reason, had cut short her stay with her grandmother in the metropolis. In the end it was none other than her new-found friend Mrs Emily Radcliff who managed to overcome the ever-increasing malcontent and persuade Isabel to accompany her to the dinner party at the end of the week.

It was only to be expected that his lordship would attend. Isabel spotted his tall figure the instant she

entered the elegant Georgian mansion's impressive drawing room. In conversation with a small group of ladies, one of whom was, yet again, none other than Charlotte Cameron, he appeared wonderfully relaxed, and didn't so much as raise his eyes when the footman announced her arrival.

Fortunately her companion Emily Radcliff came to the rescue by preventing the maelstrom of negative emotions from taking complete control of Isabel by engaging the host and hostess in conversation, and directly afterwards their charming eldest son who, in turn, made to introduce them to the only other member of the Blackwood family present that evening.

'There's no need to make me known to these two charming ladies,' Francis assured him. 'I had the felicity of making their acquaintance at my cousin's house only the other week. And am so very glad that my prediction turned out to be true,' he added, drawing Isabel a little to one side, leaving Major Radcliff's young wife to converse with another guest.

'Yes, I'm beginning to think you might possess some special powers, sir,' Isabel said lightly, desperate not to allow increasing feelings of pique towards his kinsman to completely ruin her evening. 'I had no notion I was to receive an invitation. What other predictions about my future are you able to make, I wonder?'

Although he smiled readily enough, it contained an element of smugness. 'Ah, my dear Miss Mortimer, some things are so easily foretold. You were such an overwhelming success at my cousin's party that it was unlikely you would disappear from the social scene overnight. And as for your future...' All at once he

seemed quite serious. 'Do you think it's entirely wise to know what Fate has in store for us?'

'The element of surprise would always add extra spice, I suppose,' she readily conceded.

'Yes, indeed,' he agreed. 'Besides, I think up to a point we are all architects of our own destiny, behaving in ways that ultimately have a bearing on future events.' Raising his eyes, he gazed across the room. 'Now, take my big cousin, for instance. Had he behaved with a little more—how shall I phrase it?—circumspection in his youth, he might so easily have avoided being accused of the murder of his father and brother. That said,' he added, when large grey-green eyes regarded him with keen interest, 'I, for one, never supposed the accusation was true.'

Because she didn't for a moment doubt the accuracy of what he had revealed, Isabel didn't hesitate to ask, 'Do you have any idea who might have been behind the murders?'

'One hesitates to raise doubts about a gentleman's integrity when one is a guest under his roof,' he whispered, wickedly smiling. 'None the less, it is common knowledge that Sir Montague and the late Viscount positively loathed each other, and never spoke for years, right up until my uncle's demise. Some dispute over the boundary between their respective properties, I seem to recall. Understandably, Sir Montague's dislike intensified when the dispute was resolved very much in my relative's favour.' He shrugged. 'But my uncle had altercations with numerous persons over the years. It's safe to assume, therefore, that some must surely have borne a grudge.'

It occurred to Isabel then that Francis Blackwood had been a deal more informed about the late Viscount's affairs than had the present holder of the title, and echoed this thought aloud. He merely shrugged again, however, before revealing that his cousin, after leaving Oxford, had been inclined to spend more time in the capital with his friends, well away from the comings and goings at the ancestral pile.

'And the truth of the matter is,' he went on, 'although I was closer to Sebastian in age, I had more in common with his older brother. My father died relatively young, you see, and so I came into my property before I had even left university. My home, like Blackwood Manor, boasts many acres of fine farmland, Miss Mortimer, so I often sought my uncle's advice, and Giles and I frequently discussed husbandry.'

This seemed reasonable enough, and yet a niggling doubt about this particular member of the Blackwood family had most definitely seeded itself and was growing rapidly. Francis clearly had been privy to much of what had gone on at the Manor, and therefore must have had an extensive knowledge of the general routines of the people who had resided there. Had this knowledge come merely from observations made during his frequent visits? Or had there been another revealing source? Hard on the heels of this puzzling question came the memory of certain remarks made by Lady Pimm on the night of the dinner party, which only served to increase her doubts about the trustworthiness of the man standing before her. Furthermore, a slightly more recent occurrence, that hadn't struck her

in the least odd at the time, all at once began to acquire a more sinister significance.

Although she was aware that now was definitely not the occasion to voice suspicions, especially not to someone about whom she was beginning to harbour grave doubts, some reckless imp prompted her to dig a little deeper in an attempt to discover the inmost thoughts of her companion. 'So, who in your opinion was the intended victim?'

'Why, my uncle Henry, of course! Do you not agree?'

She shook her head, all the while scrutinising his attractive features for the slightest indication of what might be passing through his mind. She was increasingly beginning to feel he knew much more about what had occurred that night than he had thus far revealed, if her suspicion about his close association with a certain other person connected with the appalling events was correct.

'At first I thought your cousin Sebastian was likely to have been the real target. After all, his graceless behaviour in bygone years is legend. Now, though, I'm convinced it was the killer's intention all along to murder both the late Viscount and his elder son, and divert any suspicion from falling on himself by implicating your cousin. Which, of course, he succeeded in doing for a number of years. Had I not intervened, the killer would by this time possibly have been rid of a third member of the Blackwood family. How he must despise me for thwarting his ambitions.'

Although he frowned, appearing genuinely puzzled, his gaze was intense and unwavering. 'He must, indeed, if that had been his intention all along,' he agreed. 'But

I do not immediately perceive why you should suppose it might have been.'

'Do you not?' Isabel raised one brow, betraying her scepticism at this response. He was an intelligent man. Surely he must have considered every possibility?

Undaunted by his lack of response she said, 'Well, let us look at the facts. Unlike yourself, I was never privy to the comings and goings up at the Manor in bygone years. All the same, even I can clearly recall observing the late Lord Blackwood and his son riding out alone on numerous occasions. It would have been a simple matter, surely, for someone with revenge in mind to lie in wait and take a pot shot at either the late Viscount or his son? But, no, the killer, at great risk of being discovered, gains entry by some means or other to the Manor and murders both his lordship and his heir and does his utmost to implicate the younger son. Either the murderer had a grievance against the Blackwood family as a whole, or he had a deal to gain by their deaths.'

'You perceive me positively agog with curiosity, Miss Mortimer! Who on earth would benefit by such a dreadful course of action?'

Isabel could only speculate on how much of his shocked amazement was assumed. 'Why, isn't it obvious…? Another member of the Blackwood family, of course! And I shall go even further by saying a member of the family who covets the title.'

Naturally enough he appeared affronted. 'I sincerely trust, Miss Mortimer, you do not include me in that offensive assumption. Might I remind you I am not next in line for the title.'

'No, indeed you are not. You are, however, a deal

closer than you once were,' she pointed out, before wiser counsel at last prevailed and she decided that if he was as innocent as he appeared, then she was going beyond what was pleasing to suggest it might be otherwise. Although privately she might retain doubts about Mr Francis Blackwood's sincerity, she was obliged silently to acknowledge it would be wrong to accuse him of the least wrongdoing without some tangible proof.

So she merely shrugged her shoulders, feigning indifference in an attempt to make light of the whole matter. 'Thankfully my slight involvement in the sad business ceased a long time ago, sir. If his lordship wishes to attempt to discover the truth, then it is entirely up to him to do so, wouldn't you say?'

When he failed to respond yet again, and continued to stare at her intently, she allowed her own gaze to stray briefly to a certain spot across the room. 'And it doesn't appear as if your cousin is exerting himself unduly in an attempt to unearth the truth of what took place. It would seem he has other things on his mind at present.'

This time when she looked back at him his gaze seemed rather more speculative. 'Yes, he does, doesn't he—the delightful Miss Charlotte Cameron.' He reached for his quizzing glass and stared through it at the young lady in question. 'Certainly pleasing on the eye, but not, I wouldn't have thought, in my cousin's usual style. Which begs the question, does it not, is he merely being courteous by paying attention to the daughter of the house, or is there some other reason for this show of preference for her company this evening?'

'I wouldn't know, sir,' Isabel managed to respond,

while manfully resisting the sudden urge to flee the room and return to the relative comfort of the farm-house. She simply wasn't herself that evening, otherwise she would never have dreamt of voicing her suspicions about the murders at the Manor to a man who was, to all intents and purposes, a virtual stranger.

'But it is only to be expected,' she forced herself to add, in yet another attempt to convey she had no real interest in the matter under discussion, 'that he will one day marry, if only to beget an heir. And he will surely look for a wife among females of his own class.'

'Perhaps,' he agreed, turning that aid to vision on to her. 'But where my cousin is concerned one would be foolish to presume too much. He has the annoying habit of behaving quite out of character on occasions. That said, it would seem his tastes have changed over the years. Seemingly he is no longer attracted to the showy beauties of this world, as he once was.'

A servant in smart livery announcing dinner spared Isabel the necessity of formulating a response, for which she was extremely grateful. None the less, the subject of the conversation was never far from her thoughts. Throughout the meal she was conscious of the laughter and light-hearted banter emanating from further down the table where Lord Blackwood was seated, sand-wiched between none other than the eldest daughter of the house and Emily Radcliff.

Lady Cameron had evidently given much thought to her table placements. No fool, she had known the happily married major's wife would prove no threat at all. Isabel began to appreciate other things too, as the meal wore on, with one excellently presented course

being replaced by another. The reason for Charlotte Cameron's early return from the capital was quite obvious now, as was Sir Montague's surprising visit to the farmhouse a few weeks before, when he had done his utmost to highlight Lord Blackwood's less favourable traits. Clearly he had refrained from warning his own daughter to be wary of such a matrimonial prize!

Although she refused to allow her attention to stray from her own immediate dinner companions, Isabel found it no easy task to maintain a light-hearted conversation, or the pretence of pleasure in the evening. The truth of the matter was she had never felt less sociable. Consequently, the instant Lady Cameron rose from the table, inviting the ladies to return with her to the drawing room, Isabel took the opportunity to slip outside to be alone with her thoughts, and—yes—attempt to soothe her battered ego.

Locating a bench in a secluded corner of the neatly symmetrical formal garden, Isabel sought to make some sense out of her tangled feelings. The truth of the matter was she was jealous of the attention the Viscount was paying to Charlotte Cameron; resented the attention he paid to any woman except her. And it was madness to feel as she did! she told herself. He had more than repaid the assistance she had rendered him in order to clear his name. Why, if it hadn't been for his show of approval and support she wouldn't be here now, in this magnificent setting. And how she wished she were not here! Life had been so simple before his lordship had entered her world. She'd been happy with the simple pleasures in life… Would she ever find contentment again?

'You shouldn't be out here by yourself, *ma belle.*'

So wrapped had she been in her own private misery that her senses, normally so acute, hadn't even registered his approach. Nor had she any notion of just how long hc'd been standing there in the shade of the tall yew hedge that bordered the shrubbery.

Very slowly she turned her head and forced herself to look up at him. With the best will in the world, though, she couldn't control the sudden surge of searing resentment at his total avoidance of her company since the night of his own splendid party. Did he suppose that she would be grateful for the smallest crumb of attention he was willing to bestow upon her now? If so, she would swiftly disabuse him! Although she might never inhabit the same privileged world as her more illustrious forebears, there was still a deal of pride coursing through her veins.

'Might I remind you, my lord, that I am my own mistress, and do as I please. I do not require advice, most especially from you.'

In one swift and lithe movement she rose to her feet and made to leave, only to have her left wrist captured and held fast in strong fingers. 'Unhand me at once, my lord!'

Even though she had managed to maintain remarkable control over her voice thus far, her right hand had instinctively curled into a neat little fist, ready to lash out should he risk importuning her further. Then she watched as strikingly blue eyes that could change in an instant from icy cool and disdainful to tenderly warm and approving travelled down the length of her arm, the look in them somewhere between the two extremes.

An unmistakable twitch at one corner of his mouth betrayed his thoughts, and only served to annoy her further. 'Might I remind you that I do not number among, nor ever shall for that matter, the doxies of your acquaintance who no doubt appreciate displays of masculine brutishness. Now kindly unhand me, my lord.'

His response was to give vent to a peal of laughter. 'My word, you can be a provoking little witch when the mood takes you, Belle!' he declared, before detecting the slight movement in her right arm. 'Ah, ah!' he warned, wagging a finger in front of her nose. 'You do not know me well enough yet to be sure just how I might respond to a cuff on the ears. So be sensible,' he advised, still wickedly smiling, 'and agree to meet with me tomorrow, and I shall release you. There are things we must discuss.'

Still miffed over his deliberate avoidance of her company in recent days, Isabel wasn't inclined to pander to his whims. 'I cannot imagine why you should suppose I might wish to discuss anything with you, my lord,' she responded, raising her chin slightly. 'Anything you have to say to me may be said now.'

'No it cannot,' he countered in a trice. 'For your own sake, Isabel, I must not be seen favouring you with my company.' He was all at once serious. 'Trust me and meet with me tomorrow.'

Although she didn't doubt he was earnestly troubled over something, and curiosity to discover just what was causing him such obvious disquiet had to a certain extent overcome her feelings of pique, she still felt unable to oblige him. 'I'm sorry I can't. I have an

appointment near Merryfield tomorrow that I would prefer not to break. And I usually see Josh on Saturday afternoons, remember? We can hardly be private with him along.'

At first he looked suspiciously down at her, as though he thought she was merely making excuses, but then he nodded. 'Very well. Sunday, then, after church?' At her assent, he added, 'Where?'

'If you wish the meeting to be private, it cannot take place at the farmhouse or the Manor,' she pointed out, after a moment's thought. 'How about the home wood, at the spot where Jem Marsh was found?'

'Very well, midday in the home wood,' he agreed, before his acute hearing picked up a sound that Isabel had yet again quite failed to detect.

His lordship then released his hold on the slender wrist before addressing the new arrival with every evidence of pleasure. 'Why, Emily, you needn't have put yourself to the trouble of coming in search of her,' he declared, thereby instantly revealing his genuine fondness for his friend Major Radcliff's young wife. 'As you see I've discovered the truant already and was on the point of escorting her back inside. My cousin Francis evinced a desire to have Miss Mortimer partner him in a game or two of whist, and I agreed to oppose him. Will you oblige me by being my partner? I rather fancy administering a sound trouncing this evening.'

Although Emily Radcliff laughingly agreed, Isabel didn't find his last remark in the least amusing. The fact that his shoulders shook slightly, when she cast him a suspicious look, before accepting his escort back inside the mansion, only went to confirm her belief that his

utterance had little to do with a determination to win at cards.

None the less, she was resolved not to let her own partner down, and for the first few hands the honours were evenly divided. Then Mrs Radcliff just happened to raise a topic that had been very much on Isabel's mind in recent days, and her concentration began to suffer as a result.

'Ah, yes!' Francis exclaimed. 'I did hear that old Cedric Walters had passed on.' Across the table he cast Isabel a half-amused look. 'Natural causes, I sincerely trust?'

'There's no need to suspect otherwise,' his lordship assured him, studying the cards in his hand.

'I cannot tell you how relieved I am to hear you say that, Sebastian!' Francis declared, before leaning in a conspiratorial way towards his cousin. 'I have it on the best authority, you see, that there is a suspicion abroad that someone is attempting to decrease the members of our family.'

Not even by the slightest movement of his shapely dark brows did the Viscount betray the least surprise at hearing this, and his eyes remained steadfastly on the cards in his hand as he said, 'May I be permitted to know from whom you gained this pearl of wisdom, Cousin?'

It was then that Isabel appreciated fully for the first time just how unbelievably imprudent, not to say downright stupid, she had been even to broach the subject of the murders with Francis Blackwood. She knew next to nothing about the man, after all. From the first, instinct had warned her against him, that, unlike his cousin, he

was not to be trusted. His openly revealing what was tantamount to a private conversation was surely proof that her instincts about him had been accurate? Or had he, perhaps, a very good reason of his own for having betrayed her to his cousin?

Once again ignoring the cards in her hand, Isabel raised her eyes to find her partner's fixed in her direction. More than assessing, they were fiercely penetrating in their regard, before they flickered briefly in his kinsman's direction. 'It was a theory put forward by none other than my delightful partner, Sebastian.'

'Indeed?' his lordship responded so coolly that Isabel could almost feel the temperature in the surrounding air plummet by several degrees. 'And why should you suppose such a thing, Miss Mortimer?'

Seemingly he wasn't best pleased, and Isabel couldn't say she altogether blamed him. Whether or not his displeasure stemmed from the suggestion that the perpetrator of the crimes might be a close relative, or for some other entirely private reason, she couldn't have said, for his expression remained annoyingly unrevealing. None the less, she was determined to try to rectify her crass blunder of earlier in the evening if she could.

'I would be the first to admit, my lord, that I do not know your cousin at all well. But I am beginning to think, increasingly, that he can be wickedly provoking on occasions.'

Emily Radcliff at least appeared to find the response amusing and her tinkling laugh went some way to dispel completely the hint of tension in the air.

'He knows full well it was a suggestion only, half-jokingly made. I was merely attempting to point out that

the murderer might have been anyone, as the motive for the killings remains a mystery. Believe me, my lord, it wasn't my intention to cause offence.'

'Rest assured you haven't offended me, Miss Mortimer,' he responded, the warmth very much back in his eyes as they turned briefly in her direction. 'I'm sure there are some very unsavoury characters among the members of my family. You'd know, Francis,' he added, turning his attention to his cousin. 'Your knowledge of the family is far more extensive than mine. I'd even forgotten that the late vicar was related to us.'

'Only very distantly, Sebastian,' Francis assured him. 'Is the new incumbent to be selected from among the far-flung branches of our family tree, I wonder?'

'A replacement for our distant cousin, Francis, has already been decided upon. The good Bishop is to return on Sunday in order to reveal our new spiritual leader to the parish at large.'

Isabel could feel her own spirits plummet. Nothing she could say to his lordship now would make the least difference. The new vicar had been selected, and there was every chance he'd wish to appoint his own curate, if he hadn't already done so. She turned her attention back to the cards in her hand, but to little avail. She and her partner lost the game quite comprehensively, and thereafter failed to regain their winning position.

Chapter Twelve

By the time Isabel set out late on Sunday morning to keep that all-important prearranged appointment in the wood, her thoughts concerning the Viscount were in stark contrast to what they had been on the night of the Camerons' dinner party.

The previous day, not only had she become the proud owner of the most sweet-natured dapple-grey mare, she had also discovered the identity of the new incumbent from none other than her cousin. Like an excited child, Clara had come bursting into the kitchen at the farmhouse with the startling news that none other than Mr Benjamin Johns had been appointed the new vicar of St Matthew's.

Isabel had guessed at once who had exercised his influence and authority over the selection and greeted him with every evidence of pleasure, after she had drawn her mount to a halt a few feet from where he was seated on a sturdy tree stump.

She received no answering smile as he rose to his feet and assisted her to dismount. Beau fared rather better and at least received an affectionate pat.

'When and where did you acquire this creature, may I ask?' he demanded to know, after running an expert hand down the mare's flanks.

Isabel was still experiencing far too much gratitude towards him to be in the least annoyed by his lofty manner. 'I told you I had an appointment near Merryfield yesterday. I bought her from a young farmer there. He assured me she was the best-natured animal on four legs. And he was speaking no less than the truth! There isn't an ounce of ill humour in her anywhere and she's so perfectly behaved!'

'Which is more than can be said for her owner!' he retorted. 'You should have known you might have use of any of the hacks at the Manor when you wished to ride. I could shake you for not consulting with me first,' he added harshly, though his expression told a very different story. 'And probably would, if I didn't adore you so very much.'

At this, she raised startled eyes. 'No, you didn't mishear me, *ma belle*,' he assured her, his voice, now, as soft as a caress. 'I've been in love with you almost from the first time I saw you.'

Stunned, it was as much as Isabel could do to gape up at him. The next moment she was in his arms, and was sampling for the first time the passion of a man of no little experience.

The suddenness of the embrace might have caught her completely unawares, and perhaps in some deep recess of her mind a tiny voice was advocating caution.

Her body, however, was encouraging a far different response, and she raised her arms a moment before his slid about her, drawing her inexorably closer.

Then she was conscious only of him, of the taste of his mouth, of the power in the muscular frame pressed against her, of the increasing desire for these moments of exquisite physical pleasure never to end. It was only when he finally raised his head to bury his lips in her hair that a vestige of common sense began to return, but even so it was nowhere near strong enough to quell the need to cling to him and have him hold her protectively within the circle of his arms. She'd experienced nothing like it before. For the first time in her life she felt safe, protected and, yes, loved. No matter what his reputation had been in the past, she had never been given reason to doubt his integrity, and she didn't doubt him now, nor the depth of his feelings for her.

'I didn't intend for that to happen…at least, not for a while.' There was a huskiness in his voice that she'd never detected before, but certainly no suggestion of regret, as his next words blessedly proved. 'But do not expect me to apologise, Belle, because I cannot be sorry it happened. It's merely the result, I suppose, of stupidly depriving myself of your company during these past interminably long and tedious days.'

This admission did prompt her to raise her head from the comfort of his broad chest and move a little away from him so as to enable her to look up into his face. 'Ah, so you were deliberately avoiding me. Might I be permitted to know why?'

With a sigh, he released her at last, and then bent to retrieve her neat little beaver hat that had fallen to the

ground at some point during their embrace. He then led her to the nearby tree stump so that she might sit, before making use of a nearby sturdy elm to rest his back.

'Until I can be sure that whoever murdered my father and brother will attempt nothing further, I intend to take every reasonable precaution. If revenge is foremost in his mind, then he could well attempt to punish me by doing harm to another.' He regarded her in silence for a moment. 'No greater hurt could he inflict upon me than to do mischief to you. I couldn't bear it, *ma belle*, if harm should befall you!'

In two giant strides he was before her again, drawing her to her feet and holding her protectively against him, as though to shield her from some hidden assailant.

'Believe me, nothing would give me greater satisfaction than to announce our betrothal to the world at large,' he assured her, after a further display of his sincere regard that left her satisfyingly breathless. 'I should derive such pleasure from parading my lovely future Viscountess before my friends.' Placing his hand beneath her chin, he very gently raised her head so that he might look down into eyes that clearly mirrored what was in her own heart. 'But for the time being our love must remain our secret. You must tell no one, my darling, no one, not even your trusty housekeeper. The world must continue to believe that I have a sincere regard for Miss Isabel Mortimer, based on respect and—yes, confound it!—gratitude, but nothing more.'

Although she quite understood his reasoning, and felt moved by the lengths to which he was prepared to go in order to protect her, she couldn't resist asking, 'But am I not to see you from time to time, my lord?'

A twitching smile was not the response she might have expected. 'Given your total compliance since your arrival in the wood, do you not think it is time you dispensed with formality, at least when we are private together?'

'Very well, Sebastian,' she returned, for the time being at least more than willing to remain agreeably submissive. 'But you haven't answered my question,' she reminded him.

All at once serious, he released her, and then took a step away. 'No, I do not wish to continue attempting to avoid you. I have found these past couple of weeks intolerable. But we must be careful, Belle—remain on our guard whenever we are together. Besides which,' he added with a rueful smile, 'my behaviour of late has not been altogether chivalrous, most especially where Charlotte Cameron is concerned. My heart belongs to you, Belle. It would be cruel to continue playing fast and loose with another young woman's feelings.'

Unexpectedly, he gave a shout of laughter. 'God, how damnably moral I sound! See what you've done to me, you witch!'

'I take no credit, sir. I have always thought you, innately, a good person.'

Once again he smiled ruefully. 'Well, I wouldn't go as far as to say that, my love. But I do believe I'm a deal better than some I could name.'

'I couldn't agree more,' she concurred softly, before her thoughts turned to their most besetting problem. 'Which makes the task before us very difficult, simply because I no longer believe you ever were the intended victim all those years ago… But you might well be now.

'Oh, no, Sebastian,' she added, cutting off the protest he had been about to utter. 'It's my future too now, remember. I intend to do all I can to uncover the truth. And I can begin by sharing certain matters that have been increasingly troubling me of late.'

As she seated herself once more on the tree stump, her expression was no less sombre than his own. 'I will begin by apologising to you for my stupid indiscretion at the Camerons' dinner party the other evening.' She could see at a glance she held his full attention. 'I discussed certain matters with your cousin Francis in an attempt to gauge his reaction. I cannot say I was even remotely successful. As you're probably aware yourself, he gives little of himself away. And that is perhaps why I instinctively do not trust him.'

The Viscount wasn't prepared to dismiss her doubts about his relative out of hand. All the same, he couldn't resist asking, 'Is this mistrust based purely on feminine intuition?'

'Not entirely, no. A little over two weeks ago, I bumped into him quite by chance in Merryfield.' She waved her hand in a dismissive gesture. 'Now, I fully accept there's no earthly reason why he shouldn't have been there. His home is situated a mere mile or two the other side of the town, after all. So I wouldn't have considered it in the least odd had I not happened to catch sight of none other than your ex-steward, Guy Fensham, coming out of the inn on the opposite side of the street a matter of a few minutes before the chance encounter with your cousin…an encounter that didn't appear to please him overmuch, though he tried his utmost to conceal the fact.

'I accept, too, their being in town on the same day might also be a coincidence, only,' she conceded, after winning no response. 'But, if not, and I'm inclined to believe a meeting between them had been arranged, it suggests an entirely different motive for the murders than has been considered before.'

'It is strange that you should mention the previous steward, Belle,' he said at length, 'because I have been going through my father's papers in recent days. He was meticulous—kept records in good order. Yet I can find nothing concerning Guy Fensham, not even a reference that might offer a clue as to where he came from, or who might have recommended him. Had I not been rather preoccupied with matters concerning the church during these past couple of weeks, I would have attempted to discover more about Fensham.'

At this her thoughts were instantly diverted, and she revealed how delighted she had been by Mr Johns's appointment. 'And my cousin Clara was doubly so. I know nothing official, but I wouldn't be in the least surprised if she wasn't the new vicar's wife within a twelvemonth.'

'I'm sure your cousin would prove to be an excellent helpmeet to a clergyman,' he responded in a trice. 'And now, my love, you must leave this place. I shall see you next Friday, if not before, for I too have been invited to dine at Emily Radcliff's home.'

After helping her to remount, his lordship watched her ride away, before turning and gazing for several minutes between the trees at the shady spot where Jem Marsh's remains had been found. Then he mounted and

headed towards that area of the estate where a row of lime-washed cottages stood bathed in the early afternoon sunshine.

As had happened on the previous occasion the elderly ex-butler betrayed how honoured he felt by his master's unexpected visit, as he invited the Viscount to step inside his humble abode.

As had occurred on the previous occasion, too, his lordship didn't waste time, once initial pleasantries had been exchanged, in trying to discover what he wished to know.

Bunting stared silently down at the rug at his feet, appearing genuinely perplexed by the question asked of him. Yet, like so many of his advanced years, his memory of happenings long past was far more acute than his recall of recent events.

'I seem to remember that it was Mr Francis who recommended him to your father, my lord.' He scratched his head. 'Now, let me see… It was a year, maybe less, after Mr Francis's father died. He was a regular visitor to the Manor back then—two or three times a month. Came to ask about land management, and the like, and your father was always pleased to give advice. Seem to recall that Mr Giles weren't at all happy about the amount of time your father spent with your cousin, though.'

This came as no surprise to the Viscount. His brother had always been a selfish, possessive devil, resenting anything their father did that excluded him. This, the Viscount mused, must surely have been one of the main reasons why he and his father had never been close.

Unlike his brother Giles, he had never attempted to vie for their father's attention or affection.

'And you're sure it was Francis who recommended Fensham to my father?'

'Positive, my lord. I remember particularly because it was one of the few times during my many years at the Manor when we were short-staffed. Three of the maids and two footmen had been struck down by the influenza that winter, and those of us who were well were having to cover. I was behind time with filling the decanters, sir, and so I was obliged to go in and out of the library on several occasions.' Bunting shrugged. 'His lordship quite understood. But I seem to recall Mr Francis wasn't too pleased by the interruptions.'

Lord Blackwood considered for a moment, before saying, 'And so as a result of my cousin's visit, Fensham was engaged.' He received a nod confirming this, before he remarked, more to himself, 'Then why was it, I wonder, I could find no written character references with regard to Fensham?'

'Because he never brought any with him, my lord,' Bunting surprisingly revealed. 'And that I do know. His lordship was impressed by Mr Fensham at the interview. I came into the library shortly afterwards, and I clearly remember your father standing by the window, saying that he thought Mr Fensham exactly right for the post. Then he muttered something about asking Master Francis for references when next he saw him. I can only suppose Master Francis had, maybe, seen the references himself, and retained them for some reason.'

'Perhaps,' his lordship agreed, staring thoughtfully down at his clasped hands. 'And there's no denying

Fensham proved to be extremely conscientious during those first years. I clearly remember my father being most impressed with him, overall. "The best steward we've ever had at the Manor", he was wont to say. Yet, after his death, everything changed. By all accounts Fensham did the minimum of work, feathering his own nest for the most part from the estate's resources.'

Clearly saddened by the last years he'd been in service, Bunting nodded solemnly. 'That's true enough, my lord, so it's no good saying otherwise. Mr Francis did his best, though, sir. He was that concerned about the Manor. Was always so very fond of the old place, I seem to remember. He took it upon himself to contact your father's man in London. Mr Goodbody travelled up from London with your good friend Mr Bathurst. They saw to it that all the valuables were locked safely away, that the house was shut up and that all the servants were given references and paid off until the end of the year.' He shrugged. 'But I don't suppose there was much else they could do, sir, without your written permission.'

'I blame no one but myself for the state in which I found the Manor upon my eventual return. I should have left instructions with Goodbody.' His lordship's wry sense of humour came to the fore. 'My only excuse is that I had other more pressing concerns on my mind at the time—namely how to save my neck from the hangman's noose.'

He was serious again, as something else occurred to him. 'How often during my years away did Francis visit the Manor, Bunting?'

'Oh, a fair few, sir—more often than not two or three times a year. Sometimes he even stayed overnight,

when he would walk about the place, candelabra aloft, making sure himself, I suppose, that the ancestral home of the Blackwoods was in good order. He was the only member of the family who ever did concern himself, sir,' the old butler added, with a rare trace of censure in his voice. 'Your uncle never came near the place, after the day of the funeral, not once.'

'No, I know he didn't,' his lordship acknowledged. 'But let us concentrate on Francis again. As far as you know, did he ever consult with the steward, Fensham, during my years away? For instance, did he ever remonstrate with him for his tardiness?'

'He may have done, sir. Mr Francis always passes the steward's lodge house when he visits the Manor, his own home being in that direction. And I seem to recall one or two things about the estate receiving attention after his visits. But it never lasted long, you understand?'

Not doubting anything the old retainer had told him, but suspecting he'd learn little more, his lordship rose to his feet. 'Thank you, Bunting. You've been of immense help. Don't be surprised if you receive further impromptu visits from me. My curiosity these days is becoming insatiable.'

As a result of the interview with the old butler, his lordship paid a visit to his cousin the following day. He was lucky enough to find him at home, and more than willing to receive him, though he did betray a marked degree of surprise at the unexpected visit.

Given what Isabel had said about this particular member of the Blackwood family, his lordship was determined to remain very much on his guard. Although

the reaction to the unexpected visit had seemed genuine enough, seeds of doubt about Francis had been sown in his lordship's mind. He was inclined to trust Isabel's judgement rather than his own. He was too close, had known Francis far too long to assess him in the way Isabel evidently could. To her Francis was virtually a stranger and, therefore, she could be entirely impartial.

'Why, Cousin!' Francis at last declared, rising from his chair, and nodding dismissal to the thin, rather stooped servant who had been employed as butler in the house for as long as the Viscount could remember. 'And to what do I owe the pleasure of this unexpected visit? Have you come to celebrate with me the wonderful news from across the Channel? Or is it merely a social call?'

'Naturally I am relieved at Wellington's success. But in truth it concerns me less than matters closer to home,' the Viscount revealed, before accepting the glass of refreshment held out to him, and making himself comfortable in one of the chairs. 'I'm here because I believe you are in a position to assist me, Francis.'

He waited only for his cousin to resume the seat opposite before, as was his custom, coming straight to the point of the visit, 'What can you tell me about the Manor's former steward, Guy Fensham?'

Light brows rose sharply in what appeared to be a further show of astonishment. 'Why, nothing, Sebastian! Why should you suppose that I know anything about the fellow?'

His lordship didn't allow his gaze to waver. 'Because I have it on the best authority that it was none other than

your good self who recommended him to my father in the first place.'

Although the hand raising the glass to Francis's lips remained perfectly steady, it undoubtedly checked for an instant. 'Did I...?' Then, after a further moment or two, 'Why, yes, I believe I did, now you come to mention it! But it was well over a decade ago, Sebastian. You cannot possibly expect me to recall every last detail after all this time.'

'Allow me to refresh your memory, then,' his lordship responded, not wholly convinced by this declaration of poor recall. Francis, he clearly remembered, had always been as sharp as a tack. 'It was over fourteen years ago to be more exact. I had just gone up to Oxford, and you had by that time come into your inheritance. Seemingly, you must have discovered about the death of the steward who had looked after the Manor estate for decades, and visited my father recommending Fensham. Bunting is convinced Fensham came on your recommendation.'

'Ah! So your old butler is the informant.' Francis stared down into his glass, smiling crookedly 'Yes, butlers do have the uncanny knack of discovering everything that goes on in their domain, do they not? And dear old Bunting was a prince among butlers, I seem to recall.'

He raised a hand to his forehead and began to rub the skin, as though to stimulate memory. 'Now, let me see. I remember advertising for someone to help me get the most out of my own acres. Really I was after a good stockman, little more. Fensham applied, and I knew at once he was far too experienced for what I required, and came highly recommended.'

'Ah! So he was armed with references, then?' his lordship returned, having quickly digested this very interesting snippet. 'Can you recall from where he came? I could find no written information regarding previous employment among my father's papers.'

'How odd!' Francis took a moment to sample his wine. 'Fensham had excellent references, I do recall that. Surely he must have produced them during his interview. I cannot imagine your father employing him otherwise.'

'From what I have managed to discover, my sire seemed to suppose that you had retained Fensham's previous employer's written assurances of good character, and would forward them in due time.'

When Francis assured him this was not so, his lordship saw little profit in pressing the matter, and decided to adopt a different tack. 'Evidently you must have been satisfied of his good character, otherwise you wouldn't have recommended him to my father. Can you recall his previous employer's name or direction?'

Francis appeared to give this some thought. 'Not after all this time, no. It was no one I knew personally. For some reason the county of Shropshire springs to mind. Whether or not Fensham was born there or merely worked there for a time, I cannot be sure.'

'How very odd,' his lordship returned, smiling faintly. 'As you are aware, Francis, I wasn't overly concerned with the running of the estate during that period in my life. But, even so, I did engage Father's steward in conversation from time to time, and clearly recall the unmistakable trace of a local accent—not strong, it's true, but there, none the less.'

'Well, what of it?' Francis returned, raising a shoulder, and appearing completely unperturbed. 'It isn't unknown for people to adopt accents so as to be accepted by a local community.'

This, too, was reasonable enough, but his lordship was becoming increasingly less convinced by his cousin's show of unconcern over the matter. The old butler had been certain that Fensham had been engaged at the Manor on Francis's recommendation, and the Viscount was inclined to believe Bunting. After all, why should the old man lie…? But, there again, why should Francis? Whether Fensham turned out to be a good or bad steward shouldn't have mattered a whit to Francis. But had it? Once again he attempted to unravel the mystery from a slightly different angle.

Leaning back in his chair, he looked for all the world totally untroubled, and even managed to summon a half-cynical chuckle. 'Well, it just goes to show, Francis, that even the most careful of men can behave rashly on occasions. My father made it a rule never to employ anyone without good character references. Evidently he thought well enough of Fensham to do so. He even managed to hoodwink you, and you are one of the most astute men of my acquaintance. Left to his own devices, Fensham proved himself to be nothing more than a lying, conniving and manipulative rogue. How it must have pricked your conscience to see how your protégé neglected his duties after my father's demise!'

Again the hand raising the glass to Francis's lips checked for a moment; all the while his gaze never wavered from his lordship's face. 'Hardly my protégé, Sebastian,' he countered. 'I was barely acquainted with

the fellow. Furthermore, you may be sure it gave me no pleasure whatsoever to see the ancestral home of the Blackwoods so shamefully neglected. I remonstrated with Fensham on numerous occasions. But sadly there was little I could do. You must appreciate I had no authority over him.'

Strangely enough the Viscount didn't doubt his cousin's sincerity over this at least. There had been a touch of bitterness and anger in his voice that had been unmistakable at mention of the Manor's neglect.

'No one blames you, Francis, over the state of the Manor, least of all me,' he assured him, striving to be fair, even though he was becoming increasingly mistrustful of his cousin's motives and actions. 'It was extremely remiss of me not to have left instructions with my man of business with regard to the family homes, before I left these shores.'

'But you have more than made up for the oversight since your return,' Francis pointed out graciously. 'The mansion has never looked so grand, not since your dear mother was mistress of the house.' A slight smile hovered round the perfectly shaped masculine mouth. 'Whose influence lies at the root of the sweeping changes, I cannot help asking myself?'

His lordship flatly refused to be drawn, and merely returned the compliment by pointing out the elegance of his present surroundings. 'You've always shown excellent taste, Francis, in dress, as in everything else. You really put the rest of us Blackwoods to shame!'

Although he appeared moderately pleased, and acknowledged the compliment graciously, Francis wasted no time in returning the conversation to the

former topic by asking, 'Why this sudden interest in Fensham again? Given the evidence Miss Mortimer eventually put before the authorities, it's clear Fensham lied about your state of intoxication on that night, when he declared that, although still a trifle unsteady on your feet, you were quite capable of committing murder. It's also very clear now just why he did lie.'

'Not to me it isn't,' his lordship countered in a trice.

Francis did appear genuinely taken aback by this admission. 'But surely, Sebastian, it was in order to extract money, by whatever means he could, from the estate. The Lord alone knows how many deer were taken during your years away, not to mention numerous other game. He must have made a tidy little profit from his various illegal activities.'

'I'm very sure he did,' his lordship acknowledged, concealing his chagrin over this extremely well. 'Just as I'm also very sure that wasn't the real reason he lied. It merely turned out to be an added bonus, as it were. Unless I much mistake the matter, Fensham expected me to be hanged for the murders, and for my uncle to come into the title and acquire everything that went with it. I also suspect that he must have retained every hope of his services being retained by the new holder of the title. You see, I happen to know for a fact that our dear uncle Horace has absolutely no interest whatsoever in the land. He would have remained in London for the most part, merely enjoying all the benefits the estate brought him, and leaving the steward to do more or less as he pleased. None the less, I still do not believe that is why Fensham lied. Oh, no—there was much more to it all than a desire to make extra money from the estate.'

'Yes, yes, you might be right about that. Fensham certainly proved himself to be a rogue,' Francis agreed, after some moments. He raised his eyes and held his lordship's gaze levelly. 'But I do not immediately perceive what you could do in an attempt to retrieve past losses. Fensham must have fled the area months back.'

'Your judgement is normally so accurate, Cousin. But in this instant it is flawed. You see, I have it on the best authority that he was seen in Merryfield a little over two weeks ago,' his lordship quite deliberately revealed, while scrutinising his cousin's every facial movement. 'As we speak I have men scouring this section of the county for any word of him,' he lied. 'It is only a matter of time before he is found… Then, it will be only a matter of time before we discover the whole truth.'

'Needless to say, if I can be of assistance, you need only call upon me,' Francis returned, as his lordship rose to take his leave.

The master of the house made no attempt to accompany his cousin round to the stables, but moved across to the study window in time to watch the Viscount ride away. He watched until the head of the Blackwood family had ridden from view, and then went across to his desk to pen a hurried note.

Chapter Thirteen

After her meeting with Sebastian, Isabel felt as though she were living in an unreal world, floating in a bubble of happiness like some charmed character who had at last found and fallen in love with her perfect prince. Sadly, though, she was far too much of a realist to continue to believe in fairy stories, and within the space of twenty-four hours prickling little doubts had burst the bubble of euphoria that had surrounded her.

True to her word she had told no one, not even her faithful Bessie, of what had passed between Lord Blackwood and herself in the home wood. Which was perhaps just as well, she decided, as she took refuge in the sitting room early the following evening to be alone with her thoughts. Truth to tell she couldn't help wondering whether she might have imagined the whole thing, that her love for Lord Blackwood had somehow affected her hearing and understanding, and that the Viscount had never proposed marriage to her at all.

Her sense of humour managed to thrust aside momentarily the ever-increasing catalogue of doubts now plaguing her, allowing a rueful smile to touch her lips. The truth of the matter was, of course, he hadn't proposed at all! she reminded herself. Arrogant demon that he was, he had taken it for granted that she would automatically comply with his wishes, and accept him as a husband. He had been so self-confident that she could only suppose he had somehow known how much she loved him.

Again she smiled. There was no denying he was damnably astute. But this hardly made him the chivalrous knight in shining armour of her girlhood imaginings. Far from it, in fact, most especially if one were to believe every story concerning his supposed past indiscretions. But he was, none the less, a viscount, and a very heroic man. No one could dispute that. Moreover, he was a peer of the realm who was becoming increasingly respected for his sound judgement and fairness, whereas she...

The opening of the parlour door interrupted her depressing thoughts and she turned to see her cousin, dreamy-eyed and smiling softly, float into the room. If anyone appeared as though they had been well and truly pierced by Cupid's arrow, then it was Clara. Almost from the moment that she had discovered Mr Johns was the parish's new spiritual leader her eyes had held a faraway look, as though she were living in a perfect world that had nothing whatsoever to do with reality.

'You're home early,' Isabel remarked, after a quick glance at the mantel-clock. A rather disturbing possibility quickly followed. Lord Blackwood was universally

liked and much respected by all those who worked for him. Nevertheless, he wasn't one to suffer fools gladly, and he expected all his employees to repay his generosity by providing good service in return. If Clara had spent her time up at the Manor mooning about like a lovesick fool, and neglecting her duties, why, anything might have happened!

'You haven't been dismissed, have you?' she queried gently.

Clara gurgled with mirth. 'Why, no, of course not! What on earth put such a foolish notion into your head?'

Brutal honesty prompted Isabel to respond. 'Well, you have been acting like a giddy schoolgirl for several days now. The sooner you and Mr Johns come to an understanding, the better it will be for all concerned.'

Clara blushed charmingly. 'Oh dear, and we've both been trying so hard to keep it a secret, at least for the time being.' All at once she brightened. 'But maybe we won't need to after today.'

Delving into the pocket of her gown, Clara drew out a letter and promptly handed it to her cousin, before settling herself beside her on the sofa. 'Lord Blackwood called in at the receiving office in Merryfield on his way home and discovered a letter there for me. You may read it if you wish.'

'Why, it's from Mr Goodbody!' Isabel declared, easily recognising the neat hand from the several communications she'd received from him when Josh and Alice had been in her charge. 'So, your stepmother wasn't speaking the whole truth when she came here. He makes no mention of her ever having been your legal guardian. Seemingly, the only provision your father

made for you was a financial one—a neat little sum that you will inherit upon marriage, or when you attain the age of five-and-twenty. I wonder now…?'

Frowning suspiciously, Isabel handed back the letter. 'No doubt your stepmother hoped to come to some financial arrangement with your erstwhile suitor Mr Sloane upon your marriage to him.'

'It seems more than likely,' Clara agreed. 'Papa left Stepmama the house, which was only to be expected. According to Mr Goodbody, though, the greater part of Papa's money was left to me. He was not a wealthy man, by any means, but he was no pauper, either.'

'Indeed not,' Isabel agreed, wondering if this unexpected windfall might induce the well-matched pair to declare their intentions quite openly. 'Are you by any chance calling in at the vicarage this evening, Clara? I believe Bessie mentioned something earlier about Mr Johns having taken up residence there now.'

'No, he's coming round here tomorrow evening, as it happens. I invited him to dinner. I hope you don't mind.'

'Not in the least,' Isabel assured her. 'But you'd best check with Bessie first. You know how she hates not being prepared.'

Clara made to leave, but Isabel forestalled her by asking, as casually as she could, how the Viscount had spent his day. 'You mentioned he'd called in at the receiving office in Merryfield on his way home. Merely idle curiosity, of course, but I was just wondering whether you happened to know where he'd gone beforehand.'

'I do, as it happens,' Clara responded. 'Josh was dis-

appointed not to be riding out with his guardian today. Apparently his lordship told the boy he would be calling on his cousin.'

'Did he, now,' Isabel murmured, when Clara left the room, closing the parlour door quietly behind her. She couldn't help wondering what, if anything, he might have discovered, or if his opinion of his cousin had altered as a result of the visit.

It might have surprised Isabel to discover to what extent his lordship's opinion of that particular member of the Blackwood family had changed in the space of twenty-four hours. The following afternoon, as he sat at his desk, the Viscount could only wonder at himself for never having noticed before certain rather unsavoury traits in his cousin's character. They had always rubbed along together reasonably well, even if they had never been particularly close. Their meetings in bygone years had always been genial enough, with Francis's home offering a welcome respite from the tensions always so prevalent at the Manor.

But now he couldn't help speculating on just how much of his cousin's affability had been feigned, a mere cover for sinister intentions. Much of it, if what he was increasingly coming to believe was indeed true, his lordship finally decided, after a further moment's consideration.

He'd been given ample time since his visit the previous day to cast his mind back over the years to several occasions when fierce quarrels had erupted between him and his father. On most every occasion an altercation had occurred during or shortly after one of Francis's

frequent visits. What had seemed at the time innocent remarks made by Francis had lit the touch-paper of both his and his father's temper. But what had his cousin hoped to achieve by resorting to such stratagems?

Leaning back in his chair, his lordship gazed unseeingly at the wall opposite, recalling quite clearly that, more often than not, a quarrel had resulted in him storming from the house in high dudgeon, and not returning until he had vented his spleen in a breakneck gallop across the park. Had that been Francis's intent? he couldn't help wondering now. Had he hoped his uncle's younger son would suffer a fatal fall from his horse? His lordship was obliged to own that it might so easily have happened. He'd been a headstrong young man, with scant regard for his own safety.

But whatever Francis's intentions might have been, his lordship no longer trusted him. He had left his cousin's Georgian mansion the previous day firmly convinced his darling Belle had been oh, so right in her belief that his cousin was concealing something. Francis definitely knew far more about the ex-steward than he had been prepared to reveal. And he had certainly betrayed a flicker of disquiet when told that a search was now being undertaken to discover Fensham's whereabouts. This hadn't been the case then, of course, but Francis wasn't to know that. Today, however, four estate workers who knew Fensham by sight were indeed scouring Merryfield and its environs for any word or sighting of him.

The sound of an arrival successfully put an end to his lordship's reverie, and a moment later none other than the subject of his thoughts was being shown into the

room. Although not unduly surprised to see his cousin again, he hadn't expected the return visit to take place quite so soon. Seemingly he had succeeded better than he could have hoped in stirring up the hornets' nest.

'Why, Francis! What brings you to the Manor?' Schooling his features so as not to betray his feeling of smug satisfaction, he rose to his feet, while dismissing the butler with a nod. 'Can I offer you some refreshment, or is this merely a flying visit?'

'It is, so I won't sample the fruits of the excellent Manor cellar, I thank you. I am here, Cousin, to request you return to my home with me.'

Very much on his guard, his lordship hadn't been deaf to the slight inflection in his kinsman's voice that had resulted in the request sounding more like a command. 'That is very gracious of you, Francis. But what makes you suppose I should wish to do such a thing?'

A sinister smile hovered around the visitor's well-shaped mouth. 'Because, Sebastian, if you do not you shall never see Miss Isabel Mortimer alive again.'

Not even by so much as a flicker of an eyelid did the Viscount betray the sudden eruption of combined rage and anxiety that consumed him. Even his voice remained remarkably composed when he said, 'If you have harmed her in any way, by the time I am finished with you, Francis, you will be unrecognisable…besides being very, very dead.'

'Oh, I'm well aware, my dear Cousin, that you are more than capable of carrying out such a barbaric feat.' Placing his hat and gloves down on the edge of the desk, Francis drew wide his perfectly tailored jacket to reveal what was beneath and, more especially, what was not

concealed. 'And that is why you perceive me totally unarmed. Believe me, I have no desire to provoke you into rash action that we might both regret. You could, of course, easily overpower me,' he readily acknowledged. 'But be sure you would never reach Miss Mortimer in time to prevent her death.'

Francis took a moment to consult his fob-watch. 'If I am not seen leaving here, quite unharmed, and with you accompanying me, within the next fifteen minutes, the lady's fate will have been sealed.'

Although nothing would have given him greater pleasure than to reach across the desk and place his fingers round his cousin's throat and slowly squeeze the life out of him, the Viscount had no reason to doubt the threat would be carried out if he did so. There were a score of vantage points dotted about the estate from where someone might adequately conceal himself and watch the house without being observed in return. He dared not chance putting Belle's life at risk. Yet, if he did as asked…?

'And if I agree to come with you, what then?'

'Then you have my word that nothing will happen to Miss Mortimer until you have seen her again.' Francis waved his hand airily. 'I'm such a romantic! It would prey on my conscience if I permitted you to leave this world without saying a fond farewell to the great love of your life, Sebastian.'

All at once his sickly fawning smile faded. 'And do not attempt to insult my intelligence by trying to convince me otherwise. You gave far too much away on the night of your dinner party. I have never seen you look at a female the way you look at her.' He shrugged.

'Sadly, I cannot spare her. She, in turn, gave away too much the other evening at the Camerons' do. A pity in a way. She's an interesting girl, and I do not dislike her. But sadly she has already guessed too much.'

Once again he consulted his fob-watch. 'You now have ten minutes, Sebastian. Attempt to harm me and you will seal her fate...without the opportunity of one last fond farewell... The choice is yours.'

For perhaps the first time his lordship realised just how much he had changed in the past ten years. Once, he wouldn't have hesitated to overpower his cousin, and then attempt to rush to Belle's assistance. Age, however, had brought not only the gift of wisdom, but also circumspection. Most important of all it had brought him the gift of love. He could so easily attempt to save himself now, and would more than likely succeed, but in so doing he would destroy the most precious thing in the world. He couldn't live without Belle; he'd merely exist. And that was no life...

'So what do you expect of me now, Francis?'

'I'm so glad you've decided to be sensible, Sebastian.' His smile nowhere near touched his eyes. 'Firstly, you may reseat yourself and pen a letter to your lady love, which I shall dictate, of course, inviting her to dine this evening at my home.'

Lord Blackwood did as bidden whilst all the while his mind worked furiously. The letter might turn out to be a godsend, his one and only opportunity to alert Belle to the danger... But how?

'Come, come, Sebastian! You must think me a moonling!' Francis declared, after leaning over his cousin's broad shoulder to study every movement of the quill.

'Dear Miss Mortimer, indeed!' he scoffed. 'I'm certain you're not still on such formal terms, at least not in private.'

'Very well,' his lordship conceded, as he reached in the drawer for a further sheet of paper to begin the letter afresh with *My darling Isabel*.

'Ah, yes, that's a great deal better!' Francis approved, much to his lordship's intense satisfaction.

He then went on to write everything, word for word, dictated to him, until he had reached the end. Then he paused for a second or two only before signing his name with a flourish.

Frowning, Francis once again studied the finished letter. 'Your writing has changed, Sebastian. It is now quite legible. Yes, it has matured into a very stylish hand. But I do just wonder about the signature. Why just Blackwood?'

Raising his head, his lordship stared without so much as a blink up into his cousin's face. 'I thought you were more observant, Francis. Didn't you notice on the night we dined with Sir Montague and his family that Isabel continues to address me quite formally? She even does so in private,' he lied, without suffering the least pang of conscience. 'But I shall rewrite the letter if you wish, and sign it in whatever way you like.'

There was a moment or two's silence, then, 'No, it will do. Come, sand it down, and seal it with a wafer! We must not delay our departure further.' Once again he cast the Viscount an unpleasant, self-satisfied smile. 'Needless to say I have taken other precautions to ensure my continued safety. So I trust you will remain sensible and do my bidding throughout the journey to my home.'

* * *

It had become almost second nature to Isabel nowadays to take very great care over her appearance, most especially when in the house. That evening she took even more care over the dressing of her hair, and her choice of gown, for not only were they to have a guest dining with them, she also had a shrewd notion an announcement would be forthcoming. In this she was proved correct, which was most gratifying. What she hadn't expected, however, was that her consent to the match would be sought.

Pausing in the act of filling glasses for a celebratory toast, it was as much as Isabel could do not to stare open-mouthed at the happy couple, sitting side by side on the sofa. 'Good heavens! What have I to say to anything, pray? You don't need my approval. You are of an age to make up your own minds,' she declared, hoping she hadn't sounded ungracious, but very much fearing by her cousin's suddenly crestfallen expression that she had.

'Oh, but you are the only family I have left, Isabel... at least the only member I care about. You looked after me when there was no one else I could turn to. I do not look upon you as a mother, or anything like that. That would be foolish.' Colour rose in her cheeks, if possible making her look even lovelier. 'But I do think of you as a much older and wiser sister. I should like to think I have your blessing.'

Having invited Bessie into the parlour in order to join in a toast to the happy couple, Isabel felt she couldn't now order her housekeeper back into the kitchen to watch over her pots. All the same, it would have given

her a deal of pleasure to box her faithful servant's ears when Bessie snickered at the backhanded compliment.

Much older, indeed! Isabel inwardly fumed. She was only five years older, for heaven's sake! Anyone listening might be forgiven for supposing she was in her dotage!

Successfully concealing her chagrin, she finished dispensing the wine. 'Rest assured I couldn't be happier for you both. Although,' she added, eyes glinting wickedly, 'I once had high hopes for you, Clara. I knew a London Season was beyond my means to provide, but I thought my purse might just stretch to a week or two in Bath. I had every expectation of marrying you off to a duke, no less!'

'Oh, heavens, no!' Clara exclaimed, evidently having taken the teasing quite seriously. 'That wouldn't have suited me at all. I am a gentleman's daughter, and was reared to behave in a ladylike manner. But I have never had designs above my station. I think it a grave mistake to marry outside one's class. One could never be oneself.'

Isabel checked for just a second before handing Bessie her filled glass. Their gazes held briefly before Isabel lowered her own. None the less, she sensed that her faithful, wily companion hadn't missed the sudden feeling of despair mirrored in her eyes.

'I expect you are right, Clara,' she returned brightly, determined to shake off the moment of sheer despondency. 'But you two, on the other hand, are remarkably well suited.' She raised her glass. 'And I wish you every happiness.'

The toast was duly drunk, and not a moment too

soon, for a loud rap on the kitchen door echoed down the passageway. 'Now, who can that be, do you suppose?' Bessie grumbled, leaving the parlour in order to answer the summons.

'I sincerely hope it isn't any visitors,' Isabel declared, seating herself opposite the happy couple. 'If there is one thing Bessie hates it's delaying dinner, especially when she's taken such care over its preparation. I'm looking forward to the feast. And to your wedding too,' she assured them. 'When is the happy day? Or haven't you decided on a date yet?'

'Ideally we'd both prefer a summer wedding,' Benjamin Johns revealed, looking adoringly at his future bride. 'But there's a deal to consider. My brother is putting up at the vicarage next week. If he is fortunate enough to attain employment at the Manor, he might need to stay with me until he's able to acquire lodgings elsewhere. Then, of course, I must accustom myself to all my duties in the parish.'

Isabel raised a sceptical brow at the latter declaration. 'You'll forgive my saying so, but I think you've been accustomed to most all of them for a considerable time now.'

Mr Johns, quite inured to the lady's plain speaking by this time, wasn't able to suppress a smile. 'Well, yes, perhaps I am. But I do take my responsibilities seriously, and shall always be willing to put the needs of my parishioners before my own.'

'I'm sure you shall. And needless to say, if I can be of assistance in any way, you have only to ask,' she assured him, before turning to Bessie, who had re-entered the parlour, with a letter in her hand.

'From the Manor, miss. Tom Clegg brought it over. He's waiting in the kitchen for a reply.'

'Oh, what a pity!' Isabel declared, after apprising herself of the contents. 'His lordship is dining over at his cousin's house, and invites me to join him there,' she added, revealing at least part of the missive's contents. 'But of course it's out of the question. I cannot possibly—'

'What is it, Miss Isabel?' Bessie's sharp eyes had detected her young mistress's sudden loss of colour. 'Is there something amiss?'

'I'm not altogether sure.' Rising to her feet, Isabel carried the letter across to the window, and read again, *My darling Isabel…* She immediately paused in her intense perusal and frowned as she raised her head to gaze sightlessly out at the front garden. He never called her Isabel, she reminded herself. Well, only rarely and then only when he was cross with her about something, she silently amended. She read on, wondering why he should desire her to join him at his cousin's house… *I have every expectation of discovering something of importance relating to the happenings at the Manor nine years ago, and should very much like you to be present to share the findings with me. My carriage is at your disposal…* On she read until finally she had reached the end, and her eyes became riveted upon the signature, most especially the formation of that all-important capital letter B, with its distinct and elaborate loop.

'Oh, my God,' she muttered, as the clear memory of the secret sign his lordship would have used to warn Wellington that the contents of a missive were falla-

cious suddenly came rushing back to the forefront of her mind. 'It's all a lie… He must be in danger.'

'Who's in danger, Miss Isabel?' Bessie, asked, after exchanging a startled glance with the couple on the sofa.

Without answering, Isabel brushed past in her headlong flight to reach the door. 'Did you say Clegg was in the kitchen?'

'Yes, but whatever's—'

Bessie broke off abruptly, deciding to save her breath in her attempt to keep pace with her young mistress, as Isabel rushed down the passageway.

'When did his lordship leave the house, Clegg?' she demanded to know the instant she burst into the kitchen to discover the groom appearing very much at home, as usual, seated at the table.

Although taken aback, he couldn't mistake the note of anguish in her voice. 'Couldn't rightly say, miss. I were working in the stables at the time with young Toby. Seemingly the master left in Mr Francis Blackwood's carriage. Is there something amiss?'

'I very much fear there might be, yes. Here, Bessie,' she added, handing over the letter, just as the newly betrothed couple also entered the room. 'You may read it aloud.'

After the missive's contents had been revealed to all, several puzzled glances were exchanged, and it was left to Bessie herself to eventually voice what was clearly in most everyone's mind.

'But what's wrong with the letter, miss?' She received no response. 'I'll admit it do seem strange that his lordship didn't want me to accompany you. Mayhap, though, he thought you'd have protection enough with

Tom, here, to care for you.' She shrugged. 'But it makes no never mind, anyway. You'll not be going, surely?'

'I have no choice. I must go,' Isabel surprised everyone by announcing before she began to pace up and down the large room, her mind working furiously. 'Lord Blackwood has done his best to warn me that something is wrong. It's my belief that letter was dictated. He never calls me Isabel, for a start.'

'Does he not?' Bessie queried, momentarily diverted by this very interesting snippet. 'What does he call you then, if you don't mind my asking?'

'Belle amongst…amongst other things, depending on his mood,' Isabel revealed, smiling in spite of the fact that she was deeply troubled. 'If my suspicions are correct, his lordship didn't go with his cousin willingly.' Her smile disappeared. 'Nor did he willingly write that letter.'

She turned to Clara. 'Didn't you say the Viscount visited his cousin only yesterday?' She received a nod in response. 'It seems strange to me that an invitation to dine wasn't issued then. Furthermore, if Francis Blackwood had any information to pass on, why on earth didn't he do so when he called to see his lordship this afternoon? No, it's all a pack of lies.' Isabel was firmly convinced she was right, as she took back the letter to read it again. 'This isn't an invitation to dine… Unless I'm very much mistaken, it's an invitation to meet my maker.'

'Oh, my gawd!' Bessie exclaimed, momentarily burying her face in her apron. 'What's to be done? You can't go, miss!'

'I have no choice, Bessie,' Isabel returned, sound-

ing remarkably composed considering the most heart-rending possibility had already occurred to her. Her throat felt suddenly constricted as though encircled in a vicelike grasp, but even so she forced herself to say, 'The Viscount might already be dead, but if not, there's just a chance he might be saved.'

Clegg was on his feet in an instant. 'What do you want us to do, miss?'

This immediate vote of confidence was exactly what Isabel needed to concentrate her mind away from the heart-wrenching unthinkable and focus positively on what might be achieved.

She went across to the small window in the west wall of the farmhouse, which overlooked the yard, to see Toby Marsh in charge of his lordship's fine horses, and talking with the elderly man she still employed to do odd jobs about the place.

'I see you've brought young Toby with you, Clegg. That will prove useful.' She turned to her housekeeper. 'Go outside, Bessie, and instruct Troake to come in here. Try as best you can to appear quite normal. We do not know who may be watching the place.

'Mr Johns, I could do with your assistance too, if you are willing?'

'Of course. Anything I can do, you only need to ask.' The young vicar's handsome face betrayed his concern. 'I could never hope to repay the kindness his lordship has shown to me.'

'You might be able to go a long way in doing precisely that before this day is over,' Isabel responded. 'I want you to return to the vicarage now, and harness your gig. It shall not be thought strange if you leave

your home at this time of day. It will be assumed you are merely paying a visit to a sick parishioner. I want you to pick up Toby Marsh, who'll be walking back to the Manor, and then go on to the steward's lodge and express my fears to him. Tell him to follow you and Toby with extra men.'

Isabel turned to Clegg as a further thought occurred to her. 'Do you and Toby both know the way to Mr Francis Blackwood's home?'

'That we do, miss. Took both his lordship and Lady Pimm out to visit when the lady were staying up at the Manor, back along.'

'Excellent, then Toby will be able to direct Mr Johns. Go out to him now, Clegg, and explain what has happened. Tell him to await Mr Johns at the Manor stables. And also tell him to arm himself.'

She broke off as her manservant followed Bessie into the room. She then learned from him that he had indeed glimpsed a stranger lurking in the spinney across the other side of the road earlier in the day. It was precisely what Isabel had feared—the house had been watched, and was possibly still being watched. Therefore it was imperative no one aroused suspicion.

After revealing more fully what she herself intended to do, she retrieved her pistol from the top of the dresser, much to her housekeeper and cousin's alarm.

'Oh, Miss Isabel, you're never taking that thing!' Bessie wailed, having found her voice first.

'I'd be a damned fool to go without it,' she returned, practical as ever. 'The question is how on earth am I going to conceal it? If I were to wear a cloak on a balmy evening such as this, it would arouse suspicion at once.

I shall just have to carry my shawl over my arm and hope that suffices. A knife I can strap to my leg.'

She glanced across at her trusty servant who was on the verge of tears. 'Come, Bessie, bustle about! You've never let me down before. Go find me the sharpest knife we have, and help me conceal it beneath my gown.'

Chapter Fourteen

In all the years he had spent out in the Peninsula, during those times he had come so close to losing his life, Lord Blackwood had never felt as he did now— almost beside himself with fear, only, not for himself.

Trussed up like a chicken, bound, gagged, and tied to a high-backed wooden chair, there was nothing he could do to warn the being who meant more to him than anyone or anything else in the world. Throughout the carriage ride he would willingly have given his own life if he thought there was the remotest possibility that Francis would spare Isabel. Yet he knew he would have been wasting his breath to try to plead for her life. Behind the refined and polished exterior there was a sinister bleakness in his cousin that, until recently, he had never realised existed. Almost from the first, Belle, bless her, had recognised something in Francis that she hadn't quite liked, hadn't quite trusted. One could only hope she had brought that innate feminine astuteness of

hers to play when reading the letter, and would realise something was very wrong. It was a forlorn hope, perhaps. None the less, it was maybe their one and only chance of coming through this with their lives.

After once again straining ineffectually against his bonds, his lordship abandoned his efforts and took a little time to catch his breath and attempt to restore some feeling back into his hands, while using those moments to stare about him. He'd been imprisoned in a room he'd never entered before. Ordered at gunpoint to mount the stairs, he had been escorted by two of Francis's henchmen to the rear of the mansion. By the position of the sun at this time of day, his lordship judged the room to be situated in the west wing, and was clearly used to store artefacts and items of furniture his cousin had evidently collected over the years.

There was a fine Jacobean desk in the far corner. Dotted about the chamber were several handsome walnut pieces of furniture, upon which stood numerous vases, ornaments and several elegant silver candelabras. There were half-a-dozen finely made chairs, all in need of re-upholstering, against one wall, whilst taking pride of place on the wall opposite was a rather eye-catching painting of three young men, all in their twenties.

His lordship frowned as he studied it more closely. One very similar hung in the long gallery at the Manor. *The Three Aitches*, his mother had been known irreverently to call the picture, because it was a likeness of his father and his two younger brothers, Horace and Hubert Blackwood. There was one fundamental difference between the two paintings, however. The one at the Manor had his father taking pride of place in the centre

of the canvas, flanked by his two brothers, whereas in this copy Francis's father, Hubert Blackwood, held centre stage.

'I'm sorry I have been obliged to neglect you for so long, Cousin,' Francis apologised, having entered the room as silently as a cat in time to catch his lordship's scrutiny of the portrait. 'But I simply cannot abide being less than well groomed at all times. And carriage journeys do so crease one's apparel.'

He then tutted, while beckoning to his butler, one of the two people responsible for making his lordship so uncomfortable. 'Really, Figg, there was no need to gag the poor fellow. Who's to hear him if he does shout? The rest of the servants will not return from the fair for some little time yet. Remove the gag at once!'

''Twere the groom gagged him, not me,' the butler grumbled while doing his master's bidding.

Francis ignored him, merely dismissing him with a nod when the servant had completed the task. 'Was that not kind of me, Sebastian, to allow most of the servants the afternoon off to enjoy the fair being held over Merryfield way?' Winning no response, he fixed his gaze on the object that had previously held his lordship's attention. 'My father had that painted. Wily demon that he was, he asked to borrow the original for a short period, soon after this house was built, and had an artist friend of his produce this splendid version.'

All at once he had the look of a rather satisfied cat. 'A far superior specimen to the one hanging back at the Manor! I might be faintly prejudiced, of course, but I always thought my sire the handsomest and most dignified of the brothers. Times without number he

would bring me in here when I was a boy,' he continued, after once again winning no response. '"Look, Francis, my son," he would say, "were there any justice in the world, I would have been head of the family, not that short-necked, chinless eldest brother of mine whose lack of taste, grace and aristocratic bearing is quite lamentable!"'

Failing to elicit a response yet again, he stared across at the Viscount. 'I must say, though, he did approve of your mother. An elegant creature, with an abundance of style, he was wont to say about her. And I must say she did produce a Blackwood of some distinction. Were it not for thee and me, Sebastian, the Blackwoods would be a very sorry lot indeed.'

'So it is your ambition to become head of the family, Francis.' His lordship made no attempt to hide the disgust he felt in either expression or voice. 'I would never have supposed for a moment that someone of no mean intelligence would have allowed his aspirations to spiral out of control, and prompt him to behave in a manner unworthy of the name he bears.'

Francis's look of smug satisfaction was all at once much less marked. 'That is one of the fundamental differences between us, Sebastian—you never had the least desire to hold the title, whereas I have dreamt of nothing else since those far-off days of my childhood.'

'But aren't you forgetting one very important fact— even if you are successful in removing me, you are still third in line,' his lordship pointed out.

Francis, however, merely waved one shapely hand in the air in a dismissive gesture, seemingly unperturbed. 'That is yet another area where we are vastly contrast-

ing, Cousin. You were always intensely headstrong, wont to act on impulse for the most part, whereas I have always tended to consider most carefully, and am remarkably patient as a rule. Uncle Horace and poor Cousin Clement are not destined long for this world, I fear. If either of them continues to survive much above two years, I shall be very much surprised. Both are destined to die from natural causes, so no possible suspicion will fall upon me.'

'You may not be so lucky where I'm concerned,' his lordship pointed out with some satisfaction. 'Too many people know where I am.'

'True,' Francis readily concurred. 'But accidents do happen, most especially at night, and on lonely roads.'

'Indeed, they do,' his lordship agreed, having now some idea of his eventual fate, should his cousin have his way. 'But, even so, my unexpected death will not pass without an investigation being carried out. Then it is likely to be considered most odd that you invite persons to dine when you have given the majority of your staff leave to visit a local fair.'

'True,' Francis agreed again. 'But it seemed less of a risk than having a member of my household whom I do not trust implicitly witnessing what takes place here this evening. Besides which, I instructed my cook to leave ample fare prepared before she left the house. And, of course, she will attest to having done precisely that when questioned. Furthermore, your deaths on the road will not arouse too much suspicion. Not so many months ago there were quite a few incidents of highway robbery in the county, one or two even ending tragically in death.'

He had sounded so smugly sure of himself that his lordship once again experienced a desire to throttle the life out of him, should he be granted half a chance.

'Strangely enough, Cousin, I shall take no pleasure in removing you from the world,' Francis went on, when the Viscount continued to regard him with enmity clearly visible in his expression. 'For a very long time I clung to the hope that you would never return, that your headstrong ways of yesteryear would have induced you to commit some act of folly in some far-flung corner of the world that would have resulted in your demise.' He sighed, sounding genuinely remorseful. 'Unfortunately, it was not to be, and you did return. Nevertheless, for a while, I was prepared to allow you to linger. But then, sadly, an unforeseen and totally unexpected event took place—you, of all people, went and fell in love.'

Moving over to the desk in the corner, Francis poured himself a glass of wine before seating himself on the edge of the handsome piece of furniture, and then swinging one leg casually back and forth, appearing totally relaxed.

'I suspected it the instant I first caught sight of her at the party. By the time I left the Manor that night I was convinced I was right—yes, the unthinkable had happened. But even so, romantic that I am, I was more than happy to allow the course of true love to run smoothly for a time. Then, the foolish chit reveals rather too much on the night we dined with the Camerons. Even though she did her best to rectify the blunder, I knew she'd discovered something, but I knew not what until your visit here yesterday.' Once again he paused to sample his wine, before asking, 'Tell me, Cousin, would I be

correct in thinking it was none other than Miss Mortimer herself who spotted Guy Fensham in Merryfield that day?'

Once again failing to elicit a response, Francis smiled. 'Of course it was! Foolishly I must have betrayed my unease when I bumped into her. I must say she's quite a sharp-witted little thing,' he continued, after staring meditatively down at a certain portion of the carpet. 'Which makes her behaviour at the Camerons' dinner party all the more difficult to comprehend.' He shrugged. 'But no matter. It was a grave error of judgement on her part, just as agreeing to meet Guy Fensham on that particular Saturday was mine... And speak of the devil!'

The door had opened, but it was a second or two before a man his lordship hadn't seen in nine long years entered his field of vision. He had changed a good deal. His hair now was liberally streaked with grey, there was a suspicion of a stoop about his shoulders, and his face was etched with many more lines. It wasn't any of these obvious changes that held his lordship transfixed for several seconds, however. It was something he'd unbelievably quite failed to detect until now, as the two men stood side by side, and the resemblance between them became so apparent.

'The carriage is about a mile away. I cut across the fields,' Fensham revealed, while all the while looking over at the Viscount in a distinctly hostile manner.

'I do believe, Guy, the son of your late employer has finally perceived the likeness between us,' Francis responded sagely. 'Yes, quite noticeable when we're standing together, is it not, Cousin? Brother Guy's

features are somewhat coarser than mine. But then you and your half-brother didn't look so very alike, either—clearly the result of having different mothers. I cannot tell you what a shock it was when he appeared on my doorstep all those years ago looking for work, and claiming kinship.' He shrugged. 'Really, though, I shouldn't have been in the least surprised. Like your good self in your youth, dear Papa was a most shocking philanderer. The Lord alone knows how many of his other by-blows litter the land. Guy, my senior by some six years, is, however, the only one my father took the trouble to have educated, as far as I'm aware. Which shows, I think, how genuinely fond he must have been of his mother. He couldn't marry her, of course. It was quite out of the question as she came from the lower orders, besides having no money. But that is another story, and one that I shall not bore you with now.'

He raised his hand when he detected what had induced his lordship's heart to miss a beat. 'I do believe a carriage approaches. Now, Cousin, if I have your word that you will not call out, Guy, here, will not replace the gag. Break your word and Figg has instructions to dispense with the delightful Miss Mortimer at once, and you shall, by your own foolish actions, be denied the pleasure of seeing her again.'

'I shall not call out,' his lordship vowed.

As the carriage rounded the sweep of the drive and the handsome sandstone mansion came into view, Isabel picked up her lightweight shawl, and folded it several times very carefully, before draping it across her left wrist and hand in order to conceal the pistol. She was

ready for whatever lay ahead. She could only pray that
the others would be too, most especially Clegg. She
didn't doubt that some attempt to overpower him would
take place soon after their arrival. True enough, he was
on the short side, but he was strong, and he had assured
her he was ready for any attack.

As the carriage slowed, she peered out of the window
and took some comfort from the fact that there was no
one about. This state of affairs changed the instant the
carriage drew to a halt before the impressive porticoed
main entrance, for an ill-looking fellow emerged from
the house to assist her from the carriage.

As much as she longed to do so, Isabel dared not so
much as look back over her shoulder at Clegg, lest something in her expression betray her fears for his safety.
Throughout the entire journey she had been plagued
by heartrending concerns over Sebastian's well-being,
and racked by remorse at having been instrumental in
placing others' lives in jeopardy. Never would she forget
the look on either Clara's face or Bessie's when she
had been obliged to embroil men they cared so very
much about in the affair. Her one small consolation was
that she had been given little choice, and both men had
offered their help most willingly.

'The master awaits you in one of the upstairs rooms,
miss,' the stooped and faintly sinister-looking servant
informed her, after closing the door against the outside
world. 'Viscount Blackwood is with him. If you'd care
to follow me?'

So far so good, Isabel mused, as she tamely did as
bidden. Seemingly the high-ranking servant had detected nothing amiss with her demeanour. Nor, which was

more heartening, had he thought to question the carrying of the silken wrap over her arm. Her only concern was whether he had lied. Was the Viscount truly there? More importantly, would she find him unharmed?

This agonising thought was successfully concealed behind the brightest of smiles as the servant threw wide a door and she saw Francis standing beside an elegant desk.

'Why, Mr Blackwood!' Tripping lightly forwards with every evidence of delight, she held out her right hand. 'How very gratified I was by your invitation to dine!' she managed to say, before stopping dead in her tracks. Unlike the assurance, her shock at finding a certain other person lurking a few yards away was not assumed.

'You are acquainted with Fensham, of course,' Francis remarked suavely, as Isabel stared from one to the other, easily perceiving the likeness between the two men now that she was seeing them close together for the first time.

For a moment or two she was undecided just how to proceed, whether or not to feign surprise at the association between the two men. Then her eyes strayed to the corner of the large room and her course was suddenly crystal-clear.

'Sebastian!' she cried, determined to reach him before anyone could stop her, and falling to her knees beside his chair.

Tears of joy filled her eyes at finding him alive, but she held them in check. Now was not the time to give way to emotion, she told herself, allowing the silk shawl

to slip from her wrist to the floor, thereby continuing to conceal the pistol beneath.

'Have you been harmed in any way?'

He shook his head, while his gaze betrayed both sorrow and joy at seeing her there.

'How very touching, do you not think, Guy?' Francis declared, only to receive a snort of derision in response. 'Oh, but it is, dear fellow!' he persisted. 'I'm so pleased to have had my assumptions confirmed. They are clearly in love, and unless I am much mistaken my dear cousin's intentions with regard to this particular female are entirely honourable.'

Fensham seemed to debate for a moment, the look in his eyes not at all pleasant as they travelled over Isabel's trim, shapely figure. 'Honourable, eh…? Are you sure? She's hardly in the same class, after all.'

At this Sebastian shot a glance in Isabel's direction and couldn't mistake the fleeting look of raw despair that gripped her features the moment before Fensham began speaking again.

'I'll say this for the wench, though, she scrubs up well. Yes, I'll give her that. I wouldn't mind half an hour with her myself. If nought else it'd repay the interfering little baggage for meddling in matters that were none of her concern.'

'Loath though I am to refuse you anything, old fellow, after all the loyalty you've shown me over the years, but I'm afraid I cannot permit you to assuage your lust in that particular quarter. I gave my word as a gentleman that no harm would befall her until her—er—execution.'

Turning on his heels, Francis reached for the decanter

on the desk once again. 'I think we might at least allow the condemned couple a final drink together. The reason I did not offer you one earlier, Sebastian, was simply because I couldn't be sure that if I assisted you to a mouthful you wouldn't spit it right back into my face. But I'm sure you would not think of doing such a disgusting thing to the delightful Miss Mortimer, if she were to assist you. Perhaps you would be good enough to carry them over, Guy?'

With lightning speed, Isabel took full advantage of those precious seconds when both men's backs were turned. Swiftly removing the knife from where it had been safely concealed beneath her dress, she successfully cut through one of the cords that bound his lordship to the chair. His eyes widened in surprise, but apart from this he remained motionless until she had achieved equal success with the cords binding his wrists. Then he nodded to confirm he had felt the slight slackening of the bonds, and accepted the knife she left between his wrists with silent gratitude.

Even before Guy Fensham had turned to carry the glasses across to them, Isabel was on her feet, standing beside his lordship in order to conceal the one loose piece of rope that now dangled against the back leg of the chair. She could do nothing about the other end, and only hoped that the men wouldn't notice if it did show. She accepted the glasses and then turned to look down at Sebastian, surprising him again by winking conspiratorially at him, and then glancing down at her shawl.

He wasn't perfectly certain what she was attempting to convey, but he could hazard a fairly shrewd guess.

His darling Belle was a damnably resourceful girl. Pray God their luck held!

As she made to place the glass to his lips, he gazed up at her. 'I'll risk it if you will, my darling. But you'd best be prepared for the wine to be drugged…or worse.'

'Do you know, Sebastian, I never considered that!' Francis declared, appearing faintly shamefaced. 'Very remiss of me, now I come to consider the matter. Truth to tell, dear boy, I've no desire to see either of you suffer unduly. I'm not a vindictive person. It shall remain on my conscience that I was kinder to your father and brother. It just so happens I did drug their wine.'

'A confession at last, my darling!' his lordship declared, much to his cousin's evident amusement.

'Not that it will do you much good, Sebastian,' he laughingly told him, before a noise from below, like that of breaking china, wiped the smile off his face. 'Now, what was that, do you suppose?'

'Figg knocking into something, I shouldn't wonder,' Fensham responded, betraying scant interest. 'You know how damnably clumsy he is. Why you continue to employ the idle buffoon, I'll never know.'

'Because he's avaricious. He'll do anything for money, and he can keep his mouth shut.' Francis sampled his wine, frowning. 'None the less, I do not intend to retain his services for very much longer, after tonight.'

'I find your complete lack of conscience quite astonishing, Mr Blackwood,' Isabel declared, her mind having woken up to a comforting possibility for the slight, unexpected noise that she too had detected. As the last thing she wanted was for Francis to insist on

an investigation, she attempted to divert his thoughts immediately by saying, 'My besetting sin is morbid curiosity. Would you be gracious enough to satisfy it one last time and reveal how you managed to gain entry to the Manor on that certain spring night, all those years ago, in order to murder both your uncle and cousin?'

'I shall be only too delighted, my dear Miss Mortimer. After all, it's the least I can do in the circumstances,' he declared, executing an exaggerated bow. 'But first, I feel I must correct you over one small matter—I did not murder my uncle, only my cousin. Guy, here, must take full credit for his late master's demise.'

By the completely bland look on the ex-steward's face it didn't appear that he was plagued overmuch by a guilty conscience. It was also impossible to judge what was passing through the Viscount's mind, for his expression was totally impassive too. Isabel guessed, though, that he had more immediate concerns occupying his thoughts. By his slight arm movements she judged he was still attempting to work completely free of his wrist restraint, so his seeming lack of interest could be forgiven.

'Now, let me see...' Francis began. 'It was such a long time ago, I must needs take a moment or two to gather my thoughts... Ah, yes, I remember! I left the Manor some time before midnight. It was a clear night with a bright moon. Guy and I rendezvoused at the prearranged spot on the estate. He'd already dispatched his first victim by then, and concealed his body in the wood.'

Isabel chanced to look down at Sebastian. Then promptly wished she had not. The look in his eyes, the

sheer, unadulterated hatred, was frightening to witness. The next moment it had faded, and she prayed she would never glimpse it again.

'You are speaking of Jem Marsh, I believe,' Isabel said softly. 'Was it necessary to murder him?'

From his jacket pocket Guy Fensham drew out a key. 'He didn't like the idea of me keeping this. He saw me return it to my pocket after leaving the house. Said I should have left it in the young master's bedchamber. I knew I couldn't trust him to keep his mouth shut, most especially concerning his young master's true drunken state.'

'I would have seen to everything,' Francis reminded him. 'You merely panicked.'

Fensham seemed unrepentant. 'But our plans changed when he didn't spend the night with that woman he kept at the time over Merryfield way,' he responded, after nodding in the Viscount's direction.

'Yes, my getting inebriated in the local inn and being returned to the Manor must have caused some disquiet. But it also offered you a most convenient scapegoat did it not?' his lordship remarked drily, and then shrugged. 'Though I don't suppose it mattered much. Even if I had spent the whole night away from the Manor, the finger of suspicion would undoubtedly have been pointed squarely in my direction.'

'Undeniably!' Francis agreed. 'But really, Sebastian, you'd only yourself to blame. Even you must acknowledge you were wild to a fault in those far-off days, quite indifferent to what was said and thought about you at the time. You were a law unto yourself.'

'Very true,' his lordship agreed, at last freeing him-

self from the last constraint about his wrist. He had no real desire to bandy words with his kinsman, but he needed to play for time—time to consider how best to protect the wonderfully gallant lady at his side. Knowing full well she would be walking into a trap, she had, at even greater risk to herself, come armed.

His lordship had every expectation of dispatching one of them—his skill with a knife had been honed to a lethally accurate degree during his years in the Peninsula. But could he possibly free his ankles in time to protect Belle from the other? He recalled her gesture towards the silk shawl, lying just behind her on the floor. Even if she did indeed have an extra weapon concealed beneath, there were still Francis's faithful servants to contend with. Time was not on their side. Sooner or later he was going to be forced to act, but until then…

'Would I be right in supposing that it was none other than your good self, Francis, who risked discovery by mounting the stairs in order to daub my unconscious person with our relatives' blood?'

The bow was answer enough. 'Yes, I surmised as much. And would I also be correct in assuming that you didn't regain entry to the house by way of the side entrance, using the very key Fensham has retained all these years?'

'You would indeed, Cousin,' Francis confirmed. 'I gained entry by way of the French windows. I had asked to see the garden shortly after we'd dined, you see. For May it was a surprisingly chilly night, as I recall. Your father and brother chose not to accompany me for a breath of fresh air. Not surprising really, I'd already

drugged their wine, and they were beginning to feel the effects. It was a simple matter for me to relock the door, and then pretend to throw the bolts before drawing the curtains.'

'And then much later you made good your escape by using, unless I much mistake the matter, that certain ill-fitting window in the same room?' This time his lordship received a nod of acquiescence in response. 'You made only a very few mistakes that night, Francis. The first was to leave the key in the lock of the French windows. It is always kept in the drawer of the bureau. The other foolish blunder was to attempt to implicate me by relying wholly on the evidence of your accomplice. In your eagerness to dispense with yet another member of the Blackwood family you conveniently forgot that there were others who witnessed my sorry state that night.'

Francis appeared to consider this criticism, and then nodded. 'Yes, I think it's fair to say that was an error of judgement on my part. From Guy I learned about the good doctor's involvement, of course, and feared all might be lost. Then I foolishly imagined all would turn out as planned again, when I discovered he had become ill. I never supposed for a moment that his written account lay forgotten in some drawer. Still…' he shrugged '…no real harm was done, after all. The four people who now know what really took place that night are in this room. Fensham won't talk, of course. To do so would be to place a noose about his neck. And as far as you two are concerned…'

He reached for his glass, and raised it as though in a silent toast. 'I'm sorry I cannot allow you a few minutes

alone together. Time is pressing, and I fear my servants will not be too long delayed in returning from the fair. Besides which, I could not trust Miss Mortimer not to attempt to release you from your bonds, Cousin.'

His protracted sigh of regret was clearly audible, though whether it was genuine was a different matter entirely. 'A pity it must end this way, my dear,' he announced, fixing his gaze on Isabel. 'I truly believe you have many quite exceptional qualities, and would have made a fine Viscountess, just like your predecessor.'

'Let's get on with it, and put an end to this charade!' Fensham urged, though whether out of consideration for the prospective victims, or because he was heartily bored, was equally difficult to judge.

'Very well, Guy,' Francis obliged him. 'Which will you dispatch? The pistols are in the drawer, ready loaded.'

'I'll see to the—'

Guy Fensham had uttered his last. The knife used at the farmhouse for skinning rabbits was embedded in the ex-steward's chest, thrown by his lordship with lightning speed, and unerring accuracy. By the time his partner in crime had assimilated what had occurred, Isabel had extracted the pistol from beneath her shawl. A moment later Francis was slumped beside his half-brother on the floor. The next moment the door had been thrown wide and to his lordship's astonishment several of his employees, not to mention his own recently appointed vicar, burst into the room.

Chapter Fifteen

Achieving a modicum of solace in the privacy of her own front parlour, Isabel went over to the window to stare out at the front garden. The view did little to lift her spirits. While Toby Marsh had worked at the farmhouse the garden had been well tended, boasting neat flower-beds and weed-free paths. Since his departure to the Manor standards had definitely not been maintained. She couldn't blame her only male employee, Troake. It was certainly true that he didn't work anywhere near as hard as he once did, but she could hardly reprimand him for that. He was well past his prime, not to mention riddled with arthritis, poor man! If anyone was to blame for the garden's neglect in recent weeks, then it was herself. She had wasted far too much time of late apeing the behaviour of those much higher placed on the social ladder, attempting to be something she was not. And it had to stop!

Instantly her thoughts turned to the Viscount, as they all too often had in recent weeks. She had seen nothing

of him whatsoever the previous day. Which had come as no very big surprise, it had to be said. He must have been fully occupied explaining to various interested parties details surrounding the deaths of his cousin and the Manor's former steward. No doubt he had done his utmost to shield her as much as he possibly could from further involvement, and having to answer a thousand-and-one unpleasant questions.

Benjamin Johns had called the previous day to see how she went on, however, and had confirmed that he had received a visit from both Sir Montague Cameron and a Justice of the Peace presiding in the locale where the late Francis Blackwood had resided.

On that never-to-be-forgotten evening his lordship had, she clearly remembered, voiced nothing but praise for the way she had attempted to organise his rescue, most especially involving the Reverend Mr Johns who, as luck would have it, had arrived in time to overhear the gist of what had been said in that upstairs chamber, and whose account of events had subsequently proved invaluable.

'A masterly example of forward thinking, my darling!' Sebastian had praised her before handing her into his carriage, where Mr Johns, designated the role of duenna, had sat awaiting her.

After a few further gentle words of farewell, he had ordered both Clegg and Toby, seated up on the box, to ensure her safe return home. That was the last time she had seen his lordship…

The next time, she felt certain, would not be long delayed, and she dreaded the encounter, for somehow

she must find the strength to tell him she could not be his wife.

The parlour door opened, making her start, a circumstance that didn't escape Bessie's eagle-eyed gaze. 'Oh, Miss Isabel, you're as nervous as a kitten! Not that I'm surprised, not after what you've been through.'

Bessie had already received a reasonably detailed account of what had taken place at the late Francis Blackwood's home on that fateful evening, when Tom Clegg too had taken the trouble to pay a visit to the farmhouse the previous evening. She shuddered at the mere thought of it all; most especially harrowing was what her poor mistress had been obliged to do in order to save the Viscount. Putting a period to someone's existence was bound to cause any right-minded person a deal of remorse. All the same, it wasn't like the young mistress to brood over matters that couldn't be mended.

She regarded Isabel's wan expression keenly. Could there be something else distressing her? Bessie couldn't help wondering. If so, there was a certain someone sure to sort it out—someone who, unless she had misread all the signs in recent months, meant a great deal to her mistress.

She raised her head as her ears detected a certain unmistakable sound. 'I do believe that were a carriage just drew up in the yard. I'd best go see who's a-visiting.'

Isabel didn't respond. There seemed little point in doing so. She had a fairly shrewd idea of the identity of the caller, just as Bessie had done. What was the point in saying she didn't wish to receive visitors? Like as not his lordship would merely brush past and demand

an audience. Besides which, what could be gained by delaying the inevitable encounter?

She knew it was he who had entered the parlour unannounced even before he declared, 'I've had the most exhausting day thus far, my darling! Been up since daybreak, and not a drop of liquid passing my lips since breakfast. I'm absolutely parched!'

Without awaiting a response Sebastian helped himself to a glass of wine, and was on the point of pouring a second glass when he checked, noting for the first time the droop of slender shoulders, and registering, too, the fact that she had made no attempt to turn from the window in order to look in his direction.

Picking up the filled glass, he sipped the contents meditatively, while moving slowly across the room. 'I'm sorry I've been unable to see you before now, my darling,' he said, assuming this must surely be what had given rise to this negative reaction to his visit. 'But, as I'm sure you can imagine, I've had the very devil of a time explaining everything to the authorities. Not only that, I'm having to deal with all Francis's affairs. I was obliged to speak to my cousin's lawyers in Merryfield, only to discover whilst there that he's only gone and named me as the main beneficiary in his will, would you believe?'

This brought her head round, as he had suspected it might, and there was nothing artificial in the astonished look she cast him. 'Why on earth should he have done that, do you suppose? I genuinely believe he didn't dislike you, but he couldn't possibly have thought that much of you, otherwise he wouldn't have planned what he did.'

'And there you have it in a nutshell, my darling,' he returned, his sharp eyes not missing the slight wince at his endearment. 'I'm not in full possession of all the details as yet. In fact the only reason I had for calling on the notaries was to apprise them of Francis's demise. It was then I discovered certain aspects of the will. Quite naturally, while enquiries are ongoing regarding the details surrounding my cousin's demise, the lawyers are being cautious. But what they did reveal is that Francis made major adjustments to his will sometime last autumn, when he discovered I'd returned to England.'

'That's all very well, but I still fail to understand why he should have done such a thing, in view of the fact that he intended to dispose of you,' Isabel pointed out, having set her own heartfelt concerns aside for the present.

'I suspect he was merely taking extra precautions for when he did arrange my demise,' his lordship responded, ever the realist. 'After all, who would suspect him of the dastardly deed when he had named me beneficiary in his will. Given that he had no wife and children to support, he was merely striving to convey the impression he was a loyal member of the Blackwood clan, sincerely attached to the head of such a noble family.'

Isabel shook her head, still finding it difficult coming to terms with what had taken place during the past days, and to what depths some people would sink in order to attain their ends.

'I wonder how long he had been obsessed with the idea of being head of the family, of owning the ancestral home and having the title?'

Sebastian shrugged. 'From a very young age, I

strongly suspect. What little he did reveal suggested the burning ambition was instilled in him by his father.'

Finishing off his wine, he placed the glass on the sill behind her, and then stared down intently, easily detecting the suddenly wary look before she lowered her eyes.

'I dare say that for a few days to come I shall be engaged far too much in dealing with matters relating to my late cousin, not least of which will be organising some kind of funeral. But for the rest of this day, I'm entirely at your disposal, my darling. So tell me what kind of a day you've had thus far. More importantly, tell me what you're planning to wear this evening at Emily's do?'

Given the trauma of recent days, it was hardly surprising that her expected presence at Mrs Radcliff's proposed dinner party had escaped her memory entirely. Isabel clasped her face in her hands, a clear indication of her genuine distress.

'Oh, Lord, I'd forgotten all about it! I must send a note at once, begging to be excused. In the circumstances I'm sure Emily will understand.'

'She might, but I most certainly shall not,' he responded, easily preventing her headlong dash across the room to the bureau by the simple expedient of momentarily grasping her elbow. 'I have no intention of playing the hypocrite by going into mourning for someone who did his level best to cut short our allotted time on this earth. Furthermore, it will be considered extremely odd if I announce our betrothal to the world at an event where my fiancée isn't present.'

There was no mistaking the heartfelt distress in the

large grey-green eyes before delicate lids lowered and she swung round to face the window again. 'You don't understand, I—'

'Oh, I think I understand perfectly well,' he countered, cutting her off mid-sentence without suffering the least pang of conscience. He recalled seeing that self-same look not so many days before, and knew precisely what was causing the anxiety. 'I suspected at the time that you had paid too much heed to Fensham's idiotic notion that our stations in life are vastly contrasting. Undoubtedly it has grown out of all proportion, resulting in your firm belief that you are unsuitable to be my Viscountess. Well, I don't want to hear anything further about it!' he continued, the annoyance and resolve in his voice unmistakable. 'It is utter nonsense, anyway! Even Francis—devil take him!—could appreciate your suitability to be my wife.'

Astute man that he was, he had calculated her misgivings in a trice, and had dismissed them as swiftly. None the less, Isabel couldn't so easily forget what Fensham and, more especially, what her cousin had said. Clara had not touched briefly on the subject of marrying out of one's class for any ulterior motive. She had merely remarked on something that she truly felt… what the vast majority of people would feel. Although Isabel had no intention of betraying her cousin as being partially responsible for her present anxiety, she felt no compunction whatsoever in using his late cousin in an attempt to try to make him see reason.

'I never supposed for a moment Francis was in earnest when he said what he did. I believe he was merely making sport of me.'

'You are utterly wrong in that assessment,' he returned, with such conviction that she instantly began to doubt her own judgement in the matter. 'Francis was ambitious, lethally so as things turned out. But one thing he was never guilty of and that was insincere flattery. From the first he recognised you for what you are—a lady of quality, a lady of integrity and sound judgement. He knew you posed a real threat because, unlike Fensham, he instantly recognised your suitability to be my wife.' He smiled ruefully. 'Ashamed though I am to admit as much, I was a trifle slower in my appreciation of your exceptional qualities. I had been in your company on several occasions before I knew you'd make me the perfect wife, *ma belle*.'

'Please do not call me that,' she managed faintly, her resolve slowly ebbing away, as he moved a step closer and she could feel the warmth of his breath fanning the nape of her neck. 'My command of the French tongue is nowhere near equal to yours, but even I know what that means. And I am no beauty, sir. Your friends would not call me so.'

A moment's silence only, then, 'Ah, but you see, *ma belle*, they are not blessed to see you through my eyes.'

This was just too much for Isabel's rapidly weakening resolve. She felt her knees buckle and would have been powerless to stop herself sinking to the floor if strong arms hadn't encircled her. The next moment she was being carried across to the sofa, where she received further corroboration, had she needed any, of the depth of Sebastian's feelings for her.

Emerging breathless from the masterly display, Isabel rested her head upon his shoulder. She didn't

doubt the depth of his regard. How could she? None the less, niggling doubts about her suitability to become his Viscountess remained.

'Of course you are bound to feel some anxiety with regard to your future role in life, my darling,' he said, once again reading her thoughts with uncanny accuracy, after raising her chin and staring long and hard into her eyes. 'It would be strange if you did not. But, remember, I shall always be there, should you need advice.'

She couldn't help smiling at this. He had clearly made up his mind that he would take her to wife, and seemingly nothing she could say would detract him from this objective. And, truth to tell, she no longer wished to try. 'It would seem, my Lord Blackwood, you are determined to have your way.'

There was a hint of smug satisfaction in the smile he cast down on her. 'Not so very long ago an astute young woman said to me that if I ever proposed marriage to a lady I truly loved, I would never take no for an answer. And how right she was! The only reason I would accept my *congé* from you, my darling girl, is if you were to say that you truly did not love me.' The self-satisfied look was all at once more pronounced. 'And that you could never do… No girl could do what you did not so many days ago and not be in love. So…'

Delving into his jacket pocket, he produced a small, square box, and after briefly displaying its magnificent contents before a pair of astonished eyes, he slipped the diamond ring on to her finger.

For several seconds it was as much as Isabel could do to stare at the exquisite gem. 'It's so beautiful,' she murmured, holding her hand up towards the window

so that the large stone reflected the light in a myriad of colours. 'Is it part of the family jewels?'

'Certainly not!' He sounded affronted, but she was not fooled. 'I purchased it in London when I was there a few weeks ago,' he then happily revealed, knowing as he did so that she would realise his regard had not suddenly manifested overnight, but had been steadily growing over many weeks. 'Mention of the family jewels is a timely reminder, none the less. One of the reasons I came over was to ask if you wished to wear again tonight that pearl set you wore at my dinner party, and very thoughtfully returned to the Manor?'

The mere thought of doing so made her smile, but then she thought better of it. 'No, no, I do not think so. It's only a small affair, after all, and I do not wish to appear vulgarly overdressed,' she said, proving that she was already considering behaviour and how she would appear to the world at large. 'I think Mama's single string will suffice, most especially as I shall be wearing this beautiful adornment,' she continued, once again staring down at her hand. 'Besides, apart from our announcement, I would imagine the evening will be slightly muted. No matter how much of a brave face Emily Radcliff puts on at the present time, she must be so deeply worried about her husband across the Channel.'

His smile was distinctly crooked. 'Evidently you haven't yet heard, my dear. In truth, I only learned earlier this week that Wellington and the allies won a great victory at a hitherto inconsequential place called Waterloo. Emily has already received word that her husband came through the battle virtually unscathed,

and will be returning within a few weeks. Apart from which, she has a further reason to celebrate. As you might be aware, she didn't accompany her husband because she thought there was just a chance she might be increasing. Now she knows for sure she is.'

Isabel was delighted with the news. Before she could voice her joy, Bessie returned to the room, wanting to know whether Lord Blackwood wished his groom to return to the Manor for any reason.

'No, Bessie, you may tell him his future mistress has wisely decided not to wear the pearls this evening, and that I shall be returning there myself presently.'

'Very good, my—' Bessie broke off, gazing in awe-struck silence for a moment or two at the couple sitting rather informally close on the sofa, before adding, 'Oh, my word, you don't say!'

'I do,' the Viscount returned with simple pride. 'So you may be the first to congratulate me on my great good fortune in becoming betrothed to your mistress.'

'Oh, I do, sir. Indeed I do!' Bessie declared, wiping a suspicion of tears on the corner of her apron.

'Of course it will mean your removal to the Manor in the very near future. My present housekeeper will be returning to London to look after the town house, leaving the position of housekeeper at the Manor vacant. Which I sincerely trust you will fill.'

Clearly overcome, it was much as much as Bessie could do to nod dumbly before Isabel dismissed her and turned to her future husband with a half-reproachful look. 'You are taking a deal for granted, my lord. What do you suppose I am to do when Bessie goes up to the Manor?'

'Do…?' He was slightly taken aback for a second. 'Why, you'll be there with her, of course. No,' he added, holding up a hand at the protest he knew was about to be uttered. 'I refuse to have a needlessly long engagement. London, of course, will be positively swarming with people wanting to celebrate Wellington's victory. I flatly refuse to attempt to organise our wedding there with all that going on. So, what I propose is a quiet wedding, here in the parish, with the good Mr Benjamin Johns officiating.'

Isabel was not in the least unhappy with that suggestion. In fact, she rather thought she would prefer it to a great society affair, held in the metropolis, where she would know so few people. Those occasions were definitely for the future, when she had acquired a little know-how. All the same, she could foresee just one slight problem.

'Well, naturally, I'm delighted to hear that your cousin and Mr Johns are betrothed. They are admirably well suited, as I've remarked before,' he responded, when she had revealed the news. 'But I tell you plainly, my darling, I have no intention on awaiting their nuptials before we tie the knot ourselves. I shall call at the vicarage in a day or two, and organise the banns. I intend we should marry within a month. Then we shall, maybe, visit Bath. I have a desire, you see, to make a return trip to the West Country to visit one or two friends.'

Isabel knew precisely who he meant, and was not averse to the idea in the least. She would like to renew her acquaintance with both Charles Bathurst and Sir Philip Staveley, and meet their wives. But she still felt

unable to go off willy-nilly on her honeymoon and ignore her responsibilities.

'But what about Clara? I can't go and leave her here on her own to fend for herself,' she pointed out.

'No one is expecting you to do any such thing,' he calmly assured her. 'Once we're married, it will be perfectly in order for her to move into the Manor, where Bessie will be in a position to look after her until your return.'

Isabel settled herself again in the crook of his arm, wondering whether all her future worries would be smoothed out so adroitly. It would be nice to think so. Undoubtedly becoming Viscountess Blackwood would bring its own responsibilities. None the less, she had the feeling she would cope very well with such a loving tower of strength to guide and protect her.

* * * * *

A sneaky peek at next month...

HISTORICAL

IGNITE YOUR IMAGINATION, STEP INTO THE PAST...

My wish list for next month's titles...

In stores from 2nd December 2011:

- ❑ The Lady Forfeits – Carole Mortimer
- ❑ Valiant Soldier, Beautiful Enemy – Diane Gaston
- ❑ Winning the War Hero's Heart – Mary Nichols
- ❑ Hostage Bride – Anne Herries
- ❑ Claimed by the Highland Warrior – Michelle Willingham
- ❑ Western Winter Wedding Bells – Cheryl St.John, Jenna Kernan & Charlene Sands

Available at WHSmith, Tesco, Asda, Eason, Amazon and Apple

Just can't wait?

Visit us Online

You can buy our books online a month before they hit the shops! **www.millsandboon.co.uk**

1111/04

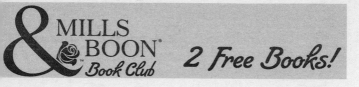

MILLS & BOON Book Club

2 Free Books!

Get your free books now at
www.millsandboon.co.uk/freebookoffer

Or fill in the form below and post it back to us

THE MILLS & BOON® BOOK CLUB™—HERE'S HOW IT WORKS: Accepting your free books places you under no obligation to buy anything. You may keep the books and return the despatch note marked 'Cancel'. If we do not hear from you, about a month later we'll send you 4 brand-new stories from the Historical series priced at £3.99* each. There is no extra charge for post and packaging. You may cancel at any time, otherwise we will send you 4 stories a month which you may purchase or return to us—the choice is yours. *Terms and prices subject to change without notice. Offer valid in UK only. Applicants must be 18 or over. Offer expires 28th February 2012. **For full terms and conditions, please go to www.millsandboon.co.uk/termsandconditions**

Mrs/Miss/Ms/Mr (please circle)
_____

First Name
_____

Surname
_____

Address
_____

_____

                                                            Postcode

E-mail
_____

Send this completed page to: Mills & Boon Book Club, Free Book Offer, FREEPOST NAT 10298, Richmond, Surrey, TW9 1BR

Find out more at
www.millsandboon.co.uk/freebookoffer

Visit us Online

0611/M1ZEE

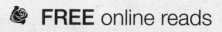